THE GIRL WHO SEES

SASHA URBAN SERIES: BOOK 1

DIMA ZALES

♠ MOZAIKA PUBLICATIONS ♠

Copyright © 2018 Dima Zales and Anna Zaires
www.dimazales.com

Published by Mozaika Publications, an imprint of Mozaika LLC.
www.mozaikallc.com

Cover by Orina Kafe
www.orinakafe-art.com

e-ISBN: 978-1-63142-351-2
Print ISBN: 978-1-63142-352-9

CHAPTER ONE

"I'M NOT A PSYCHIC," I say to the makeup girl. "What I'm about to do is mentalism."

"Like that dreamy guy on the TV show?" The makeup girl adds another dash of foundation to my cheekbones. "I always wanted to do his makeup. Can you also hypnotize and read people?"

I take a deep, calming breath. It doesn't help much. The tiny dressing room smells like hairspray went to war with nail polish remover, won, and took some fumes prisoner.

"Not exactly," I say when I have my anxiety and subsequent irritation under control. Even with Valium in my blood, the knowledge of what's about to come keeps me on the edge of sanity. "A mentalist is a type of stage magician whose illusions deal with the mind. If it were up to me, I'd just go by 'mental illusionist.'"

"That's not a very good name." She blinds me with her lamp and carefully examines my eyebrows.

I mentally cringe; the last time she looked at me this way, I ended up getting tortured with tweezers.

She must like what she sees now, though, because she turns the light away from my face. "'Mental illusionist' sounds like a psychotic magician," she continues.

"That's why I simply call myself an illusionist." I smile and prepare for the makeup to fall off, like a mask, but it stays put. "Are you almost done?"

"Let's see," she says, waving over a camera guy.

The guy makes me stand up, and the lights on his camera come on.

"This is it." The makeup girl points at the nearby LCD screen, where I have avoided looking until now because it's playing the ongoing show—the source of my panic.

The camera guy does whatever he needs to do, and the anxiety-inducing show is gone from the screen, replaced by an image of our tiny room.

The girl on the screen vaguely resembles me. The heels make my usual five feet, six inches seem much taller, as does the dark leather outfit I'm wearing. Without heavy makeup, my face is symmetric enough, but my sharp cheekbones put me closer to handsome than pretty—an effect my strong chin enhances. The makeup, however, softens my features, bringing out the blue color of my eyes and highlighting the contrast with my black hair.

The makeup girl went overboard with it—you'd

think I'm about to step into a shampoo commercial. I'm not a big fan of long hair, but I keep it that way because when I had it short, people used to mistake me for a teenage boy.

That's a mistake no one would make tonight.

"I like it," I say. "Let's be done. Please."

The TV guy switches the screen back to the live feed of the show. I can't help but glance there, and my already high blood pressure spikes.

The makeup girl looks me up and down and wrinkles her nose minutely. "You insist on that outfit, right?"

The really cool (in my opinion) borderline-dominatrix getup I've donned today is a means to add mystique to my onstage persona. Jean Eugène Robert-Houdin, the famous nineteenth-century French conjuror who inspired Houdini's stage name, once said, "A magician is an actor playing the part of a magician." When I saw Criss Angel on TV, back in elementary school, my opinion of what a magician should look like was formed, and I'm not too proud to admit that I see influences of his goth rock star look in my own outfit, especially the leather jacket.

"How marvelous," says a familiar voice with a sexy British accent. "You didn't look like this at the restaurant."

Pivoting on my high heels, I come face to face with Darian, the man I met two weeks ago at the restaurant where I do table-to-table magic—and where I'd impressed him enough to make this unimaginable opportunity a reality.

A senior producer on the popular *Evening with Kacie* show, Darian Rutledge is a lean, sharply dressed man who reminds me of a hybrid between a butler and James Bond. Despite his senior role at the studio and the frown lines that crisscross his forehead, I'd estimate his age to be late twenties—though that could be wishful thinking, given that I'm only twenty-four. Not that he's traditionally handsome or anything, but he does have a certain appeal. For one thing, with his strong nose, he's the rare guy who can pull off a goatee.

"I wear Doc Martens at the restaurant," I tell him. The extra inches of my footwear lift me to his eye level, and I can't help but get lost in those green depths. "The makeup was forced on me," I finish awkwardly.

He smiles and hands me a glass he's been holding. "And the result is lovely. Cheers." He then looks at the makeup girl and the camera guy. "I'd like to speak with Sasha in private." His tone is polite, yet it carries an unmistakable air of imperiousness.

The staff bolt out of the room. Darian must be an even bigger shot than I thought.

On autopilot, I take a gulp of the drink he handed to me and wince at the bitterness.

"That's a Sea Breeze." He gives me a megaton smile. "The barman must've gone heavy on the grapefruit juice."

I take a polite second sip and put the drink on the

vanity behind me, worried that the combination of vodka and Valium might make me woozier than I already am. I have no idea why Darian wants to speak to me alone; anxiety has already turned my brain to mush.

Darian regards me in silence for a moment, then pulls out a phone from his tight jeans' pocket. "There's a bit of unpleasantness we must discuss," he says, swiping across the screen of the phone before handing it to me.

I take the phone from him, gripping it tight so it doesn't slip out of my sweaty palms.

On the phone is a video.

I watch it in stunned silence, a wave of dread washing over me despite the medication.

The video reveals my secret—the hidden method behind the impossible feat I'm about to perform on *Evening with Kacie.*

I'm so screwed.

"Why are you showing me this?" I manage to say after I regain control of my paralyzed vocal cords.

Darian gently takes the phone back from my shaking hands. "You know that thing you went on about at the restaurant? How you're just pretending to be a psychic and that it's all tricks?"

"Right." I frown in confusion. "I never said I do anything for real. If this is about exposing me as a fraud—"

"You misunderstand." Darian grabs my discarded

drink and takes a long, yet somehow elegant sip. "I have no intention of showing that video to anyone. Quite the contrary."

I blink at him, my brain clearly overheated from the adrenaline and lack of sleep.

"I know that as a magician, you don't like your methods known." His smile turns oddly predatory.

"Right," I say, wondering if he's about to make a blackmail-style indecent proposal. If he did, I would reject it, of course—but on principle, not because doing something indecent with a guy like Darian is unthinkable.

When you haven't gotten any for as long as I haven't, all sorts of crazy scenarios swirl through your head on a regular basis.

Darian's green gaze turns distant, as though he's trying to look through the nearby wall all the way into the horizon. "I know what you're planning on saying after the big reveal," he says, focusing back on me. In an eerie parody of my voice, he enunciates, "'I'm not a prophet. I use my five senses, principles of deception, and showmanship to create the illusion of being one.'"

My eyebrows rise so high my heavy makeup is in danger of chipping. He didn't approximate what I was about to say—he nailed it word for word, even copying the intonation I've practiced.

"Oh, don't look so surprised." He places the now-empty glass back on the vanity dresser. "You said that exact thing at the restaurant."

I nod, still in shock. Did I actually tell him this

before? I don't remember, but I must have. Otherwise, how would he know?

"I paraphrased something another mentalist says," I blurt out. "Is this about giving him credit?"

"Not at all," Darian says. "I simply want you to omit that nonsense."

"Oh." I stare at him. "Why?"

Darian leans against the vanity and crosses his legs at the ankles. "What fun is it to have a fake psychic on the show? Nobody wants to see a fake."

"So you want me to act like a fraud? Pretend to be for real?" Between the stage fright, the video, and now this unreasonable demand, I'm just about ready to turn tail and run, even if I end up regretting it for the rest of my life.

He must sense that I'm about to lose it, because the predatory edge leaves his smile. "No, Sasha." His tone is exaggeratedly patient, as though he's talking to a small child. "I just want you to not say anything. Don't claim to be a psychic, but don't deny it either. Just avoid that topic altogether. Surely you can be comfortable with that."

"And if I'm not, you would show people the video? Reveal my method?"

The very idea outrages me. I might not want people to think I'm a psychic, but like most magicians, I work hard on the secret methods for my illusions, and I intend to take them to my grave—or write a book for magicians only, to be published posthumously.

"I'm sure it wouldn't come to that." Darian takes a

step toward me, and the bergamot scent of his cologne teases my flaring nostrils. "We want the same thing, you and I. We want people to be enthralled by you. Just don't make any claims one way or another—that's all I ask."

I take a step back, his proximity too much for my already shaky state of mind. "Fine. You have a deal." I swallow thickly. "You never show the video, and I don't make any claims."

"There's one more thing, actually," he says, and I wonder if the indecent proposal is about to drop.

"What?" I dampen my lips nervously, then notice him looking and realize I'm just making an inappropriate pass at me that much more likely.

"How did you know what card my escort was thinking of?" he asks.

I smile, finally back in my element. He must be talking about my signature Queen of Hearts effect—the one that blew away everyone at his table. "That will cost you something extra."

He arches an eyebrow in silent query.

"I want the video," I say. "Email it to me, and I'll give you a hint."

Darian nods and swipes a few times on his phone.

"Done," he says. "Do you have it?"

I take out my own phone and wince. It's Sunday night, right before the biggest opportunity of my life, yet I have four messages from my boss.

Deciding to find out what the manipulative bastard

wants later, I go into my personal email and verify that I have the video from Darian.

"Got it," I say. "Now about the Queen of Hearts thing... If you're as observant and clever as I think you are, you'll be able to guess my method tonight. Before the main event, I'm going to perform that same effect for Kacie."

"You sneaky minx." His green eyes fill with mirth. "So you're not going to tell me?"

"A magician must always be at least one step ahead of her audience." I give him the aloof smile I've perfected over the years. "Do we have a deal or not?"

"Fine. You win." He gracefully sits on the swivel chair where I went through my eyebrow torture. "Now, tell me, why did you look so spooked when I first came in?"

I hesitate, then decide it will do no harm to admit the truth. "It's because of that." I point at the screen where the live feed from the show is still rolling. At that precise moment, the camera pans to the large studio audience, all clapping at some nonsense the hostess said.

Darian looks amused. "Kacie? I didn't think that Muppet could frighten anyone."

"Not her." I wipe my damp palms on my leather jacket and learn that it's not the most absorbent of surfaces. "I'm afraid of speaking in front of people."

"You are? But you said you want to be a TV magician, and you perform at the restaurant all the time."

"The biggest audience at the restaurant is three or four people at a dinner table," I say. "In that studio over there, it's about a hundred. The fear kicks in after the numbers get into the teens."

Darian's amusement seems to deepen. "What about the millions of people who'll be watching you at home? Are you not worried about them?"

"I'm more worried about the studio audience, and yes, I understand the irony." I do my best not to get defensive. "For my own TV show, I'd do street magic with a small camera crew—that wouldn't trigger my fear too much."

Fear is actually an understatement. My attitude toward public speaking confirms the many studies showing that this particular phobia tends to be more pervasive than the fear of death. Certainly, I'd rather be eaten by a shark than have to appear in front of a big crowd.

After Darian called me about this opportunity, I learned how big the show's studio audience is, and I couldn't sleep for three days straight—which is why I feel like a Guantanamo Bay detainee on her way to enhanced interrogation. It's even worse than when I pulled a string of all-nighters for my stupid day job, and at the time, I thought it was the most stressful event of my life.

My roommate Ariel didn't give me her Valium lightly; it took a ton of persuasion on my part, and she only gave in when she could no longer bear to look at my miserable face.

Darian distracts me from my thoughts by fiddling with his phone again.

"This should inspire you," he says as soothing piano chords ring out of the tinny phone speaker. "It's a song about a man in a similar situation to yours."

It takes me a few moments to recognize the tune. Given that I last heard it when I was little, I up my estimate of Darian's age by an extra few years. The song is "Lose Yourself," from the *8 Mile* movie, where Eminem's character gets a chance to be a rapper. I guess my situation is similar enough, this being my big shot at what I want the most.

Unexpectedly, Darian begins to rap along with Eminem, and I fight an undignified giggle as some of the tension leaves my body. Do all British rappers sound as proper as the Queen?

"Now there's that smile," Darian says, unaware or uncaring that my grin is at his expense. "Keep it up."

He grabs the remote and turns up the volume on the TV in time for me to hear Kacie say, "Our hearts go out to the victims of the earthquake in Mexico. To donate to the Red Cross, please call the number at the bottom of the screen. And now, a quick commercial—"

"Sasha?" A man pops his head into the dressing room. "We need you on stage."

"Break a leg," Darian says and blows me an air kiss.

"In these shoes, I just might." I mime catching the kiss, throwing it on the floor, and stabbing it with my stiletto.

Darian's laugh grows distant as my guide and I

leave the room, heading down a dark corridor. As we approach our destination, our steps seem to get louder, echoing in tune with my accelerating heartbeat. Finally, I see a light and hear the roar of the crowd.

This is how people going to face a firing squad must feel. If I weren't medicated, I'd probably bolt, my dreams be damned. As is, the guide has to grab my arm and drag me toward the light.

Apparently, the commercial break will soon be over.

"Go take a seat on the couch next to Kacie," someone whispers loudly into my ear. "And breathe."

My legs seem to grow heavier, each step a monumental effort of will. Hyperventilating, I step onto the platform where the couch is located and take tiny steps, trying to ignore the studio audience.

My dread is so extreme that time flows strangely; one moment I'm still walking, the next I'm standing by the couch.

I'm glad Kacie has her nose in a tablet. I'm not ready to exchange pleasantries when I have to do something as difficult as sitting down.

Knees shaking, I lower myself onto the couch like a fakir onto a bed of nails (which is not a feat of supernatural pain resistance, by the way, but the application of scientific principles of pressure).

Time distortion must've happened again, because the music signifying the commercial break comes to an abrupt close, and Kacie looks up from her tablet, her overly full lips stretching into a smile.

The pounding of my pulse is so loud in my ears I can't hear her greeting.

This is it.

I'm about to have a panic attack on national TV.

CHAPTER TWO

"BY DAY, Sasha works for the infamous Nero Gorin at his hedge fund," Kacie says, reciting the intro I've prepared. The words reach me as if I'm in an underground bunker. "By night, she performs at the sumptuous, Zagat-rated—"

The sips of Sea Breeze churn painfully in my stomach. It's going to be my turn to speak in a couple of seconds.

The crowd looks at me menacingly.

The cliché of picturing them in their undies just makes me want to gag, so I picture them sleeping— which doesn't work either.

Without Ariel's medication, I might've run out screaming.

Scanning the audience again, I admit what should've been unsurprising: Mom didn't come. When I sent her the invitation, I knew this was likely, but on some level, I must've still been holding out for her to show up. I only had one invite to give out, and I now wish I'd given it to someone else. Mom has never approved of my passion for "silly tricks," as she puts it, probably because she's worried that my income could fall drastically if I pursued magic as a career. And since she benefits from that income—

"Sasha?" Kacie repeats, her smile extending almost to her ears. "Welcome to my show, dear."

I swallow and choke out, "Thanks for having me, Kacie." If I hadn't practiced it a million times, I would've messed up even this basic greeting. "I hope I can add a little mystery to everyone's day."

"I'm certainly intrigued." Kacie looks from me to the camera and back. "I understand you're going to predict the future today. Is that right, Sasha?"

Damn Darian. Why did he put me in this situation? Before he asked me not to end the show with a disclaimer, I had my act and speech perfectly planned out. Now I have to tread carefully and pick only the "safe" lines from the patter I've rehearsed so many times.

Kacie is looking at me expectantly, so I nod and plunge ahead, steadying my voice as I say, "My day job at the hedge fund requires me to predict how the market and individual investments might behave. I do so by absorbing a lot of financial and political data and using it to make my forecasts. As it turns out, I'm very good at this."

Though magicians often lie in their patter, every word I just said is the truth. As much as I hate my job, I do excel at the forecasting aspect of it. I'm so successful at it, in fact, that my boss Nero puts up with my crap.

Having said that, the only reason I bring up my job at all is because every book on magic performance instructs you to make your material personal. Comedians use the same trick. And since nothing is more personal to me than my current purgatory, into the patter it went.

"Well then." Kacie turns to the camera. "Sounds like a demonstration is in order."

"Definitely," I say, and hoping nobody notices the tremor in my hands, I casually roll up my sleeves—a move every magician worth her salt does before performing to rule out suspicion of the go-to "something up your sleeve" explanation.

Swallowing to moisten my dry throat, I say to Kacie, "Two days ago, you and I spoke on the phone, and I asked you to think of a playing card. Did you choose one?"

I hold my breath, my heart thrashing in my chest. What she says next will determine how amazing my first trick will seem to millions of people.

"Certainly," she replies. "I have a card in mind."

I exhale in relief, most of my nervousness melting away. She didn't accidentally rat me out—which means I messed with her memory as intended. What I actually told her on the phone was, "Think of a card in the deck that represents you, or one that feels personal to you."

There's a world of difference between "think of a

random card" and "think of a card that represents you." One is a free choice; another is a directed choice.

From my experience, most women will think of the Queen of Hearts when confronted with my carefully worded instruction. This psychological ploy works doubly well for extroverts like Kacie, especially ones who use as much red lipstick as she does.

"It's very important that the viewers understand that you had an absolutely free choice," I tell her. I really enjoy saying that line, given how evilly false it is. "Please also confirm to everyone that I offered you a chance to change your mind if you so desired."

The second part is true. I did tell her she could change the card, but I said it offhandedly, as an afterthought, not giving her a chance to really think it through. It was a risk, of course, but people almost never change their minds after they have a card picked, especially if they are stuck on the idea that the original card "represents them."

"That's exactly what she said." Kacie is on the verge of clapping her carefully manicured hands together in excitement. It's amazing how magic can turn this polished woman into a little girl again.

Deciding that fortune favors the bold, I say, "This is your last chance to change your mind. If you want, you can do so now."

Kacie shakes her head, clearly in a rush to know what happens next.

Great.

She's sticking with her choice.

"For the first time, please name your card out loud." I make a sweeping, go-ahead gesture with my right hand and prepare to not look disappointed if I have to resort to plan B.

"The Queen of Hearts," Kacie announces triumphantly.

I swallow a grin. Showing my excitement might hint at my method, just as revealing disappointment would.

Slowly, I turn my outstretched arm toward Kacie. "Remember, you could've changed your mind at any time."

She gasps, her spidery eyelashes fluttering in rapid blinks.

"Is that real?" Her voice is full of awe. She obviously forgot the selection process and believes she genuinely had free choice of any card.

"I got this a few months ago," I say, keeping my arm steady to make sure it remains within everyone's sight.

Someone in the audience whispers one of my favorite phrases: "There's no way."

The camera zooms in on my forearm.

The big screen behind us shows my pale skin and the intricate tattoo adorning it.

The Queen of Hearts.

"Would you like to touch it?" I slide all the way to the edge of the couch and thrust the tattoo at Kacie. "Make sure it's not just drawn on there."

Kacie's cool fingers massage the tattoo, and she

slowly shakes her head, whispering in amazement under her breath.

I now allow myself a huge grin. Every time an effect succeeds like this and I see the awe on people's faces, I get a huge rush.

This is why I'm pursuing this career of honest deception despite my fear of public speaking.

Risking a glance at the crowd, I notice that they're even more impressed than Kacie—as they should be. As far as they know, I told Kacie to "think of any card."

"And of course, this is the only tattoo I have on my body." I turn my ink-free left arm toward the camera and lift my hair up to display the back of my neck. I debate showing my tramp-stamp-free lower back, but since that requires getting up on still-unsteady legs, I decide not to risk it and quip, "At least the only tattoo in a place I could show on national television."

The joke bursts the pent-up tension from the revelation, and everyone laughs.

I beam at them.

I'll remember this moment forever.

The act has gone perfectly.

Of course, there's a slight problem. The people who have seen me perform at the restaurant—like Darian— might catch on to the fact that I always reveal the Queen of Hearts.

I meet his inscrutable green gaze in the VIP section of the first row and wink. Is he any closer to figuring out the method behind the effect, having seen it twice?

Hopefully, he thinks I'm a careful manipulator who

can make people think anything I desire—which I guess isn't *that* far from the truth. The question that should be eating at Darian now is: "What if Kacie *didn't* name the Queen of Hearts?"

The answer to that question is very simple: I'd go to plan B. I have a deck of cards in my right pocket—something I never leave home without. If Kacie named the wrong card, I'd try not to look disappointed and would use my already-extended right hand to retrieve the deck from my pocket. I'd ask Kacie to name a number between one and fifty-two, and I'd count to that number from the top of the deck to "magically" reveal her card—an effect that feels like a prediction, and for other magicians might seem like a bigger miracle than the tattoo version. No one—besides Darian—would be the wiser.

Enthusiastic clapping brings my attention back to the audience.

"Thank you." I bow slightly, ignoring the sweat trickling down my spine. "That was just a small appetizer before the main event."

Kacie, the crowd, and even Darian (who knows the method of what's about to come) are hanging on to my every word. Maybe it's presumptuous, but I can picture the people at home scooting closer to their TV screens.

After all, they just saw me predict, via a tattoo no less, a free thought that occurred in a human mind, yet I call it an appetizer.

My pulse is still too fast, and I become aware of an odd sensation—like I'm filling up with warm energy. Is this the Valium kicking in? I hope it's not the cocktail mixing with the medicine.

Pushing the worry aside, I focus on my performance.

"A few weeks ago," I say evenly, "I mailed an important letter to Kacie." I actually mailed it to her assistant, but she doesn't correct me, so I proceed. "Kacie, do you have that letter now?"

Kacie triumphantly picks up a large sealed envelope.

"This envelope was at the studio at all times, was it not?" I ask and lock eyes with Darian.

A horrific idea just popped into my head.

What if he doesn't want me to deny being a psychic so he can play the cursed video and make me look like a fraud?

Debunking a fake psychic might make for good TV.

Shoving that awful thought away, I refocus on Kacie as she says, "Yes, and it's sealed. There's no sneaky business here."

I could kiss her. Now I don't have to emphasize how untampered the envelope was and how impossible it was for me to access.

"Great. Thank you," I say. "Now, before we get to the envelope, can you please put up the front page of *The New York Times* on that big screen behind me?"

The familiar page appears on the screen, with the biggest story of the day prominently featured. The headline reads: *MAJOR EARTHQUAKE HITS MEXICO; DOZENS KILLED.* Under the article is an image of a tall building lying on its side, with people digging in the rubble.

This is my moment, but I can't help a huge pang of guilt. What I'm about to do is going to seem that much more dramatic because of this terrible tragedy. Of course, I had no control over today's headlines, and this sort of outcome is always a risk with this illusion. One mentalist accidentally predicted Elvis's death like this, and to this day, he's stalked by conspiracy theorists.

Swallowing the guilt, I say in my most authoritative tone, "Kacie, please open the envelope and show everyone what's inside."

"I'm not sure I want to open this," Kacie whispers, but her fingers are already ripping at the paper in front of her.

She reaches into the envelope gingerly, as though it has anthrax inside. Pulling out the big sheet of paper, she looks at it, and blood leaves her cheeks.

I want to kiss her yet again. Her reaction is fueling the audience's anticipation.

Finally, the entertainer inside Kacie takes over, and she turns the paper toward the camera with a flourish.

On the paper, there's a hand-drawn recreation of the newspaper still on the screen behind us. In the neatest script I could manage, I wrote *MAJOR EARTHQUAKE HITS MEXICO; DOZENS KILLED.* Using my shoddy artistic abilities, I also drew a big building on its side and a couple of matchstick people next to some splotches of ink that represent the rubble.

One of the studio's graphics people puts my prediction letter side by side with *The New York Times*, and the visual is very powerful.

I prepared a spiel about the difficulty of predicting earthquakes, but I don't go into it. There's no need. The audience is in the rare state of silent shock, and I don't want to ruin it with words. This is the coolest reaction a magician can hope for—frightened awe.

Alternatively, the audience might be sucking in a breath to start booing me off the stage.

Darian breaks the spell by beginning a slow clap, like in a teen movie.

The roar of the applause that follows is the best thing I've ever heard. I jackknife to my feet and take a bow.

"Bravo," Kacie says, her voice still uneven. Into the camera, she says, "We have to take a quick commercial break and will be back in a moment."

The commercial music turns on, and I'm glad. If I freak out now, at least it won't be broadcast live.

The audience slows their clapping, and I notice a few people in the crowd who didn't react at all. One is a sickly looking older gentleman in the third row, and the rest are pale men in aviator sunglasses and black suits who remind me of security guards. They're all the way at the back of the studio.

I look at Darian. He's stopped clapping and is staring at the unhealthy-looking senior citizen. Something about the man must upset him because Darian's face darkens. Bringing his finger to his ear, he mouths something, and one of the men in black repeats the gesture.

Is he talking to the studio security, and if so, why?

Concealing my puzzlement, I glance at Kacie. She's fanning herself with the envelope, clearly still recovering from my prediction.

I remain on my feet, waiting for the applause to cease. As honored as I am by the ovation, I hope it ends soon because my knees feel weak, and the odd, warm-energy sensation is back, but much stronger this time. It's like I'm being flooded with it, and my pulse accelerates further, my breathing quickening uncontrollably.

What's happening?

Is this the panic attack I've been trying to stave off?

My nails dig into my palms. If I didn't keep them so short for dealing with cards, I'd be bleeding.

Another tsunami of oddly pleasant energy rushes into my body, making my extremities tingle.

My toes curl inside my high heels. Did I just orgasm in front of a hundred people?

The pleasure lasts only a moment, and as intensity builds, the sensation morphs into pain.

The bright studio lights turn into suns, and my vision blurs. I squeeze my eyes shut, my muscles locking up as I begin to shake uncontrollably.

Am I having a seizure? A stroke?

The intensity of the experience is now beyond pain. I'm going into shock, like the day I got my tongue pierced, only infinitely worse. It's as though my whole body has turned into a nerve ending that someone zapped with a billion volts of electricity.

If I weren't feeling the ground under my feet, I'd be convinced I'm levitating, with lightning striking me, Highlander style.

I bear the sensation for only a few short moments before something short-circuits in my brain and I collapse, my consciousness winking out.

CHAPTER THREE

I'M ON THE COUCH, my awareness diamond sharp.

The commercial tune is still on, so I must not have been out for long.

The sickly older man in the audience leaps to his feet, causing everyone to stare at him and his gray skin.

"Stop him!" Darian screams, and a pale man in black starts running toward the stage.

The sickly man is painful to look at as he moves. He must have brain damage or a muscle disease because his limbs are uncoordinated as he wields them in jerky trajectories. Yet despite the apparent motor difficulties, the guy has enough energy to propel himself forward.

People shriek as he jumps onto the shoulders of the audience members in the second row.

Then his nondescript black shoes land on two women in the first row.

They scream, but the old man just uses his perches to leap onto the stage.

I'm too stupefied to move.

The black-clad security guy is moving like an Olympic sprinter, but he's too far back and the crowd is in his way.

This would be a great time to run away screaming, but I'm still too petrified to move a muscle.

"Sir," Kacie yells, her voice panicked. "You can't be up here!"

The guy's rheumy eyes glance at Kacie, but he must not find her worth his time because his gaze zeroes in on my neck.

The man in black and some of his colleagues are almost here, but it's clear they won't intercept the gray-skinned weirdo before he reaches me. I have no idea what he wants, but I don't like the blank expression on his sickly face. He might be on something like meth.

One of the camera guys on stage leaps into the sicko's path. "Sir! Excuse me, sir—stop. You can't be here."

The gray-skinned man flings the camera guy aside with shocking strength. I catch a glimpse of him rolling on the stage, and I go into a pure fight-or-flight response, tunnel vision and all.

I only have moments to decide what to do.

As a relatively small person, I ideally need a weapon for the fight option.

I have no conventional weapons, but a thrifty magician can always improvise. Maybe I can use the lock picks that constitute the stud in my tongue to stab him in the eye? Or create a card waterfall from the deck in my pocket as a distraction?

Settling on a more mundane option, I frantically slip off my right stiletto and jump to my feet, channeling Buffy by holding it in front of me like a stake.

I'm face to face with the guy now, and the most horrific odor assaults my nose. It smells as though I plunged head first into roadkill. The fumes are so nauseating I almost pass out.

Instead of fainting, I swing my makeshift stake at his face, aiming for his eye.

I've only stabbed playing cards before, and I've never done it with one high heel on. As a result, my weapon lands way off the mark—in the middle of the man's chest.

To my utter shock, the heel penetrates a couple of inches into him, as though there's a hole there already. His clothing is intact, yet I hear a rip of some kind.

Could there have been stitches in his chest? He does look sick enough to be post-heart surgery, though he's way too spry.

Ignoring the shoe protruding from his chest, the man wraps his foul-smelling hands around my neck and starts to squeeze.

My hands fly up to claw at his strangling fingers, but he's bizarrely strong, and I can't inflict much damage with my short nails. So I knee him in the groin, using all my strength. Pain shoots through my knee, but I take solace in knowing no man could withstand such an attack.

I'm wrong.

The fingers around my neck don't loosen, and through my blurring vision, I see his glassy eyes staring at me without blinking.

I claw at his face next, but with a similar lack of success. My lungs are now screaming for air, and though I've practiced holding my breath in order to one day perform a Houdini-like underwater escape, panic overwhelms me.

My body thrashes mindlessly, and my head feels like it's about to explode through my ears as the world grows more distant.

With the last remnants of consciousness, I realize that this is it.

Blackness overwhelms me, and I die.

CHAPTER FOUR

I GASP, and as air fills my non-exploded lungs, I realize I've just had a nightmare.

And what a weird nightmare it was. My heart is still thrashing in my chest as though the strangling fingers are squeezing the life out of me.

This sucks. There's no way I'll be able to go back to sleep with this much adrenaline coursing through my system.

What time is it? Do I have to get up for work?

Wait a minute. Am I actually in my bedroom? Now that I'm calmer, I can feel bright light pummeling my eyelids, and I always close the extra heavy curtains at night.

Distant voices speaking nonsense are also inconsistent with the bedroom theory, as is my half-sitting position.

I open my lids by a micron, but it's enough to show me that I'm still in the TV studio.

Crap.

Did I just black out in front of all these people?

The concerned faces around me support that hypothesis.

As I sit up straighter, memories slowly trickle in.

I was having some sort of an episode and collapsed onto the couch. After I passed out, I had a weird dream —the most vivid dream of my life.

A dream about dying.

I blink my heavily mascaraed eyes in an effort to reorient myself.

The commercial music is playing somewhere, so I couldn't have been out of commission for long.

As I scan the crowd, a strong sense of déjà vu hits me.

The sickly guy from my dream leaps onto his feet.

His skin is a purple shade of gray, his eyes are blank, and his cheap-looking blazer and over-starched shirt look like they're being worn for the first time. Just like in my dream, the way he moves is highly erratic.

Also like in my dream, the audience's attention swings to the strange man.

"Stop him!" Darian screams again, and the nearest man in black starts the sprint that didn't reach me in time.

Every detail of what's happening is so familiar to me that I begin to doubt my sanity. Could I be dreaming now?

That would imply that the first dream was a dream inside a dream, like in the movie *Inception*.

The studio audience all react with the same horror as the gray-skinned guy once again jumps onto the shoulders of the audience members in the second row.

Dream or delusion, I'm not waiting for him to choke me. I take off my heels, but this time, with the intention of fleeing.

"Sir." Kacie's voice is just as panicked as I recall. "You can't be up here!"

As the guy's rheumy eyes glance at Kacie, I jump to my feet and dash toward the corridor that led onto the stage. The floor is icy under my bare feet, but I scarcely register the discomfort, my body firmly back in fight-or-flight land.

The door I came through is closed.

I grab the handle, rattling it frantically as an abominable smell reaches my nostrils. It's the roadkill stench from my dream, and I gag, barely stopping myself from projectile vomiting at the door.

The handle doesn't budge.

The door must be locked.

I spin around.

My attacker is already reaching for my throat—and I know how that will end. Operating on pure instinct, I slam my back against the door and slide down, making my neck harder to reach.

His hands meet with a loud smack where he missed his target.

I take advantage of his momentary distraction by punching him in the groin, which is currently at my eye level. My fist connects with spongy flesh, but just like in my dream, the guy doesn't react to what should be a debilitating hit for any man.

Instead, he takes a lumbering step back and bends over me, hands still reaching for my neck.

I'm about to lunge in desperation at the small gap between his legs when I see another pair of legs behind my attacker.

My run wasn't a waste of effort.

It gave the black-clad security guard time to catch up with us.

Pulse hammering, I watch as pale, neatly manicured fingers grasp my attacker's shoulder.

The gray-skinned man's bending action stops, his shoulder compressing as though the fingers of the security guard are a hydraulic press.

What happens next makes me question the reality of this moment. Maintaining his graceful grip on the gray-skinned man's shoulder, the guard grabs the man's arm with his free hand and rips it out of its socket with a ghastly tearing crunch.

The stench of rotting flesh intensifies, but all I can think is that there's not enough blood.

Not much blood at all, really.

If this is a dream, I blame Ariel. She's a huge fan of fighting games, and this is eerily reminiscent of how she ended my character in *Mortal Kombat* last week—minus the fountains of blood in the game.

Adding to my sense of unreality, the gray-skinned man reacts to the loss of his arm with the same aplomb as to my groin assault. Staying on his feet, he tries to reach me with his remaining arm.

The black-clad guard uses the arm he's holding to club his opponent on the head. There's a sickening crack of bones breaking, though I'm not sure if it's the skull or the arm.

I clap my hand over my mouth. I'm not particularly squeamish, but this is beyond what I can stomach.

My attacker staggers, but incredibly, he remains on his feet, glassy eyes as blank as always.

Another black-suited guard leaps into the fray, grasping the wounded man by his still-intact shoulder on one side and by the gory remnants of the detached arm on the other. Then, grunting from the strain, he rips my attacker in half.

Literally.

My stomach heaves, and I bite the fleshy part of my palm to hold back a scream.

This is even more impossible than ripping out the arm. If this were the classic "cutting a lady in half" stage illusion, I could think of a number of ways it could be done. But to do it for real, the force required would be staggering.

This must be a nightmare.

But why am I not waking up?

The guard throws the two halves of the old man on the ground, and the nightmare continues as the half with the head keeps twitching, eyes blinking as though alive.

"End it," the other guard hisses at his partner, and I

watch in dazed disbelief as the first guard stomps on my attacker's skull, crushing it like an egg.

He keeps stomping on parts of the corpse until the twitching stops.

Numbly, I stare at the brains splattered on the floor like a grisly modern art painting.

It takes a moment to remember where I am, and when I look back at the crowd, they're scattering like quail.

All the exit doors must be locked, however, because I see people struggling with them to no avail.

Kacie is hiding under her desk, and Darian is approaching us, his face livid with anger.

"Do the Mexican earthquake coverage *now*," he says into a walkie talkie. "We have a small malfunction here at the studio."

A small malfunction?

I suppress a maniacal giggle.

"What about the lady magician?" the woman on the other end of the walkie talkie asks, her voice slightly staticky. "She wasn't done."

"Have Juan say that Sasha tried to warn the Mexican authorities about the earthquake—that should tie the segments together. Then say the politicians she warned were skeptical of an American psychic, and then proceed to the earthquake coverage," Darian says and clicks off the device.

I'm too stunned to be annoyed at him for making me out to be a psychic.

Crinkling his nose at the ripped-up body on the

floor, he says, "Gaius, what the hell? I was hoping for more subtlety."

The guy who did the halving—Gaius—shrugs. "You wanted the girl alive, and she is," he says, the cadence of his speech oddly hypnotic.

I finally recover my voice. "What's happening? Who was he? How did you rip him apart like that?"

Darian pays me no mind. "Wipe everyone," he says to Gaius and my other rescuer, and then he repeats the instruction into his earpiece. "They're to remember that Sasha was amazing, and that she had to run to another big performance," he adds as pale security guards start grabbing people in the audience and forcing them into what looks like staring contests.

"And her?" Gaius points at me.

"She's a Cognizant, though not under the Mandate," Darian says as though I'm not there. "Even your illustrious leader wouldn't be able to fully glamour her. Or would he?"

"If it's time for inappropriate questions, shouldn't *you* have foreseen all this?" Gaius's hypnotic voice drips with honey-laced malice. "And how are you planning to stop the Council from killing her for this?"

Darian's eyes narrow. "Just do your best with her."

"That I will," Gaius says with the same arrogant confidence that the traders at my day job possess.

He kneels so that his eyes are parallel to mine.

I try to scramble back, but with the closed door behind me, there's nowhere to go.

Gaius takes off his sunglasses.

der if the Army gave her special drugs to turn her a super soldier.

Do you need help with your clothes?" she asks she lays me on the bed.

Unable to think of a good reply to such a difficult ndrum, I blink at her and plummet into sleep as as my head touches the bliss of my memory foam w.

He has the kind of pretty face that some women swoon over, but I'm not a fan. His eyes are the color of arctic sky. Then they start to change. The pitch-black pupil turns reflective silver and begins to expand, first covering the iris, then the white of the sclera.

My breath evens out. The mirrored orbs that are Gaius's eyes each reflect a distorted image of me, my face translucently pale and my pupils the size of dimes.

A drunken serenity steals over me. Analytically, I know it's something to do with his gaze, but no matter how hard I try, I can't close my eyes or look away.

My consciousness sinks into a dark, underground place. The closest I've ever come to feeling this way was when I was drunk on a dozen shots of tequila.

Through the haze, I register only slices of events.

The guards, if that's what they are, finish their odd stare-down of every person in the crowd. Gaius picks me up like a feather, and a blink later, I'm half-lying in a limo that's zooming down West Side Highway.

Just as my mind begins to clear, Gaius peers into my eyes again, and the haze envelops me once more.

When I next come to my senses, I'm inside my building's elevator, propped up by a body so hard it might as well be made of marble.

"Almost home," says the familiar hypnotic voice as the mirrored eyes stare into mine. "You're amazingly resilient to glamour. I'm truly impressed."

I must black out again, because in the next instance, I'm standing by my apartment door with a strong arm holding me upright. Gaius's pale finger is on the doorbell, and I'm too out of my mind to chastise him for waking up my roommates when I have the key to the place.

The door opens, revealing Ariel in her silk nightgown.

The arm around me tenses, and I can't blame Gaius for his reaction. Even when she's wearing hospital scrubs—clothes designed to make nurses look less sexy —Ariel looks like a supermodel, and in this skintight nightgown, men would gobble fish oil with a spoon for her attention.

When I look at beautiful people, I often philosophically ponder what it is about a person's face and body that makes it so appealing. Is it symmetry and proportions? If so, Ariel's is among the most symmetric faces I've ever seen, and her body's 0.7 waist-to-hip ratio is pure mathematical perfection. On top of it, her skin is melted-candy smooth, even now, when she's not wearing any makeup. And, whereas more traditionally pretty faces have infant-like, small facial features, Ariel's Greek nose and jaw are strong, yet both are sublime on her face, giving her a touch of the exotic.

Her dark brown eyes stare at me with worry, then focus on my chaperone with undisguised hostility.

"What's going on? What are you doing with her?" Ariel's voice is melodious even when angry.

"Sasha isn't feeling well." Lowering his shades a couple of inches, Gaius scans Ariel up and down, his gaze lingering on her ballerina-long neck instead of

her breasts. "I'd like to put her to bed. invite me in?"

"Hell no. I've got it from here, thank me, she loops a toned arm around my ba

"Suit yourself," Gaius says and stej Ariel support me fully.

She's about to drag me into the apa says, "Just one other thing." Reaching hair from my head around his finger, or I can protest, he yanks it out.

I flinch but feel nothing—I flabbergasted to feel such minor pain.

Pocketing the hair, he says, "Sh remember any of this in the mornin not want to cause her unnecessary gr her."

Instead of answering, Ariel pu apartment and slams the door shut, a pale man in the face.

"What happened?" she asks, turnir Her eyes hone in on my neck as tho hickey. "Did he—"

I sway on my feet. "I just need wake up."

"Good idea," Ariel says, and thoug same size, she picks me up like a carries me to my bedroom without a

Anyone watching this would be used to this sort of thing with Arie herself "Army Strong," and I somet

CHAPTER FIVE

I'M DISEMBODIED. This reminds me of playing a virtual reality game, one where I look down and, instead of my breasts, see a futuristic gun, or whatever else the game designers decided. In this case, I see a wall with a large clock above rows upon rows of gray metal squares. It's a sight CSI shows regularly feature—the inside of a morgue.

Unlike the disembodiment of VR, though, I can smell my surroundings, though I wish I couldn't. The chlorine and faint perfume scents aren't masking the stench of death, and the worst part is that I recognize the putrid fumes from somewhere.

According to the digital clock on the wall, it's 5:29 a.m. on Monday morning. Does this mean I have to get up for work soon? And if so, wouldn't I need to locate my body first?

A woman enters the room. She has a heart-shaped face, and the outline of her lips mirrors it, though her mouth reminds me more of a spade (as in, playing cards)—in part thanks to the blackness of the lipstick. Her eyes and hair are also black, with metallic undertones in the fluorescent lights. With her black skirt and white lacy top, her outfit is more fitting for a cocktail party than the morgue, but her earlobes are adorned with dangling earrings that end in little skulls.

Reaching into her tiny black purse, she takes out a smartphone and begins to look around.

I guess she doesn't find whatever she's looking for, because she grunts disapprovingly and reaches for the nearest metal square, pulling it out with a screech.

Unsurprisingly, there's a dead body inside.

It's a man in his forties. His gray skin hue looks oddly familiar and has something to do with the smell. I can't recall what, though. My memory must not work as well without my physical brain.

The woman studies the corpse intently. Walking up to his head, she opens his mouth and puts her phone there, as if that were a perfectly reasonable perch for it.

The phone doesn't stay put in the corpse's mouth, and the woman's lips purse in obvious annoyance.

With an angry motion, she reaches into her purse again and takes out a knife. It's butterfly style, where the blade sits between two handles.

With a whoosh, she stylishly opens the knife with a well-rehearsed flourish that the performer in me can appreciate.

Knife in hand, she examines the body in front of

her for a moment and then slices into the dead man's chest—across the scars left from the embalming.

With my body gone, so is my ability to feel nauseous, it seems, because I watch in calm fascination as she finishes cutting a hole and jams her phone into the macabre holder, propping it up so it sits vertically inside the dead flesh.

She stares at the phone, then looks up at the digital clock, and the disgruntled look on her face deepens. She seems to be impatiently waiting for something.

Turning around, she pulls out another drawer with a body, this one a man in his nineties. Gently, she brushes the tips of her fingers over the man's bald head and sagging muscles. She seems to dislike something about this corpse, though, because she closes the drawer and pulls out another one.

This guy is in his fifties and has a purplish tint to him.

She looks him up and down and nods approvingly.

Her phone begins to play the notes of *Piano Sonata No. 2* by Chopin, commonly known as the *Funeral March*.

She stalks back over to the first corpse to face her grim phone stand and presses the screen to accept the call.

"Hello, Beatrice," says an amused voice. "As I keep telling you, we don't have to have a video conference every time. Especially when you're in your natural habitat."

"You're late." Beatrice's voice is surprisingly perky.

"I wanted to get a head start; the fresher the body, the better my lovelies turn out."

"You must've used a very old one last night." The amusement in the stranger's tone is joined by a note of scorn. "I assume that's your excuse for failure?"

"You never told me a seer would be involved in this." Beatrice uses her knife to carve something on the skin of the corpse in front of her. "And you particularly failed to mention the vampires."

"I'm offering you the chance to go under the Mandate and settle here in peace." His voice is mocking now. "Did you think that would be easy? And besides, why should *you* worry about vampires? I thought they hated your kind because *they* fear what you can do."

Beatrice's face darkens. "I just don't like having mortal enemies around. Since I'm new to this Mandate business, tell me, can it really make it so that they won't try to kill me on sight?"

"No, it can't pull off that kind of a miracle. But the Mandate makes it so that anyone who harms you will pay with their life. It marks you as one of us, and that provides you with something like the human rule of law. But nothing can undo their fear and hatred of your kind. Despite the Mandate, the seers still hate my kind and vice versa." From the tone of his voice, you'd think he's happy about the state of affairs he describes. "But, the Mandate does take the sting out of such hate. The vampires despised all werewolves back in the day, but look at things now. After centuries of the Mandate, there are marriages between them. Isn't that what appeals to you here—our liberal attitudes?"

If I had eyebrows, I'd want to raise them at the mention of vampires and werewolves, but since I don't, I just keep hanging.

"You're a smooth talker, even for one of your kind." Beatrice carves another symbol into the dead flesh. "Tell me, how am I supposed to outwit a seer?"

"He won't risk involving himself after what she did on TV," the voice on the phone responds, sounding serious for the first time. "He took a big enough risk setting it up. At least I assume he set that up, but I have no proof, courtesy of the vampires."

"But isn't *she* also a seer?" Beatrice stops her grisly work and makes eye contact with the phone's camera. "Won't she see me coming?"

"Even he didn't see you coming," the mystery man replies. "What can an untrained newbie hope to foresee? Despite what they want you to think, seers aren't omniscient. If they were, free will would be but a distant memory. Keep in mind that by working for me, my powers rub off on you—which is why you're not as dead as your 'lovelies.'"

"Death doesn't scare me." Beatrice looks around the morgue as though it's her living room. "It's the only real mystery left in the world."

"Is it? Well, I can help you uncover it if you keep failing like this."

"How about instead of threats, you wire me another

five hundred grand?" Her smile is all teeth. "Plus the expenses, obviously."

"Anything else?" he asks sarcastically. "A key to a whorehouse full of virgins? Soup made from kittens?"

"There is something else," she says, unruffled. "If I die on this job, I need you to take care of my body. I want it turned into fertilizer. I'll email you the exact instructions." Beatrice wipes her knife on the nearest corpse's skin before folding it and stashing it in her purse. "It's the ultimate recycling. When I think of how many nutrients are locked up in the ground instead of going back into—"

"I don't have a lot of time." The voice on the phone sounds amused again, but the command in it is clear. "Whatever you want, you will get. Just. Do. Your. Job."

Instead of replying, Beatrice stands straighter and raises her arms toward the ceiling, as though she's praying for sprinklers to rain down.

Multi-colored bolts of energy illuminate the room as they shoot from Beatrice's fingers into the two dead bodies.

The lightning spreads through the corpses. They convulse like frog legs in Galvani's electric experiments, and the chest carvings she's made light up from the inside, as though she implanted bright LED lights under the skin.

After a moment, the bodies go still, but the carvings still shine.

"I know I'll regret asking, but why aren't they

getting up?" the voice on the phone asks, and though I can't see his face, I can tell there's a smirk on it.

"These symbols are there to program in a little delay." She points at one of the bright carvings. "I do this when I can afford the luxury."

"Why?" It's odd to hear an adult man sound so much like a teasing five-year-old. "Wouldn't you want to be present when your lovelies get up? I thought you'd want to consummate the relationship when they rise to the occasion. No, wait, I'm thinking of another kind of necro."

"This conversation is clearly over." Beatrice slings her purse over her shoulder, grabs her phone, and without saying goodbye, hangs up.

She then looks at the two corpses with an unreadable expression and leaves the room.

I float for another second until I realize something that should've occurred to me in the beginning of this strange episode.

This has to be a dream.

As soon as I think the word 'dream,' I wake up.

CHAPTER SIX

WHAT A WEIRD NIGHTMARE.

Sitting up in bed, I rub my irritated eyes and wonder if I slept with mascara on.

As the dream clears from my groggy brain, I recall the much stranger happenings that preceded it. The details of last night's performance slowly come back to me, and I feel sure that most, if not all, had to be a dream or a hallucination.

The key question is: how much?

Did the show itself happen?

Grabbing my phone, I find that it's dead—I was too out of my mind to charge it.

My nightstand clock shows that it's 5:20 a.m. on Monday morning, ten minutes before my alarm is supposed to go off and nine minutes before the time in my morgue nightmare.

I get up, put my phone on the charger, and pull back the curtains.

Examining myself in the mirror, I confirm that I have heavy makeup on—evidence that I was at a TV studio, and that I came home too messed up to wash my face.

Though I'm dying to get on my computer and get some answers, I put on a robe and head to the bathroom to freshen up. Once I feel semi-human, I hurry back to my room and dress for work.

Buttoning my blouse, I open my laptop and load YouTube.

Evening with Kacie already posted last night's show, and when I see the four million views it has gathered overnight, chills race down my spine.

Frantically, I skim the comments below the video. While a few trolls have made some sleazy remarks about my looks, most people were blown away by my performance. The comments run the gamut from "the psychic girl was incredible," to "what a great magic show," to "she just got lucky"—and a bunch of stuff in Spanish.

My bare feet are cold, so I tuck them under my butt as I fast-forward the video.

"By day, Sasha works for the infamous Nero Gorin at his hedge fund," Kacie says on the screen before going into the spiel about my restaurant side gig.

Nero, my day-job boss, might be pissed about the "infamous" bit, but the management of the restaurant is going to be thrilled about the TV plug.

With a critical eye, I watch myself perform the Queen of Hearts effect, followed by the Headline

Prediction. It's amazing how calm I look in this video, given how I was freaking out. Is it due to Ariel's Valium, or all that hard work I put into rehearsals?

After the Headline Prediction, unsurprisingly, I don't come back on the air. Instead, a reporter named Juan takes over with the Mexican earthquake coverage. He calls me a psychic and claims I warned Mexican authorities about the earthquake—which couldn't be further from the truth and is probably behind some of the YouTube comments in Spanish.

That BS Juan says sounds familiar, though. It's what Darian said, in what I hoped was the dream portion of last night's events—the part that's still hazy.

If it wasn't a dream, can something else explain some of the things I saw last night?

It started with me having pleasant sensations and then passing out, which, if it happened for real, could be explained by a brain issue, such as a stroke.

Biting my lip, I Google "strokes" and "pleasure" and don't find many results. Still, figuring it doesn't hurt to be proactive, I navigate to the NYU hospital website and request an appointment with my primary care physician. If something is wrong with my brain, I want to get it checked out as soon as possible. On the other hand, if the problem is psychosis, my primary care physician can probably refer me to the right specialist also.

Thinking of doctors gives me an idea of what else could explain last night's fogginess and strange memories.

Valium.

That explanation would be infinitely preferable to having had a stroke or going insane.

I eagerly type in some related search phrases, hoping for validation.

When the results of my query pop up, I'm both relieved and terrified. The drug's side effects indeed include hallucinations, psychoses, delusions, and nightmares—leave it to me to get all of the above. Upon further study, I also learn something that Ariel should've warned me about: you're supposed to avoid grapefruit with benzodiazepines such as Valium. Apparently, grapefruit blocks an enzyme called CYP3A4, thus increasing both the levels of the drug in the blood and the severity of the associated side effects. And the scariest part is that you're not supposed to mix the medication with alcohol at all, as doing so enhances the most dangerous effects of both substances.

I definitely should've rejected the Sea Breeze Darian offered me.

Actually, if I'm magically rewriting the past, I should've never gotten tempted by Valium in the first place. No matter how much I want to be a TV magician, using a drug that messes with my neurotransmitters isn't the way to do it. Looks like I'll have to put on my big-girl panties and overcome my stupid fear of public speaking. Somehow.

Also, and this might be a longer-term project, I need to figure out a way to get Ariel off this poison. When she served in the Middle East, my roommate saw some things she doesn't ever talk about. Though I'm not a shrink, I suspect she has PTSD—something she vehemently denies. She claims her bouts of anxiety are brought on by the stress of med school, and have nothing to do with the Army.

Since I'm on the computer already, I submit some forecasts to the Good Judgment Project. I first learned about it in one of my favorite non-magic books, *Superforecasting.* The stated mission of the project is "harnessing the wisdom of the crowd to forecast world events."

The idea here is not very different from what I do for my day job, except these forecasts can actually bring some good to the world, instead of just making my boss and his obscenely rich clients richer. All participating forecasters read publicly available information and make educated guesses about a future event, such as who will win an election, or whether the country so-and-so will develop nukes by such-and-such date. I'm one of the top forecasters in this project, and I'm as good at it as I am at forecasting the market for Nero. The top forecasters in this project, as a whole, are reportedly "30% better than intelligence officers with access to actual classified information."

As a New Yorker who lives near where the Twin Towers once stood, I find that little factoid very scary.

Realizing that I'm getting sidetracked by the internet and using up my breakfast time with things I can do from my desk at work, I shut the laptop, my stomach rumbling at the idea of food. I threw up what little dinner I could stomach last night in the studio bathroom before getting into makeup.

First, though, I need to feed my favorite creature in the world—my pet chinchilla, Fluffster.

It's actually surprising he didn't greet me when I woke up. Maybe he's upset I didn't spend Sunday night with him. Then again, he could be playing hide-and-seek.

Assuming the latter, I get up and look around. My room is decently sized for New York, which means that an eleven-inch-tall (without the fluffy tail), one-pound creature can hope to hide here, at least for a little while.

A poster of Houdini looks at me with eyes that seem to think very little of people who play hide-and-seek with their pet, especially if said pet is a type of rodent.

I walk up to the bookshelf to see if Fluffster is hiding in the same spot as last time and pull out a book —*Bobo Modern Coin Magic*. But the only sign of my chinchilla is the corner he chewed off out of boredom that day.

I check behind Corinda's *13 Steps to Mentalism*, followed by Erdnase's *Expert at the Card Table*, with the same lack of results.

Next, I look behind my keyboard plant prank since Fluffster has been eating it on occasion, but there's no chinchilla there.

The keyboard plant is a project I'm preparing for when my roommate Felix goes on vacation. He uses a fancy mechanical keyboard for his coding, so I got a broken version of the same keyboard on eBay and planted chia seeds in the gaps between the keys. Since the grass has grown, whenever I need a smile, I picture the look on Felix's face when he gets back from that future vacation and sees his keyboard sprouting greenery on his desk.

The smell of coffee and pancakes wafts in from the kitchen, and my stomach does another somersault.

"Fluffster, sweetie, I'm too hungry for games," I say pleadingly. "I'll give you three raisins if you come out right now."

The chinchilla doesn't show up, though I hear an excited chirp from under my bed.

I reach for the top of the bookshelf and grab a little plastic house filled with white powder.

"I'm just going to set this dust bath here," I say and place every chinchilla's favorite object at the foot of the bed. "It's only going to be there for a count of five. One."

Fluffster loves his dust bath so much that you'd think it's filled with cocaine (which is what it looks like) and not fine pumice (which is what it is).

A large ear shows up from under the bed, then whiskers. Then the rest of Fluffster torpedoes into the dust bath house, and he begins to roll in the white powder with movements finely tuned to be as adorable as is chinchillaly possible.

Originally from the high-elevation regions of the Andean mountains, chinchillas look like bunnies crossed with squirrels and kangaroos, but are fluffier than all of them combined. The only creature with denser fur is a sea otter, but chinchillas beat the otters on cuteness. In my (possibly biased) opinion, they are also cuter than kittens, puppies, young Leonardo DiCaprio, and babies. Touching a chinchilla is an almost spiritual experience, as their fur is softer than clouds—a feature they sometimes pay for with their lives, as Cruella de Vil types make expensive coats out of them.

After a minute, Fluffster's nose pops out of his dust bath house, and his facial expression seems to say, "There was a mention of raisins."

"You didn't come out when I said, so you only get two, and *only* if you promise to eat your pellets and some hay," I say sternly. "Also, grind your teeth on that chalk I got you."

Fluffster gets out of the bath, runs up to his bowl, and stares at it demonstratively, ready for the pellets.

I know pet owners always anthropomorphize their fur-children and think their animals are the smartest ever, but in my case, it must be true. Fluffster is a genius chinchilla, cleverer than any dog—and some people—I've met. He's potty trained, and he understands at least a couple thousand words. He knows not to drown himself in the toilet (getting wet can give them fungus, thanks to that super-thick coat), not to chew through electrical wires (at least, now he does), not to leave the apartment without my supervision (meeting a cat in the hallway taught him that), and he knows to stay away from a New York City rat, should one invade our apartment again. He tried to hump the first one he met, and let's just say NYC rats live by prison rules.

Once Fluffster is satiated, I make my way to the kitchen.

Ariel is sitting at the table in her faded Batman t-shirt. She clearly just woke up, yet she looks amazing anyway. I'm not too proud to admit to some jealousy, particularly of Ariel's unshakeable confidence in her looks. When I was a teen, I was a mess of contradictory insecurities, going from, "Oh no, where are my boobs?" right into, "Oh no, everybody is staring at my new boobs." Ariel, on the other hand, seems to have always been at ease in her skin. Whatever costume she wears for Halloween inevitably gets a "sexy" prefix before it, even the year she was a toaster.

We met as lab partners in biology back in college. She graduated first and found Felix on Craigslist (hopefully under housing>rooms/shared and not personals>rants & raves). It was the greatest find ever; not only do we get fed every morning, but the three of us are now great friends.

Felix is fussing at the stove, putting finishing touches on pancakes. A head taller than Ariel but about the same weight, from the back, he looks like a "before" image for gym commercials.

"*The Matrix* is a better movie than *Batman Begins*," he says to Ariel over his shoulder, rehashing an old argument of theirs. "It has a 73 on Metacritic while

Batman Begins has a 70, and it's higher rated on IMDb and Rotten Tomatoes."

"Those scores are inflated because people who review movies online are more likely to prefer *The Matrix*." Ariel pulls her hair into a ponytail and secures it with a scrunchie. "Can you at least agree that the directing and acting in *Batman Begins* was better? It was Christopher Nolan's masterpiece and the best performance of Christian Bale's career."

"Morning," I say from the doorway. I want to ask Ariel about last night, but I'm not sure how to approach it, so I say instead, "Can I settle this cinematic debate for you once and for all?"

"There you are," Felix says without turning. "I made some pancakes with bananas just for you."

I walk over to the fridge and get a carton of orange juice. Looking at Felix's back, I say, "The best movie ever made is actually *The Illusionist*—and I don't care what any scores have to say about that." I look provokingly at Ariel. "And Christopher Nolan's *real* masterpiece was *The Prestige*, which is also where I saw the *real* best performance of Christian Bale's career."

"You're fixated on those movies because there are stage magicians in them." Ariel shakes her head in the negative when I offer her the OJ.

"That's like saying Felix likes *The Matrix* because he's a programmer/hacker, and so was Neo in the film." I pour myself a glass of juice and plop into a kitchen chair.

"Exactly." Ariel beams at me. "My Batman addiction, on the other hand, is pure."

"If lust for Ben Affleck, George Clooney, Val Kilmer, and Michael Keaton can be said to be pure." I sip my juice, and the rush of cold sugar calories hits the pleasure centers of my brain.

"Don't forget the older versions with Adam West, Robert Lowrey, and Lewis G Wilson," Felix says. "Besides, she lusts for every Robin as well, and maybe even some of the villains."

"What kind of slut are you making me out to be?" Ariel says in mock horror. "I don't lust for George Clooney—even *I* didn't like *Batman & Robin*."

"Even if we exclude movies with magicians, Sasha's opinion on films shouldn't count." Felix upturns the skillet full of pancakes onto a large plate. "She always foresees all the plot twists, so she can't enjoy them on the same level as everyone else."

"I'm right here; you don't need to speak about me in third person," I object. What he says is actually kind of true. I prefer documentaries and nonfiction books because when a story involves an unexpected twist, which much of fiction does, I usually see it coming. Defensively, I add, "Most people who've read and watched a lot can predict what will happen in a movie; if anything, you should value such wise opinions, not dismiss them."

"Wise. Sure." Felix grabs the big plate and walks to the table.

Felix's parents moved to the United States from the

Soviet Union just as it was collapsing. Their home country of Uzbekistan is, as his dad says in his thick accent, "a land rich with many ethnicities." Felix's face is a mathematical average of all those ethnicities. He's got Slavic cheekbones, Ariel's suntanned look without ever going into the sun, a black unibrow, and—and this has nothing to do with his heritage—a freakishly long ring finger. He looks vaguely Middle Eastern when he frowns (which he rarely does) and Asian when he smiles (which he does a lot, including now).

"You're the best roommate ever," I say when Felix puts a couple of banana pancakes on my plate. "Thank you so much."

Felix nods, and I attack the first pancake with the ferocity that Fluffster unleashes on raisins.

"How are you feeling today?" Ariel asks me carefully, putting down her fork. "You seem to have had an eventful night."

I nod, grateful she's bringing it up herself. "Yeah, about that... Things are kind of hazy in my mind." Thinking about what to say next, I cover my pancakes with a thick layer of the miracle honey Felix's grandparents regularly ship to him from Uzbekistan. "Did a security guard escort me home last night? I think you opened the door, but—"

"Yes, you came with an escort." Ariel picks up her fork.

At the mention of a guy, Felix frowns, making me wonder again if his feelings toward me are as platonic as mine are toward him.

"Promise me you'll avoid that guy in the future," Ariel says as she violently stabs a pancake, and Felix almost imperceptibly nods.

"That should be easy, since I have no idea who he is. His first name might've been Gaius, but that's all I—"

"Did he say or do anything to you?" Ariel's dark eyes regard me with worry.

"I don't think so, but I don't remember for sure." I swallow a small piece of honey-smothered pancake as relief appears on Ariel's face. "Your Valium kicked my ass big time. I had hallucinations and nightmares thanks to that poison. I don't think you should take it under any circumstances."

She frowns and stuffs her mouth with a whole pancake—probably her way of not responding to my plea.

"You should try shrooms for your anxiety," Felix says to her with his mouth full.

"Great idea," I say sarcastically. "Psilocybin will be an excellent substitute for Valium. That way, you'll be seeing things by design instead of by accident."

"There are studies that explored mushrooms as a treatment for PTSD," Felix says. Seeing Ariel's frown deepen at the mention of the condition she denies having, he hastily adds, "It's useful for many other things too, and unlike Valium, mushrooms are naturally occurring."

"Uranium is also naturally occurring," I retort. To Ariel, I say, "Until the FDA approves something as medicine, I'd steer clear of it, especially if it's recommended by Doctor Felix."

She shifts in her seat. "I'm actually trying some alternative treatments. I have a Reiki appointment next week."

Felix kicks my foot under the table, but I don't need his reminder to stay quiet. Though I'm deeply skeptical of Reiki's no-touch massage premise, I keep my opinion to myself. As a med school student, Ariel knows all about controlled studies, so who am I to take away a safe placebo like this? Let someone wave his hands around her body if that means she doesn't take an extra Valium.

"That's a great idea." Felix gets up, grabs a coffee pot, and places it in the middle of the table. "Shrooms can give you a bad trip, but that won't."

"Your performance was amazing, by the way," Ariel says to me in an obvious attempt to change the subject. "Does that mean you'll get the TV show you want so much?"

I grin. "Not yet, but it's a good start."

Ariel sighs. "I still don't get why you want to be a TV magician so badly. You're great at magic, don't get me wrong, but you have such a promising career in finance, and you're just as good at that."

Some of my excitement deflates. For whatever reason, neither of my roommates are particularly supportive of my TV career aspirations. They're not as obvious about it as my mom, but I've always caught a subtle undercurrent of disapproval from them every time I talk about wanting to be a famous magician. I don't get it, because they're my best friends, but it's always been that way. If one of them had gone on TV the way I did last night, that would've been the first thing I would've asked them about, but they're acting like it's just another morning, almost as if they'd like to forget that the biggest break of my performing career happened last night.

"You know I hate working for Nero," I tell Ariel and realize that my phone is still on the charger in my room. As though it were waiting for me to remember it, it rings at that exact moment. Suppressing the instinctual urge to run over and pick it up, I wave my hand toward my bedroom. "See that? It's not enough that I have to be at work by seven a.m.; they're already calling me—and someone even called me last night, on a Sunday."

"But that's just because your boss is an asshole," Felix says. He knows Nero personally, having freelanced for our fund a few times. "What Ariel means is, why not just get a different job, in a bank or another fund?"

I grimace. "Working in finance makes me feel like a cog in a machine that's completely useless to human society." I pour myself a cup of coffee and spoon some sugar into it. "When I perform, I feel like I make people's lives better, even if in a small way."

"So? You could do that without being on TV." Felix blows on his coffee. "You have your restaurant and—"

"Let me ask you a question," I say. "As quickly as possible, name some TV magicians for me."

"David Blaine. Copperfield." Felix says without hesitation. He rubs his dimpled chin and adds, "Also those two German dudes with the white tigers, that British guy you told me about, plus your favorite, Criss Angel."

"See? You didn't name a single woman. In fact, if you put the phrase 'famous magicians' into Google, you'll get a long list of names and pictures, but not one of them will be female."

Ariel sighs again. "So you want to be the first famous female magician."

"I wouldn't exactly be the first." I sip my coffee. "There are some semi-famous female magicians already, but I want to be the first who becomes a household name, like the guys Felix mentioned. I want to inspire more girls to go into magic. It's crazy that in this day and age, a woman can run for president and head up corporations, yet not a single one has become a big name in magic. In any case, it's not all about my ego. I love the expression of awe on people's faces, and—"

"And it's a way for her to safely channel her incessant desire for cons and pranks." Felix chuckles. "Sasha and magic is a match made in heaven."

"I get all that, I guess." Ariel uses her butter knife to cut up another pancake. "It's just that if I could beat the market as she can, I'd sell out and work in finance in a heartbeat."

"No one can beat the market," I say. "Everyone who seems to beat the market is just lucky, including me. Do you know how scary it is to have a job where you always expect your luck to run out?"

"I don't think it's luck in your case," Ariel and Felix both say, almost in unison.

They look at each other and laugh.

Felix gestures for Ariel to speak, so she says, "By the way, how did you know about the earthquake in Mexico? Did you really warn the Mexican government about it?"

"I think I know how she did it," Felix says.

"And you will not say anything." I shake my butter knife at him in a mock threat.

It's actually spooky how good Felix is at guessing the methods behind my effects. He claims he can do so because as a programmer, he's very logical, but I think he secretly watches the twelve-year-olds who expose magic methodology on YouTube, just so he can occasionally show off in front of us.

"But I really want to know." Ariel pouts and makes puppy eyes that would make any male magician give in on the spot. "You have to tell me how you do your tricks."

"Tricks are what hookers do," I say for the tenth time. "I perform effects."

"Fine." Ariel rolls her eyes. "Then can you explain some 'effects?'"

I put the last piece of the pancake into my mouth

and debate if I want to do the effect I prepared for this very occasion.

"I'll make you a deal." I rise to my feet. "I'll show you something, and if you guess how it's done, I'll admit it."

"What about me?" Felix asks. "Can I guess too?"

"No." I put my plate into the dishwasher. "Only Ariel."

"Then I'll just have to guess how you did your TV prediction." Felix wipes his hands on his sweatpants. "And I'll do my guessing in front of Ariel."

"That's blackmail." I rinse my own hands in the sink and demonstratively wipe them with paper towels. "But fine. If Felix guesses how it's done, I'll own up to it as well. But you have to nail it exactly on the very first guess. If you get even one detail wrong, the deal is off."

"This is so exciting." Ariel shovels the rest of the food into her mouth and chews rapidly.

"I'll go get my cards from my room," I say as I head out of the kitchen. "Felix, can you please clear the table? Ariel, can you get your M9 knife?"

"Ooh, a trick using my knife." Ariel jumps to her feet. "I mean, an effect."

In my room, I grab my phone and what I need for the demonstration and return to the kitchen.

Handing Felix a deck of cards, I order, "Shuffle."

He mindlessly shuffles the deck, overhand style.

"I got it," Ariel says, returning to the kitchen. She displays the big Army knife as though she wants to sell it on TV. "Please tell me the trick involves stabbing

Felix. Or how about I puncture his hand, and you make the wound go away?"

"I'll have to work out a method to do that one." What Ariel just suggested would indeed be a great effect, maybe even better than the one I'm about to show. Shoving the idea aside for later, I say, "This will have something to do with those cards in Felix's for-now-intact hands. As Hofzinser, one of the great magicians of the nineteenth century, once said, 'Cards are the poetry of magic.'"

Felix continues to shuffle, and we both look at him sternly, Ariel's eyes beginning to roll.

"Give Ariel a chance to mix those," I say when it's clear he'd keep shuffling until lunch if he could.

Felix grudgingly gives Ariel the deck, and she puts the knife on the table so she can give the cards a fancy riffle shuffle she learned from an ex back in the army.

"Now." I turn my back to her so that Felix can't accuse me of reading secret marks on the cards or reflections in her eyes. "Choose one."

With my peripheral vision, I see Felix's bushy unibrow rise. He knows that this selection process is much fairer than if I were holding the cards in my own hands, as other magicians usually do.

"I got one," Ariel says excitedly.

"Commit it to memory." I catch myself reaching for the knife but stop just in time, not wanting Felix to accuse me of tampering with the weapon.

"Memorized," she says.

"Put it back in the deck and shuffle again," I say

without turning. "Even you shouldn't know where it is."

I hear the riffle of a couple of Ariel's shuffles before she says, "Okay."

Turning around, I point at the center of the table. "Put the deck there."

Ariel complies.

"Now take the knife," I say imperiously.

Ariel looks at Felix and whispers, "No way." She picks up the knife and stares at me, awe already in her gaze.

"Stab the deck." I mime the motion made famous by slasher films. "Use all your strength. Let the knife cut through as many cards as possible."

Hand steady but eyes gleaming with excitement, Ariel raises her arm and brings the knife down on the deck so hard the table nearly topples over.

Her long lashes flutter in surprise at her handiwork.

The knife has only penetrated about halfway into the deck.

She frowns, then glances at the knife still in her hand. "I thought I'd pierce the whole thing and ruin the table."

"Even *you* don't have enough strength for that." I debate whether I should tell them about the research I did on this subject—like the fact that you can stop a .9-millimeter bullet with slightly less than ten decks—but I decide against it, saying instead, "Please take the knife out."

She does.

"Find the first card from the top that doesn't have a knife mark in it, and put it right here, face down." I casually gesture at the same spot where the deck was—center of the table.

Ariel fans out the cards in her hands, locates the card in question, and places it on the table.

Without saying a word, I extend my hand, and she puts the rest of the deck in it.

"What card did you memorize?" Instinctively, I square the deck that's now in my hands.

"The Seven of Hearts." Ariel's eyes are drilling a hole in the card on the table.

"Please turn over that card," I say, my muscles tensing in anticipation.

Both Felix and Ariel bend over the table, and Ariel does as I ask while I take advantage of their distraction.

When the card on the table is revealed as the Seven of Hearts, Ariel squeals like a teenage girl at a Justin Bieber concert.

"And of course"—I spread the deck face up across the table—"you stabbed about twenty cards here. If it was one more or one less card, this wouldn't have worked."

Ariel stares at the faces of the cards and slowly shakes her head.

"I know how you did that," Felix says when Ariel is calmer. "The deck Ariel handled consisted of fifty-two copies of the Seven of Hearts."

I get myself a glass of water and slowly take a sip;

this way, it won't be obvious if I don't comment on what Felix says.

"They're right there and all different," Ariel says, pointing at the cards on the table. "Half are stabbed, half are still whole."

"She switched decks," he says. "While we were distracted by the card on the table, I bet she reached into her pocket with one deck and pulled out another."

I take another sip.

"But the stabbed cards—"

"Pre-stabbed before the trick started." Felix tries to echo my earlier stabbing motion, but it comes out looking like in-air masturbation. "She must've estimated how many you'd be able to pierce, or she asked some buff guy at the gym to do it for her to emulate your freakish strength."

Ariel takes her knife and puts it into the hole of one of the cards on the table. The card and the knife are a perfect fit.

"She must've snuck into your room and borrowed your M9 knife," Felix says preemptively. "Remember, she didn't just say, 'Bring any knife.' She specifically asked you for that one."

I take a larger sip.

"Is he right?" Ariel already looks disappointed—a major reason why the methodology of effects must *always* remain a secret.

I point at the water in my mouth and shrug.

"If it's not how you did it, how about you let one of

us pat your pockets?" Felix says, his cheeks reddening —probably at the thought of him patting me down.

Ariel scratches her head. "You really went through all that trouble just for a trick?"

I take another, smaller—and hopefully noncommittal—swig of water and resist chastising her for using the "t" word again.

"I think you'd better go clubbing with me this Friday," Ariel says, chuckling. "You desperately need to get laid."

A loud snort tries to escape my mouth but only causes most of the remaining water to spray out, though some gets painfully into my nose.

I begin coughing and laughing at my own reaction, but also at the beet-red expression on Felix's face. I didn't think it possible, but he's about fifty shades redder than before. My theory is that he just thought about helping me with the "getting laid" problem— though if he did, I don't know why his blood flooded in the wrong direction.

When I feel semi-normal, I give Ariel a narrow-eyed stare that tries to say, "There's teasing, and there's talking about my nonexistent sex-life in front of Felix. Not cool."

She just looks at me, eyebrows wagging, and I know she wants to reply, "You're just cranky because you haven't gotten any in two years."

And it's true. The last time I had sex was with my college ex-boyfriend, and it seems so long ago that I sometimes worry things might atrophy down there.

Clearly, sharing this factoid with Ariel was a big mistake, and not only because getting laid is so easy for her that she can't relate to my troubles. I bet all she needs to do is crook her index finger at any guy, no matter how hot.

Seeing no dignified way out of this situation, I reach into my pocket and take out my phone. "Oh no," I say, demonstratively looking at the screen. "Someone from work is desperate to reach me."

Unfortunately, I'm telling the truth. Staring me in the face is a text from Nero Gorin himself—and he almost never contacts me at home directly, letting his assistants do the dirty work.

Call me NOW, the text says.

"So, did she switch out that TV prediction too?" Ariel asks the still-blushing Felix, her words reaching me as though from a distance.

I ignore her, my heartbeat speeding up as I look over the record number of missed calls and texts. Something big must be going on at the office, and I'm probably in a lot of trouble.

Dimly, I register Felix saying, "She didn't touch the envelope. Kacie opened it," as I frantically read the first text.

Mr. Gorin is going to present at One Alpha Conference Monday morning. He needs you to get him up to date on RANR.

"Did she ask you to hack into *The New York Times* to get the headline?" Ariel asks as I scan the other messages.

"She mailed that prediction weeks ago," Felix says, but I tune him out, my mind not on my magic for once.

Gorin's assistants wanted me to come into the office on Sunday to bring Nero up to speed on a stock I was researching. It's for his 8:00 a.m. presentation at the Alpha One Conference, a gathering of hundreds of the most important hedge fund honchos. After they couldn't reach me on Sunday, they wanted me to come in at 6:00 a.m. this morning. Then 6:30—an impossible task as it's already 6:37 on my phone, and my commute is half an hour.

I'm late for my regular start time, much less for making it into the office early.

"Then how did you do that, Sasha?" Ariel asks as I slip the phone into my pocket and rush to grab my bag and keys.

"Very well, hopefully," I say automatically, using my rehearsed response. Mentally, I'm plotting the fastest route to the office and trying to come up with excuses for missing all the earlier correspondence.

"I'm so sorry, guys, but I seriously have to run to work," I say as I open the front door. "See you later."

What I don't say is they might see me sooner than they think—if Nero fires me over the phone in the next few minutes. And as much as I'd like to one day leave this job, that day is not here yet.

I still need it to pay the lion's share of our obscene rent.

CHAPTER SEVEN

AS I REPEATEDLY STAB THE elevator down button, I debate if I should call Nero now or face his wrath when I get to the office.

The elevator doors glide apart, postponing my decision.

There's no cell reception in the metal box.

I have one foot inside the elevator when my phone dings with an incoming text.

I check the message instantly.

To my relief, the text is from Darian.

Amazing job last night, it says.

Thanks, I speedily text back. *I'd love to come back if Kacie would have me.*

"Sasha," a familiar breezy voice says from behind me. "I'm so glad I caught you. I need your help with the *direst* emergency."

It's Rose, an older lady I first befriended by helping her recover her lost cat—a sneaky creature that ended up on one of the yachts at the marina down in Battery Park.

Damn Darian and his text. Another second, and Rose would've missed me. But now that I hear the worry in her voice, I can't just leave, so I turn around.

As usual, Rose's makeup is as heavy as it is skillfully applied, her hair expertly colored and her jewelry impeccably chosen to disguise both her age (which I'd estimate as eighty-plus) and her frailty. I'm not fooled by this veneer of vitality, though. Rose has good days and bad; sometimes, she seems as active as a young girl, and other days, she has trouble walking. Judging by her walking stick, this is not one of the good days. In fact, though she usually plasters a mysterious smile on her face, today she looks so troubled that wrinkles show up on her forehead—and I could've sworn she had Botoxed it into submission long ago.

She grabs at the wall, as if to steady herself, and I rush to her, worried. "What's wrong?"

"It's Luci," she says, almost crying. "She's dying."

Of course, it's the damned cat again. She causes Rose nothing but trouble, which is why I mentally renamed the thing Lucifur. Well, because of that, and because she almost ate Fluffster when they met in the hallway on that fateful day. The only reason my little friend survived is because I ran out of the apartment just in time. Before I spooked that evil monster, the look on her face said, "Right there is a noble feast worthy of our majesty."

Lucifur is a Persian with a misleadingly cute

appearance. Her bright green eyes and angelic face are similar to the ones that adorn the Fancy Feast line of cat food. According to her papers (and yes, this cat has papers), her color classification is Chinchilla/Shaded—which must be why she thought Fluffster was destined to be her prey.

"Where is she?" I ask grudgingly. "What has she done now?"

"She's there." Rose lets me lead her into her apartment, and as I enter, I notice that the usual Chanel perfume aroma of the place is spoiled by a faint undertone of feline stomach acid. "She had diarrhea Sunday evening and has been vomiting all night," Rose says. "She was vocalizing previously, but now she's catatonic."

In the middle of the living room, the cat lies curled into a tight little ball.

"Luci," Rose calls out, but the mound of fur doesn't reply.

"Hey you," I say soothingly as I examine the little creature.

The cat doesn't reply.

I know there's no way she could be pretending to be sick, but just in case, I try a gambit that would settle it once and for all, saying, "We have to take her to the vet."

Lucifur must not be faking because the word "vet" would usually send her into a psychotic frenzy. I learned this the hard way when I helped Rose put the beast into her special carrier for her annual checkup.

We now never utter the v-word under any circumstances, just like we never say, "It's time for your bath."

Her last bath is how I got the scars I covered up with the Queen of Hearts tattoo.

Kneeling carefully, I put my hand on the cat's back. Though her fur isn't as heavenly soft as that of a real chinchilla, it might be the softest that a cat's genes are capable of producing. The poor thing is damp and feverish, and this close up, I can hear very faint meow-like sobbing that makes pity claw at my heart.

"When did this start?" I whisper.

"Last night as I was watching you on TV—which was amazing, I meant to tell you. Things got worse later in the night." Rose seems to be on the verge of crying again. "Can you take her to Dr. Katz, please?"

I'm so bummed out by the cat's condition that both Rose's praise and the humor of the vet's name just fly by. I'm as worried about Rose as I am about the cat; if something happens to Lucifur, I'm not sure Rose would be able to handle it.

I have to run to work if there's any chance of salvaging my job, but I can't abandon Rose in this situation. The cat has to get to the vet, of that I'm certain, and I can't ask Felix or Ariel to go in my stead because they have their own Monday morning responsibilities. It would be unfair to get them in trouble. Besides, Rose doesn't know either one of them enough to trust them with her baby. That only leaves

Rose herself, but she must be unable to go; otherwise, she'd be there already.

"I can't locate my door key," Rose says, as though reading my mind. It's clear she'll use any excuse, no matter how lame, rather than admit that she's not feeling well.

"It's not a problem, Rose." I grab the cat carrier. "I'll take her right now."

The cat meows piteously as I gently place her into the cage-like contraption and carry her out of the apartment, with Rose trailing worriedly next to me.

"Thank you so much, Sasha," she says when I enter the elevator. "Call me as soon as you know what's going on."

"I will," I say and press the parking lot button.

Though I usually cab it to work, I decide to take my Vespa to avoid traffic and get the cat to the vet before it's too late. The ride might be slightly more rocky, but I'm an excellent driver—one of the best in the city, in my not-so-humble opinion.

I stick my phone into a special holder attached to the wheel and secure the cat carrier in the back. Poor Luci is looking even more miserable.

"Almost there," I croon. "Please don't die on me."

I make sure my helmet-compatible Bluetooth headset is paired with my phone, put on the helmet, and start the Vespa.

Breaking the speed limit, I zoom through the garage parking lot and fly out onto the street.

The Oculus—the famous downtown four-billion-dollar train station—looms a few blocks away to my right. From this angle, it looks like a dinosaur carcass, though from the windows of our apartment, it resembles the winged dove it was intended to be.

I dodge a killer yellow cab and a couple of suicidal pedestrians as I make a right turn. For as long as I can remember, I've had an uncanny ability to anticipate traffic behavior and adjust accordingly. Like some of my other, similar abilities, I imagine this is just a well-honed skill that began to feel instinctual—a bit like what Malcolm Gladwell describes in *Blink: The Power of Thinking without Thinking*. Hopefully, my traffic Spidey sense will keep me and the cat safe.

Letting a stream of pushy pedestrians pass, I contemplate the swiftest route to the vet, who's located on Canal Street, just as you enter Chinatown. When the flow of people subsides, I resume moving.

Ignoring everything I've read about using phones while driving, I prepare to ask the phone's AI to call Nero.

Before I get a chance to say anything, though, my phone lights up with an incoming video call.

The caller ID shows it to be Makenzie Ballard, or as I know her, Mom. It takes me an extra moment to realize that's who it is, because I'm still not used to her maiden name outside of the credit card security questions. Mom started talking about changing her last name from Dad's—Urban—back to her family name as soon as my parents divorced, but it took over a decade for her to get around to doing it legally.

THE GIRL WHO SEES

Five minutes after her official name change came through, though, Mom started hounding me to do the same, and she refuses to understand that I'm keeping the old last name because of inertia and laziness, not as some subtle way to favor Dad. I could tell her that I haven't spoken with him in forever now, that I ignore his attempts to reconnect, but for some reason, I haven't said anything—partly because I don't want her to delude herself into thinking that I do it for her.

I let the call go to voicemail and pray that Mom butt-dialed me by accident.

No such luck.

The phone rings again, the caller ID displaying Mom's name.

If I don't pick up before I call Nero, Mom will call again, over and over and over. My phone will make an annoying beep each time, and I'll probably crash when I reach to decline her call for the hundredth time. It might be easier to just pick up and dismiss whatever she wants, so I accept the video call.

Keeping my eyes on the road, I view the screen with my peripheral vision—a skill I practice for mentalism, so I can always sneak a peek at something. Mom is wearing her brown pair of horn-rimmed glasses today, her discreetly colored blond-gray hair neatly tucked behind her ears. As usual, she gives off an aristocratic vibe, which makes sense. Her family came from very old money—something she never lets anyone forget despite the fact that the money ran out years before she met and married my dad—who had *new* money.

"Sasha." Even with the headset, I can barely hear her with the clatter of the New York streets around me. "Why did it take you so long to pick up?"

"Can you see around me, Mom?" I stop at a red light. "I'm on my Vespa."

She looks up at my helmeted head. "That explains the abominable noise."

"Is this urgent?" I ask impatiently. "I can get a ticket for driving and talking on my phone."

No cop would be able to tell that I'm on the phone, thanks to my headset, but Mom doesn't need to know that.

"Do you remember my friend Zamantha, with a Z?" she says, unsurprisingly ignoring the not-so-subtle hint that I don't want to talk right now. "Zam Durand?"

How can I forget? As I once wrote in my pre-teen diary, "Zam iz one of Mom'z mozt pretentiouz friendz."

"I remember her," I reply, wondering if Mom will at least acknowledge that last night's TV performance happened, let alone give me some praise.

"Zam invited me to her Paris chateau," she says, and even in my peripheral vision, I see her cheeks flush with an excitement that usually only appears when she buys expensive jewelry. "I was hoping you wouldn't mind me going."

Translation: "you wouldn't mind me going" is Mom speak for "if you wouldn't mind paying for my trip to France." She's not going to ask for money outright unless she's really desperate, but we both know what this is about.

As soon as I graduated from Columbia and moved out of Mom's Upper West Side townhouse, Dad finally stopped sending her checks. Though it might be a bit unreasonable, given how long they'd been divorced by that point, I'm still mad at him about that. As the owner of a booming tech company, he's in a much better position to throw money at Mom than I am.

"Another vacation?" I ask cautiously. "Didn't you just go to your yoga retreat?"

Translation: "Didn't I just pay for your yoga retreat?"

"That was two months ago," Mom says without blinking an eye. "I was dreadfully stressed out. Still am. Zam's chateau is exactly what I need. Don't you remember how peaceful it was? I took you there the year after... you know..."

Nice. She just *had* to remind me that I indeed went to France with her and Dad the year after they adopted me.

She might as well have stimulated the guilt center of my brain with an electrical wire.

"How much is the ticket?" I ask, figuring I can skip putting money toward my "Quit Nero's Fund" savings for a month.

"Twelve," Mom says with distaste.

For someone who spends so much money, she sure doesn't like to talk about it.

"Twelve what?" I nearly run over an old man who

decided to jaywalk across Broadway. "Thousand American dollars?"

She looks at me with an unreadable expression and nods.

"Is it so much because you're going last-minute, or first class?"

Dad had an expression about Mom that went, "When in doubt, pout." And pout is exactly what she does, saying, "Well of course it's for first class. You wouldn't want me to fly with the—"

"I will send you a check for two thousand." I put as much firmness as I can muster into my voice. "You should be able to get a business-class ticket for that. Alternatively, you can fly coach, like most of humanity." I debate if I should tell her that this very conversation increases the chance that I will lose my job and she'll lose her Sasha-shaped piggy bank, but I decide against provoking her into hysterics. Instead, I pleadingly say, "I'm not made of money, Mom."

"Okay." Mom still looks upset but accepts her defeat with grace. "Just please, don't tell anyone I'm flying business class," she adds in a hushed whisper.

"Deal." I pause at a stop sign and wonder with whom I'd share such a vile rumor. Needing to end the conversation, I say, "I really have to get off the phone, Mom."

"That's fine, dear," Mom says. "I'm going to have to call my travel agent and see what she can finagle."

I sigh. Naturally, Mom doesn't use Expedia, or Orbitz, or Priceline, or any one of a million budget traveling sites. She'd risk actually saving money if she used such plebeian modus operandi.

"Bye, Mom."

"Bye," she says and disconnects.

I finally initiate a video chat with Nero, and to my shock, my boss picks up the call personally—I fully expected to be vetted by at least one assistant.

He's standing by the whiteboard in his enormous office, making notes with an erasable marker. His back is to the camera and far enough away that I can see his lean, broad-shouldered frame. His chestnut-colored hair is extra short—he must've just gotten a haircut—and though I can't see his face, I can easily picture his strong chin and prominent cheekbones.

"If it isn't the busy bee finally deigning us with her attention," he says in a deep, low-pitched voice that makes his female assistants ovulate—though if you ask me, it sounds like a blend between a dinosaur roar and a bear growl. "You go on TV once, and that's it? Are you calling to tell me you quit?"

"No," I reply, trying not to give him the satisfaction of sounding defensive. "An emergency came up."

He turns from his writing, and almost instantly, his face fills the screen. He's looking right at me now, and I can't help but notice that despite the upcoming conference, his typical devil-may-care heavy stubble still adorns his face.

"What emergency?" he asks, and if I didn't know any better, I'd swear I saw worry in those blue-gray eyes—but I dismiss such fanciful imaginings. Nero would only worry if the fund lost a bunch of billions overnight, which will never happen, given how shrewdly he runs the place.

I consider coming up with something better than the truth, but Nero is famous for his ability to detect lies. Word is, all he needs to do is hear a company CEO on a quarterly conference call, and he'd know how well the company is really doing. More importantly, Nero loathes BS to such a degree that the risk of getting fired is always lower if you tell him the worst kind of truth.

If he catches you in a lie, you're dead to him.

"My elderly neighbor had a big emergency," I say. It's the truth, but only half of it. I hope he doesn't dig deeper.

"What happened?" There's no empathy behind the question, just mild curiosity.

"It's her cat." I stop on a yellow light so I can lean to the side and show him the carrier behind me. "She's sick."

"The *cat* is sick." Nero makes the question sound like a statement, but I nod anyway.

He stares at me for a moment. His limbal ring—the circle around the iris of the eye—is oddly dark and thick, making the whites of his eyes whiter and the blue-gray deeper. I only notice this due to a magician's fascination with visual illusions, of course—not because I enjoy looking into those eyes, and definitely not because I feel like a rabbit caught in the gaze of a snake.

"You let people take advantage of you," he says, and

I snap out of my daze as the light changes to green. Gritting my teeth, I yank my eyes away from the phone and rev up my gas.

I always knew he was cold, but this just highlights it. Of course he considers helping a nice elderly woman as being taken advantage of.

"Can I bring you up to speed on RANR over the phone?" I ask, ignoring his prior comment.

He looks at his million-dollar Patek Philippe watch and frowns. "We don't have much choice, do we?"

I'm about to launch into my spiel about the company I've researched, starting with their revolutionary new product, when my automotive awareness screams in panic.

Though I don't know what the danger is yet, I do know I've never felt this strong of a warning before.

Momentarily ignoring Nero, I laser focus on my surroundings in the hope that I can prevent whatever it is that's setting off my alarms.

The last thing I want is to kill myself and the cat in a horrible car crash.

CHAPTER EIGHT

THOUGH THE INTERSECTION is bursting with vehicles and people, two targets stand out in my hyperawareness.

An express bus and an ancient Ford Crown Victoria.

The ginormous bus is hurtling toward me in the opposite lane, the driver clearly overeager to pass under the green light while the pedestrians are standing on the sidewalk for a change.

The beat-up Crown Vic is in the lane perpendicular to mine, going so fast that it's bound to run over a few people on the red light—and then T-bone my Vespa.

Without fully understanding what I'm doing, I jerk on the handlebars as I max out the gas.

As my scooter turns, I catch a glimpse of the Crown Vic's driver. It's a man in his fifties, his skin oddly gray with a purplish tint. Something about his face rings a very distant bell, but I quickly lose sight of him, the express bus taking over my whole field of vision.

The bus driver doesn't know he needs to slow down yet.

If my panicked brain miscalculated my current maneuver by just a tiny fraction, in a moment, there will be a Vespa/Sasha/Lucifur-shaped tortilla on the front of the bus—a tortilla the Crown Vic will then scrape off and turn into a human-and-cat-stuffed metal burrito.

In my haste, I pay no mind to any obstacles on the pavement, so I don't realize I've run over the manhole cover until after it happens.

Like a bull at the rodeo, the scooter tries to throw me off.

My heart tries to jump off the Vespa without me.

I squeeze the handlebars with all my might and tighten my thighs until they cramp. When I don't fly off, I vow to buy Ariel another year of gym membership for forcing me to use that gynecological-exam-chair-inspired machine.

Luckily, the carrier with the cat stays on too, but my phone isn't so fortunate—it flies out of its holder and lands somewhere behind me.

Also, I have no idea if the bump has slowed me down enough not to hit the bus.

A second later, I clear the bus by the width of a soap bubble, but before I can exhale in relief, there's a shriek of metal and plastic colliding.

The Crown Victoria has just slammed into the bus.

If I hadn't acted as fast I did, I'd now be sandwiched between them.

Slowing down, I debate what is morally and legally required of me in this situation. The idiot in the Crown Vic is likely dead, but the folks on the bus should be fine, just inconvenienced. Someone should call 911, but my phone is in pieces under the bus.

Seeing at least a dozen people using their cells and gesticulating at the crash, I assume emergency vehicles have been summoned. If I want to save Lucifur, I have to get going again—she just got a shake-up on top of whatever is going on with her, and the vet's office can't come soon enough.

I speed up, and the rest of my path to Dr. Katz's office is blissfully free of collisions.

One advantage of a scooter is that it's easier to find parking for it. I leave my Vespa between two parked cars and unhook the carrier, ignoring a strange fishy smell from a giant puddle nearby.

"Almost there," I whisper to the unresponsive cat. "Please hang on."

The trip up the elevator and through the corridors happens in a blur.

Entering the vet's office, I run up to the receptionist and rattle out, "My name is Sasha, and I have Rose's cat here. She's dying. You have to help me. Please."

The girl launches into action. Before long, the tall and lanky Dr. Katz asks me about the cat's symptoms and takes the carrier away, promising that he'll let me know what's going on after some testing.

I breathe out a sigh of relief. This office is pretty impressive. They've reacted to the emergency better than some places that cater to humans.

"Can I use your phone?" I ask the receptionist.

"Sure," the girl says. "Come around."

I walk over to her desk and realize I have no clue what Nero's phone number is.

"I'm sorry, can you do a search on your computer for me?" I ask. "I need the main number for Gorin Fund."

The girl gets me the number I need, and I call, only to learn that asking the lowliest phone operator to connect me with the head of the fund is not such a simple task.

First, I get an assistant of an assistant, who is an assistant to one of Nero's lowest-ranked assistants. I get bounced around from there, and I'm up two layers of assistants when Dr. Katz comes out, so I ask the grumpy assistant I'm speaking with to hold on for a moment.

The bastard hangs up on me.

"It's a Gastric Foreign Body," the doctor says to me, waving the black-and-white X-ray in his hand. "It's consistent with the symptoms you described."

"A what?"

"Here." He holds the X-ray up to the light.

There's a ghostly outline of a cat—with a key-shaped object in its stomach.

"You're kidding me," I say. "She swallowed Rose's door key?"

"We see this a lot with dogs—with a wide range of objects." Dr. Katz lowers the X-ray. "But it happens with cats too."

It's hard to imagine anything or anyone eating a key, but if I had to nominate a cat who could do something like that, Lucifur would be at the top of my list. The rest of the list would all be cats that look like Hitler.

"So, what now?" I ask. My insides feel cold, as though I myself have a metal object in there. "Will you need to cut her up?"

"No, nothing that serious," Dr. Katz says, a crooked smile spreading over his narrow face. "We'll get it out endoscopically."

When I was younger, Dad had an endoscopy to diagnose an ulcer, but I didn't know it could be done to a cat.

"She will need to be anesthetized," Dr. Katz says when he sees me relax. "There are risks associated with that."

"Is there any other solution?" I ask. "Can she just poop it out?"

Dr. Katz frowns. "I'd highly recommend the endoscopy."

"Okay," I say. "I'm convinced, but this is Rose's decision to make."

"Actually, she filled out a pet care emergency authorization form in your name," the receptionist says, brandishing a paper from her desk.

"That's if we can't reach her," Dr. Katz says. "We need to try."

Fortunately, they have Rose's number in Lucifur's chart—yes, cats have medical charts, and of course, this cat has a thick one.

It takes all but a few seconds of explanation to get Rose to agree to the procedure.

"I knew I didn't just lose that key," Rose says through the speakerphone after Dr. Katz leaves to prep the cat.

"How long will you keep Luci here?" I ask the receptionist while we still have Rose on the line.

"Every patient is different," the girl says. "But we're probably going to keep an eye on her for a few hours after the anesthesia."

"But she'll come home today?" Rose's voice cracks.

"Yes," the girl replies. "We'll keep you both up to speed on her progress."

"I killed my phone on the way here," I say to both of them. "Call my office number if you need to reach me, and I'll get myself a new cell as soon as I can."

"Will do," the receptionist says, handing me a business card with the phone number of the practice on it.

I write Rose's number on the back of the card while Rose herself asks several more questions.

After we hang up on Rose, I excuse myself and rush to my scooter. There's a tiny chance I can still get to the office before the 8:00 a.m. presentation, and I'm determined to try.

When I exit the doctor's building, it takes me a moment to recall where I left my Vespa, but once I do, I run to it and jump on—at the exact moment when a yellow cab drives over the fishy-smelling puddle and sprays the foul substance all over me.

Dark, smelly splotches are all over my pants and shirt.

On any other day, I'd go home to change and get to work late, but right now, I don't have that luxury.

Hopefully, the stuff will dry out and be less disgusting as I ride.

The rest of my drive to the office is like a scene from *The Fast and the Furious*, only on a scooter with a top speed of forty miles per hour.

My clothes don't seem to smell anymore, but the stains remain. If I get to my desk, I could at least cover my shirt with the jacket I keep for days when the office AC spins out of control. Except it's now 7:43 a.m., and Nero needs me to bring him up to speed on the stock before eight.

I sprint through the security desk and keep running until I get to Nero's office.

Venessa, one of Nero's assistants, looks me up and down without bothering to hide her overwhelming contempt. "There you are," she says in a tone many bitchy women think exudes friendliness but really does the opposite. "Mr. Gorin left instructions in the unlikely case you arrived."

I look at Venessa expectantly as I try to catch my breath.

"Since there's no time for you to prep him, you're going to need to personally present at One Alpha." Venessa hands me a laptop, and since I'm too stunned to think at the moment, I just clutch the computer like a life raft. "Use that to prepare what you need on the way to the auditorium."

I'm tempted to use the laptop to do more research on Valium and the nightmares it can cause, because it seems like I've been dropped into my worst one yet.

The building's auditorium can house three hundred people, and One Alpha gatherings always leave the room packed with financial movers and shakers—plus members of the media who usually have to stand.

Venessa marches toward the elevator.

I stand frozen, my feet filled with lead. Aside from my disheveled state, I'm simply not prepared to speak about this stock. I rehearsed my TV act for at least fifty hours, and that was just a couple of lines. Not that being prepared would matter. The mere thought of speaking in front of all those people—

"Why are you standing there?" Venessa snaps, turning to look at me as she punches the elevator button. "Are you going to do your job or not?"

I drag my heavy feet to the opening elevator.

As I step inside, the reflective surface inside the car confirms the stains are still on my clothes.

The doors close.

Venessa wrinkles her nose. "Do you smell fish?"

"I have to prep," I say and open the laptop, hiding my face as I frantically launch PowerPoint and think of what I'll say if I don't freeze up when the moment comes—which I probably will.

RANR is the ticker for Rapid Rabbit Biotech LLC, or (and this is a good joke to mention in the presentation) Rabid Rabbits, as industry insiders have nicknamed them. RANR will soon announce a new product called Focusall, a substance that will make Adderall seem like a sedative in comparison. I reviewed a lot of data on the drug, interviewed test subjects, and even managed to get my hands on a sample. It was when I was on the drug myself that I decided that we definitively, absolutely must get as much RANR stock as we can, high valuation or not. While on Focusall, I finished my usual analysis in a fraction of the time it usually takes, then worked on and completed a dozen other projects, all the while staying as focused as a Zen monk and as happy as a clam.

It was so good, in fact, that instead of flushing the rest of the sample down the toilet, I kept the pills for a rainy day. And as soon as the drug hits the market, I'll find a way to get more—unless they discover side effects, which thus far seem to be mild to nonexistent.

It's a testament to Nero's respect for my analytical skills that he had our traders go on a buying spree of RANR as soon as I recommended it, and without me explaining any of the details. Now it's one of our largest positions, and once—or rather, if—I give this presentation, the stock will likely go through the roof. Undoubtedly, that's why Nero decided to include it in his presentation last minute: because part of the reason for these conferences is to create a sort of self-fulfilling prophecy. If you sway other savvy hedge funders with your pitch, they will jump on the stock and drive up the price, making your investment that much more valuable.

Of course, the main reason for the conference is to shout, "Look at how smart we are at Gorin's fund. Invest with us. Work for us. Don't think about regulating us. Resistance is futile."

Venessa drags me from the elevator and through the corridors, my nose buried in the laptop.

By the time we get to the backstage of the auditorium, I have a couple of very basic slides ready and, more importantly, a rudimentary idea of what I will say. However, none of this silences the insane heartbeat in my ears or slows my ragged breathing, and the world takes on a surreal tint.

Nero is already speaking on the stage. He's introducing me with praising words, and his deep voice seems so amplified in my head that my brain threatens to explode through my eardrums.

"Go." Venessa pushes me onto the stage, and as I walk to the podium on jelly-like legs, the lukewarm applause sounds deafening in my ears.

"You got this," Nero whispers as he vacates the podium.

He must see something he doesn't like in my face, because he takes the laptop out of my numb hands and plugs it in for me.

The hilarity of Nero Gorin doubling as an

audio/video tech doesn't penetrate my dread; all I can focus on is the debilitating conviction that I'm about to have a heart attack.

I take my place behind the podium and try to stand straight. Through the haze of panic, I realize that Nero is still standing next to me—and though I'm too pumped up with adrenaline to be sure, I think his muscular arm might be surreptitiously holding me up.

I'd sell my soul for some Valium right now. The fear I felt on TV is but a tiny echo of what's happening now.

"H-hello," I stutter into the microphone as I behold the crowd.

Three hundred hungry eyes stare back at me from the abyss beyond the stage.

The walls of the auditorium shrink, suffocating me.

Darkness closes in.

CHAPTER NINE

I WAKE up in the air.

Am I flying?

Opening my eyes, I realize that I'm being carried like a bride again. This time, the strong arms belong to Nero, and before I fully understand what's happening, he lowers me onto a gray leather couch backstage.

Is this another inappropriate dream about my boss? Until now, there's only been that one about a kiss—but this looks like a full-on wet dream.

My abstinence is really messing with my head.

He pulls out a phone and dials. "We need an ambulance to—"

Tuning him out, I gather my thoughts. This is *not* a dream. I was on stage and passed out. He's calling 911, but I'm certain what just happened was a panic attack, not a real medical emergency.

"I'm okay now," I say weakly and attempt to sit up.

"You're not," Nero says, hanging up on 911. "Hold on."

He dials another number and says, "Lucretia, join me backstage." He pauses, listening to some reply, then adds, "That's great. Please walk and talk; this is urgent."

He then proceeds to explain to her what happened to me, and it's clear that he also suspects I had a panic attack.

Lucretia Rossi is a shrink, and her job at the fund (as I see it) is to help traders get more confidence—which is a bit like teaching cockroaches survival skills. Analysts rarely, if ever, see her, so the only reason I'm even aware of her existence is because a couple of people have told me I remind them of her. I take that as a compliment since Lucretia is quite striking and is admired at the fund for her intellect. Personally, though, I don't see any physical resemblance between us, aside from hair and eye color, and perhaps the pastiness of our skin.

"Lucretia is almost here." Nero gives me a thorough once-over. "You look like you should be fine, for the moment at least. I'm going to go salvage your presentation."

Before I can reply, he strides back onto the stage, steps onto the podium, glances at my slides on the laptop in front of him, and says, "As this slide suggests, and as many of you already know, we have a long position in RANR."

Still stunned, I listen to Nero speak and fill up with envy. If I didn't know for a fact that Nero is winging this talk from my just-created slides, I wouldn't have ever guessed it. If I could be that comfortable in front of a large crowd, the sky would be the limit for my career as an illusionist.

How do I get to this level of self-assurance?

How do I learn to face a crowd that big?

"Sasha," whispers a female voice to my right. "I didn't alarm you, did I?"

Apparently ninja skills are part of a psychologist's toolkit. That, or Lucretia is a better magician than I because she just pulled off an appearing shrink illusion.

"Hi," I say, hoping that missing time and visual delusions aren't part of whatever is happening to me.

Her red lips curve in a toothy smile. "Forgive me for skipping the pleasantries, but Nero brought me up to speed and I would like to go straight into the therapy, if you don't mind."

I nod bemusedly, feeling a wave of relaxation at the slightly odd cadence of her voice. It's as soothing to my ears as Fluffster's fur is to my palms.

"What sensations do you feel in your body right now?" she asks, studying me with an enigmatic expression.

Damn. The office legends about this woman must be true—she *is* good. I feel a deep compulsion to do exactly as Lucrecia says, so after a moment of introspection, I tell her, "I have an irregular heartbeat and shortness of breath."

"Splendid," she says. "Empty your mind and listen inward. List as many sensations as you can."

"I'm sweaty," I say softly, amazed at how comfortable I am sharing something so embarrassing with a woman I'm speaking with for the first time. "My chest hurt before, but it's better now."

"It's fortuitous that you remember the chest sensations," she says, and I realize she has a faint accent of some kind. "Can you list more?"

"I thought I was going crazy," I say, and she nods encouragingly. "I also thought that I could be ill."

"How about your musculature?"

"My lower back is stiff," I say, realizing just now that it's the case. "Overall, I'm pretty tense."

"Focus on these sensations." Lucretia's jet-black hair covers her right eye, so she hides the stray strand behind her pale, unpierced ear. "Study them. Commit them to memory. Awareness of these changes in your body helps you stay in control. It tells you that you're not irrational, and that you're not having a heart attack. You're merely experiencing symptoms that you can learn to mitigate."

I sit quietly and follow her instructions. Aside from all the sensations I've already described, I'm tired and a little lightheaded, so I share that with her.

"Now I want to coach you." She puts one hand over her breasts and another on her belly. "Put your hands like this."

I do as she says.

"Not quite." Lucretia scoots toward me on the couch until our sides almost touch. She takes my right hand and moves it closer to my belly button. And though I usually would find a stranger's touch disturbing, with her, it seems perfectly natural—her ice-cold fingers are actually pleasantly refreshing on my skin.

"Close your eyes so that you can focus on your breathing and on the movement of your stomach under your left palm. Your right palm should soon become stationary," she murmurs almost into my ear, her voice hypnotic. "You're breathing into your lower abdomen. This is called diaphragmatic breathing."

Closing my eyes, I do as she says. Some of my symptoms, especially the ragged breathing, improve.

"Gently slow your breathing," she says, her voice even softer and more melodious. "Count mentally to five as you inhale, and count to five as you let the air out."

I follow the directions, amazed at how effective this is. The mumble of Nero's presentation and the applause from the crowd seem distant now, as does my fear.

"Now we'll work on your muscles," Lucretia says. "Curl your toes as you inhale; relax them as you exhale."

This reminds me of a visualization meditation a hippie counselor had us do at camp. The similarity grows stronger as Lucretia names more muscles around the body to contract and relax.

By the time she has me relax my forehead muscles, I'm as calm as an underground lake.

The serenity lasts a few minutes before I start to get

antsy from just sitting and breathing, and I wonder how she isn't bored with this already.

"This is great," I say after another couple of minutes, when I can't keep still anymore. Opening my eyes, I ask, "What's next?"

"In order to get proper privacy, it would be preferable for us to go to my office," Lucretia says. "Can you walk?"

I nod.

"Good." She gets up. "Try to breathe slowly as you walk. Treat it as exercise."

Getting up, I follow her suggestion. Rather than treating it as exercise, something I associate with "pain and gain," I tackle this the same way as I learn new sleight-of-hand techniques. Whenever I need a new finger-flicking move for a routine, I rehearse it over and over, until the move becomes second nature and I can do it in my sleep. In this case, it might be literally true; if I practice breathing slower for long enough, my breathing overall, including during sleep, might slow down.

Breathing slowly while walking is extremely challenging, though, and by the time I plop onto a brown leather chaise in Lucretia's office, I take great pleasure in ignoring my breathing completely and examining my surroundings instead.

Unlike the rest of the building, which screams "ultra-modern," Lucretia's office has a last-century feel to it. Across from me is an antique-looking bookshelf filled with paper books, and instead of blinds, intricate curtains cover the glass walls of the office.

Lucretia pulls those curtains closed, creating a theater-like ambience, and gracefully lowers herself into her large, throne-like chair.

"Anything you say to me is protected by doctor-patient confidentiality," she begins, and proceeds to explain my privileges in detail, with the key point being that no one—not even Nero—can make her disclose what I share.

"Got it," I say, wondering what kind of secrets she expects me to tell her.

"Splendid." She steeples her fingers and looks at me like I'm the most interesting person in the world. "In that case, I'd like you to tell me why you think you felt so anxious."

Like earlier, I'm overwhelmed with an almost unnatural ease in her presence. Though I intellectually know that you're supposed to confide in a therapist, I never thought I'd be so eager to do it. I feel almost a compulsion to share with her my deepest and darkest secrets—things I don't even like to think about, let alone speak out loud.

"My earliest memory is at JFK airport," I say, listening to my own words in surprise. "I was lost. Scared. I had to ask someone, anyone, for help, but I was too afraid to do so. There were just too many people. They were all so big. They spoke so fast."

Pausing, I realize that my elevated heartbeat and a

few more of the troubling symptoms are back, so I slow down my breathing as she taught me.

The empathy on Lucretia's face is so genuine it's easy to forget that this is merely her job. "Why were you lost?"

"I don't know. My parents—my adoptive parents, that is—think that my biological parents lost me at the airport that day, but I can't be sure."

"So what happened?" she asks. Yet again, something about her piercing gaze makes me want to share this with her, even though I've never spoken about it with anyone, not even Felix and Ariel.

"I was overwhelmed. Curled into a ball at one of the terminals," I say, my breathing speeding up despite my attempt at control. "Mom—the woman who ended up adopting me—saw me. She and Dad were going on vacation. She talked to me, calmed me down, and initiated the search."

Lucretia sits utterly still, as if she thinks that even taking a breath might spook me—and perhaps that's true.

"Mom convinced Dad, her then-husband, to cancel their Fiji trip and help me," I continue. "At first, everyone thought my biological parents were flying somewhere—this was an airport, after all. However, no none could figure out who they were. Every couple traveling with a child my age had their kid with them, and nobody reported me missing. Later, when the police got involved, they couldn't figure out who I was either. I was probably three years old, because I held up three fingers when someone asked me my age, and the only other thing I knew was that my name was Sasha. I didn't know my last name or where I lived. My parents aren't even sure I'm an American. The name Sasha is more popular in Eastern Europe, and I enunciated English words very deliberately when I spoke. But then again, many kids speak funny—"

A phone rings, bringing me out of the trancelike state.

It's Lucretia's office phone, and she gives it a look so scathing it's a wonder the thing doesn't melt.

Shifting uncomfortably in my seat, I practice the slow breathing again as I try to figure out why I overshared with the therapist. I guess getting the truth out of me is her job, but still, I can't believe I blathered on like that. Could that incident at the airport really be the root cause of my fear of public speaking? It was the first thing that popped into my head when she asked about it, but if that's the case, does that mean this realization will help me eventually speak (and more importantly, perform effects) in front of large groups of people?

The phone doesn't stop ringing, so Lucretia picks up.

"It's the ambulance," she tells me, and the way she says it, it sounds like she just barely omitted an f-word.

"Oh, I don't think I need that anymore," I say, my face heating up with remembered embarrassment.

"I concur, but Nero insists."

"Fine," I say, getting up.

"Before you go…" She stands up and looks at me intently. "You should see me again, so we can finish this session. And please, consider seeing me regularly going forward."

"I thought you only saw traders," I blurt out.

"My services are available to everyone in Nero's employ," she says, arching her sharply defined eyebrows. "I'm here to make sure everyone functions optimally—especially the people he takes interest in."

"Okay." I look into the depths of Lucretia's lapis-blue eyes and wish we really did look alike.

The phone rings again, and with the look she gives it, I half expect her to rip it out of the desk.

"I'd better go," I say, careful not to commit to returning. I have to think long and hard about whether I'm comfortable seeing a therapist on a regular basis, especially at a job I consider transient.

"I hope to see you soon," she says instead of a goodbye. She must've detected some of my reluctance.

In a daze, I make my way downstairs before the ambulance people come up. I hope I can get them to go away before the whole firm learns about my embarrassing incident.

Nero is downstairs, talking to an EMT guy. I catch Nero's gaze, and I could swear he momentarily looks relieved. Then his usual arrogant expression is back, and I decide I must've imagined it.

"I don't want to go to the hospital," I say, doing my best not to sound like a petulant child.

"You fainted in front of half of Wall Street," Nero

THE GIRL WHO SEES

says. "If I don't send you to get checked out, my lawyers will never let me hear the end of it."

"Well, why didn't you say that before? Making lawyers happy is my life's ambition. I've been slipping them Zoloft for months now, but if they require me to go to the hospital too…"

The EMT guy chuckles, and Nero gives him a stern glare.

I'm not sure why I'm even fighting Nero on this. Even going to the hospital is more fun than my usual day here at the office—and here is my boss, pretty much ordering me to slack off. Then I remember one reason why I need to be by my desk.

"I destroyed my phone earlier, when I tried to bring you up to speed on the way here," I tell Nero.

"How can I forget?" he says, his face noticeably darker. "I thought you crashed at first; then I realized what really happened."

"Well, the vet might call my desk number and—"

"Right. The cat." He sounds like a zealot charging me with heresy.

I frown at him. "Yes, the cat. What, are you allergic?"

"I'm allergic to absurdity." Nero reaches into his pocket, takes out a phone that's a replica of the one I broke, fiddles with it for a minute, and hands it to me.

I reluctantly take the phone. It's the same Android model that everyone at the fund gets on their first day at work—something to do with securing our correspondence. Like everyone else, I use mine for calls outside of work in order to avoid carrying multiple phones.

"But this is yours," I tell Nero, looking at the EMT guy for support and getting none.

"I'll have Venessa get me another." Nero waves his hand dismissively, like the two grand these phones cost is but a penny to him. "She will also route your desk calls to this number."

"Sounds like I'm going to the hospital then," I say and surreptitiously check if he left any of his emails or texts in the phone. Unfortunately, the device is reset to factory defaults, which must be what Nero did when he was fiddling with it.

"Here." He hands me a wad of bills. "Hospitals are expensive."

I gape at the money in shock. "I have health insurance."

"There's a deductible," Nero says, his eyes narrowing. "Take the cash."

I stuff the money into my pocket, mumble a thanks, and storm out of the building, the EMT guys on my tail.

Before someone can suggest I get on a stretcher or something equally humiliating, I beeline for the ambulance, jump into it, sit down on a bed, and practice the breathing technique Lucretia just taught me.

———

THE TRIP to the hospital is as useless as I expected it to be. My heart and brain are scanned via various methods, and the verdict is that I'm as healthy as a grass-fed, free-range, organic, non-GMO horse.

On my cab ride back to the office, I make the new phone completely mine by logging into all accounts to set up my email and other minutia. I then call the vet and learn that the key is out of Lucifur's stomach and she's now recovering from anesthesia. They assure me they'll call when I can pick up the cat after work.

Back at work, I run to the cafeteria and grab a giant salad for lunch, so I can eat it at my desk as I research a couple of pharmaceutical companies we're thinking about adding to our portfolio.

The call from the vet comes at 8:30 p.m. as I'm eating a bean burrito for dinner.

Lucifur is finally ready for pickup.

I quickly wolf down my food and head for the elevator, ignoring the half-envious, half-dirty looks of my coworkers. They're probably going to work for at least a couple more hours, but then again, they care about their careers and I don't.

Obeying speed limits and traffic lights, I zoom on my Vespa toward Chinatown. I'm a few minutes from my destination when the Spidey sense that saved me earlier raises a new alarm.

My breathing turns fast and shallow, but I don't utilize Lucretia's calming techniques—if I'm about to crash, I want to be alert so I can avoid it.

The problem is that I don't see any dangerous scenarios in front of me.

I drive super carefully for a couple of frantic heartbeats until I realize what's going on.

The danger is behind me.

A silver Dodge Charger is following me much too closely.

CHAPTER TEN

IF I HAD to bet my life on it, which is sort of the case right now, I'd say that the driver of the Charger is trying to catch up with me so he can steamroll over my scooter.

Hoping that I'm just being paranoid, I switch lanes.

The Charger switches into my lane.

Figuring a little detour would be a small price to pay to lose the idiot, I make a sharp right turn.

In my mirror, I see the Charger appear behind the corner.

Could this still be some weird coincidence?

Speeding up, I feel the bean burrito like a cold piece of granite in my stomach.

The car behind me revs its engine.

I make a left.

The Charger follows.

Ignoring the red light, I turn back onto Broadway,

hoping the larger street will provide more opportunities to lose my pursuer.

With a screech of tires, the Charger turns onto Broadway, squelching any remaining doubt that he's following me.

Maxing out the gas again, I cut in front of a yellow cab, ignoring the angry honking.

My pursuer switches lanes and soon lines up with me.

I catch a glimpse of the driver's face. It's a man in his forties, his skin sickly gray. He looks vaguely familiar, but there's no time to dwell on how and why I might know him.

It might be my imagination, but I could swear the guy is about to swerve into me.

To avoid the possible collision, I decide on a desperate maneuver. There's a tiny gap between an SUV and a Lexus to my right, so I twist the handles and pump the gas, hoping the Lexus driver is alert enough not to flatten me.

The smell of burned rubber hits my nostrils as the Lexus driver hits the breaks, shouting obscenities. But as I'd hoped, the gap between him and the SUV is much too small for my pursuer to squeeze through, so I lose sight of the Charger—which hopefully means he loses sight of me.

Taking advantage of my short reprieve, I swerve onto the sidewalk, weaving between confused and annoyed pedestrians as I scream, "Excuse me," over and over.

If this were rush hour, I'd have run over someone's foot already, but even as is, I can't get too far this way.

I notice a thick oak nearby and turn toward it. Getting to the tree, I stop completely and jump off, leaning the scooter against the trunk before running to the Duane Reade pharmacy that's a dozen feet away.

The guy at the register must be extra slow because there's a long line. I push my way through until I'm deep inside the store, and then I look back at the road through the giant storefront window.

This is when I see something that will probably make the evening news.

Ignoring the cars and pedestrians in its way, the Dodge Charger is flying at my parked scooter.

Hairs stand up on the back of my neck as I watch the car hit a large man—who flies over the hood and rolls over, landing on the pavement.

The grill of the Charger hits the back tire of my scooter with a nails-on-chalkboard screech.

Pedestrians scatter as the scooter flies at the window that I'm currently staring through. The Charger doesn't slow, though—not until it catches the poor Vespa mid-rotation and pins it against the window like a butterfly.

Vespa parts rain onto the sidewalk, and the glass shatters into a shower of shards.

The gray-skinned guy's fate is a lesson in the importance of buckling your seatbelt. Like a crash dummy, he flies out of his broken windshield and topples the Hallmark shelf in front of us as if it were a house of cards. A jagged piece of glass is sticking out of his eye socket—there's no doubt he's a dead man.

A woman to my right screams.

I lose my dinner burrito on the floor. When my heaving stops, acting on strange autopilot, I head for the exit, elbowing my way through the gawkers. The idea to leave the pharmacy must enter everyone else's mind too, so before I'm halfway out, I'm caught in a stampede that carries me out to the street and away from the crash.

Sirens are already blaring in the distance, so I don't bother calling 911.

Without a firm plan in mind, I jaywalk across the street and sprint toward Canal Street without looking back at the site of the crash.

Two blocks later, I realize I'm not in good enough cardio shape to keep up this pace all the way to the vet, so I rudely steal a cab from a guy in a suit.

When the cabbie tries to say something snide, I thrust a crisp hundred from the stack Nero gave me earlier and tell him, "No change if you can get me to Canal Street in four minutes."

I don't get to catch my breath, in part because the cab makes it to my destination in three minutes—clearly an overachiever.

"Please wait for me," I say as I slam the door behind me. I imagine he will, hoping to get another huge tip.

As I vault over the steps of the vet's building, I let myself fully register what happened.

A guy followed me, and I think he wanted to ram into me.

Why would someone want to do that?

Maybe it was a case of mistaken identity. Could this guy hate a woman who rides a Vespa, someone I just happen to look like?

With the helmet on, this is semi-plausible.

No, that doesn't seem right. Plus, I did have the feeling that I'd seen his face before—and now that I'm not in a high-speed chase, I even know where.

He was one of the corpses in the nightmare about the morgue.

That's insane, of course, but there could be a logical explanation. Perhaps this guy is a serial killer who likes to kill via car crashes à la Tarantino's *Death Proof*. For whatever reason, maybe because of the Vespa, he chose me as his victim and has been following me for days. I might've seen him in my peripheral vision a few times, and the dream I had earlier was a warning my subconscious mind decided to send to my conscious one.

Something else occurs to me. The pale driver who almost crashed into me this morning also looked very similar to a corpse in the morgue nightmare.

Does this mean I'm facing a team of serial killers? Do they even work as teams?

Whatever their reasons, one man is dead for sure—that glass shard in his eye will haunt me forever. The other should at the very least be hurt, and possibly dead, too—depending on whether he buckled his seat belt, and whether his ancient Crown Vic had air bags. Still, I should call the police and explain what happened to me in case the first guy survived, or the hypothetical serial killer team is larger than two members. But if I do call the cops, will I get in trouble for leaving the scenes of these accidents?

I'll need to research this when I get home, and maybe call a lawyer.

I open the vet's office door and greet the receptionist.

A couple of minutes later, Dr. Katz hands me a carrier with Lucifur. The cat is still sedated, but nevertheless looks a million times healthier than this morning. "Our Majesty is weary," she seems to say with her green eyes. "Quickly, my vassal, take us home, and you may yet avoid the lash."

"Here." The doc gives me a small plastic bag with the key inside.

I take the bag with the tips of my fingers and, without overanalyzing, stick it in my pocket. "Thank you for saving her."

"You're welcome," Dr. Katz says. "I've already talked to Rose about how to take care of Luci, so you're good to go."

I leave the office and find that the cabbie did indeed wait for me.

When we arrive at Battery Park, I give him a great tip, though not as exuberant as before.

On the elevator ride up, I can't help but come back to the attempt on my life. I've dismissed my hazy memory of the attack in the TV studio as a delusion, a nightmare, or a hallucination brought on by Valium— but what if at least some of it was based on reality? Something about that attacker was similar to the guys in the Crown Vic and the Dodge Charger. Also, assuming I did dream up the studio attack, could that dream have been brought about by my subconscious trying to tell me that there's a third man in the hypothetical serial killer club?

I decide to call the police as soon as I hand over the cat, consequences be damned. Also, I will call Darian and ask him what happened last night. He'll probably think I'm crazy, and I'll have to kiss future help from him goodbye, but I need to know.

In any case, would Darian be wrong to think I'm crazy? I feel fine, but people with mental illness don't always realize it. True, my brain scans were exemplars of perfection, but I don't think most mental illnesses show up on such scans. And yes, I also talked to a shrink today—but I only told her about the symptoms related to my fear of public speaking. She'd have to be psychic to diagnose me on what little she had to go on.

Ultimately, it comes down to this: if I'm so crazy that I imagined those accidents so vividly, I'm too far gone. I might as well act as though I'm normal until I wake up in a padded room.

It's a bit like free will and consciousness. As an illusionist, I find the idea of free will being an illusion —something some scientists and philosophers postulate—very appealing. Minor examples of this abound, such as this morning, when Ariel thought she had a free choice but could really only select the Seven of Hearts for the deck-stabbing effect. On a larger scale, the laws of physics predetermine the state of my brain at any given time, and a powerful enough quantum supercomputer could theoretically predict what state my brain might be in. And yet, I think we ought to act as though we do have free will—like with the "crazy" scenario, it's the only way to exist that makes sense.

Similarly, some scientists state that consciousness is another illusion. What I think they mean is that our brain is a chemical computer, and what we think of as consciousness is what it feels like for the meat computer to run its computations. But again, in everyday life, the only logical way to behave is as though consciousness is real.

The elevator doors ding and bring me out of my *Intro to Philosophy* musings. I pick up the carrier and make my way to Rose's door, realizing I've never visited her after work before. What if she goes to sleep at nine p.m., like my mom? But no. Even if she usually goes to bed early, today she'd certainly wait for the cat to return.

I ring the bell.

There's no response for almost a minute. Maybe my early-to-bed theory was spot on after all?

The door opens.

Rose isn't at the door. A man stands there instead.

A man I'd expect on a cover of a magazine, not in the apartment of my elderly friend.

He has an imposing brow, and his pale face is extremely symmetrical, as if carved out of ivory. Nothing this mathematically flawless can be biological, can it? His shiny black hair flows down to his shoulders, the waves reminding me of posters at salons, and his eyes are so dark that they seem to absorb the light of the hallway, like black holes. His alluring lips are set in a disapproving line as he stares at me. It's as if nature wanted to practice that dark and brooding look on his face and came close to perfection.

I clear my suddenly dry throat. "I'm here to see Rose." I raise the cat carrier as explanation. "Who are you?"

"Sasha," Rose says over the man's wide shoulder. "I thought you'd just be getting off work right now."

The handsome stranger turns to let Rose see me.

"I left as soon as I got the call from the vet," I say, and when I catch her gaze, I look very pointedly at the chiseled face that should be our main topic of conversation.

"Oh, where are my manners?" Rose takes the carrier and looks worriedly inside it, then glances up at us. "Vlad, meet Sasha. Sasha, this is Vlad."

"Hi, Vlad," I say, giving him the charming smile I use to put spectators at ease before blowing their minds with a particularly devious effect.

"Hello, Sasha. It's a pleasure to meet you." He pronounces my name with the same hard "sh" as Felix's parents—which they tell me is the Russian, not Uzbek, way of saying it. Despite that, and his Russian-sounding name, he has no detectable accent. "Rose told me a lot about you," he continues.

I'm tempted to say, "She never mentioned you," but depending on who he is to her, that might sound rude.

"Vlad is my nephew," Rose says, discerning my confusion. "He goes to Whole Foods for me."

Until now, I thought she was using an online grocery delivery service, like my roommates and I. Whole Foods —or "Whole Paycheck," as Felix insists on calling it—is indeed more Rose's style, so I'm glad she has this secret nephew to help her out. Though if he is her helper, where was he this morning, when the cat needed the vet?

Rose steps away from Vlad and lets the cat out of the carrier. Lucifur stumbles out drunkenly, hisses viciously at Vlad, and heads toward the kitchen.

Okay, so maybe Rose didn't ask Vlad to help because the cat hates his guts? Then again, I don't think the cat is a huge fan of me either.

"You should join us for dinner," Rose says before I can head back to my place. "I have the table all set up."

A new theory occurs to me. Is Rose playing at matchmaking?

She's asked about my love life a few times in the past, so maybe she's disappointed by my lack of a boyfriend and has decided to take matters into her own hands. If that's what's happening, I have to hand it to her—Vlad is an impressive specimen. Though Rose should've realized that a guy this good-looking wouldn't settle for a non-supermodel me.

Could this be why he looks so morose? Because he's disappointed with her matchmaking?

I'm about to politely refuse the offer of dinner when my treacherous stomach rumbles so loudly that the cat comes back to give me a narrow-eyed stare.

Oh, well. My dinner burrito did escape before I got a chance to digest it, so even though I don't feel particularly hungry, I should probably force a meal into my stomach—else I risk waking up to rummage through the fridge in the middle of the night.

When we enter the kitchen, the table is set with candles and a vase with fresh flowers—a romantic ambience that supports my matchmaking theory. On Rose's left is a barstool, and Lucifur is sitting there. A tiny tea saucer with Fancy Feast on it indicates that this is Her Majesty's personal eating space.

Rose makes me sit to the left of the cat, with Vlad to her right. Being so far apart from Vlad doesn't support the matchmaking theory, but maybe Rose has some reason for this.

Without asking, she puts a mound of something on my plate.

"It's buckwheat with an assortment of mushrooms," she explains as she gets some for herself. "The herbs are from my mini-garden."

She doesn't give Vlad any food, and when she notices my glance at the empty space in front of him, she rubs her intricate pearl necklace and says, "Vlad already had his meal."

Vlad grunts disapprovingly for some reason. Are his eating habits a state secret?

"Do you like history?" Rose asks me. "Vlad was just telling me fascinating stories about Catherine the Great." She gives her nephew an adoring look. "He's a huge Russian history buff and tells it so vividly—as if he were there." She chuckles at something that I assume must be an inside joke, but he looks even more somber.

"Sure." I taste a spoonful of the grain, enjoying the flavors exploding on my tongue.

"Her Russian was horrible in the beginning." Vlad puts his pale hand on the table in front of him, his eyes firmly on Rose's face, as though I'm not in the room.

"You have to give Sasha context, dear." Rose puts her hand over Vlad's and looks at me. "In case you didn't know, Catherine wasn't Russian; she was born Sophie von Anhalt-Zerbst."

"And she allowed those close to her to call her by that name." Vlad looks distant as he says this. "One of the many rewards she bestowed upon her lovers."

The word "lovers" makes Rose frown for some reason, but Vlad just delves into a story of how Catherine the Great gifted one lucky ex a thousand serfs—which leads into a history lesson about the Russian serfs of that era, and how they could be treated like slaves and gifted among the nobles.

As I listen, I wolf down the buckwheat with

undignified gusto, my appetite having returned with a vengeance. I also observe a strange pattern of behavior that becomes more obvious throughout the history lesson.

Rose and Vlad are acting way too incestuously for aunt and nephew.

She touches his hand a lot, he actually smiles at her (which looks out of place on that grimly handsome face), and there's a chemistry between the two that's not platonic at all. Did I misread the whole thing as matchmaking in a bout of wishful thinking?

Could they be together?

Despite the evidence, I find it hard to accept. Their age difference is huge. He looks to be in his late twenties or early thirties, which makes Rose old enough to be his grandmother. Also (and I know it's a shallow logic), Rose looks great, but not Vlad-great. Going by the photos on her walls, she was in his league when she was young, but no matter how well she has taken care of herself (and it's clearly an obsession of hers), there comes a point when the decades stack up and entropy catches up with us.

It briefly occurs to me that this could be a fetish hookup for Vlad, but as I study them closer, I dismiss the idea. They mesh together like best friends, reminding me of an old married couple who's lived a long "happily ever after." Does this mean they've been together for a while?

Could Rose have seduced him when he was in high school?

I begin to feel like a voyeur in the middle of what Rose clearly keeps as a secret relationship. So I finish my plate, look for a pause in the Russian history lesson, and say, "That was so yummy, Rose, but I hope you don't mind if I go. I've had a crazy day, and I want to be in bed when the food coma hits me."

"Of course," Rose says, looking so startled I wonder if she forgot I was there for a moment.

"It was nice to meet you," Vlad says in the friendliest tone he's used with me tonight. Clearly, he loves the idea of me leaving. "Thank you for taking Luci to the vet."

"No problem, and thank you for dinner," I say. "And for the entertainment."

"Get some good sleep," Rose says as I head out of the apartment. "We'll talk soon."

Exiting out into the hallway, I plod toward my apartment, my legs heavy with the encroaching food coma and the post-adrenaline slump.

As I pass by the elevator doors, the light above it lights up, indicating an arrival.

I stop to look at the door because it could be Ariel—she arrives around this time. It could also be Felix, though it's a bit early for him.

The doors start to open, and a putrid stench hits my nostrils. It's so strong that I'm instantly on the verge of losing my second dinner.

The doors slide farther apart, and I gape at the arrivals in shock.

The gray-skinned driver from this morning, the

one from behind the wheel of the Crown Victoria, is inside—and he is not alone.

The Dodge Charger driver, the second guy who tried to kill me, is there with him.

The shard of glass is still sticking out of Mr. Charger's left eye, while his right one stares at me emotionlessly.

I stagger backward.

The two men leap into motion.

CHAPTER ELEVEN

LEGIONS OF THOUGHTS fight for my attention.

How can the guy with the chunk of glass in his eye be alive?

How come no one stopped him on the way here? Did they think Halloween came early?

How can both of them be walking after what they've gone through?

And why do both look exactly like the guys in my morgue dream?

Suppressing these mystifying questions for the moment, I prioritize survival and spin around, my hand diving into my pocket for the keys to my apartment.

Shuffling steps echo in the corridor behind me.

The hallway becomes a tunnel as my vision desperately zooms in on my apartment door.

Without attempting to even out my ragged breathing, I sprint.

I reach the door in two leaps, but my hands shake when I try to insert the key.

The horrible stench intensifies, and all my muscles tense as something brushes my shoulder.

I sink into a squat as I pivot, key clutched tightly in my fist.

Mr. Crown Vic's hand whooshes by my shoulder as I slice at my attacker's body with the key.

The tiny piece of metal doesn't even scratch his shirt.

Before I can straighten my legs, Mr. Charger flanks me on the right.

I stab at his leg.

The key doesn't pierce his pants, but it should at least hurt a little. Then again, we're talking about a man who shows little cognizance of the shard of glass sticking out of his eye.

Instead of reacting to the tiny prick of the key, Mr. Charger grabs my neck with his left hand. Dimly, I notice that his right arm is hanging limply at his side, as though broken.

The guy must be a powerlifter because his grip on my neck is stronger than if Ariel were to have me in her clutches. I claw at his hand with all my strength, but no matter how much I try to pry his fingers apart, his hold on my throat just gets tighter.

My feet slide on the floor as he drags me toward the opposite wall.

Through the heartbeat pounding in my ears, I hear a door slam. Maybe a neighbor just saw what's happening and called the cops? Even if that were the case, if my attacker keeps choking me like this, I won't survive long enough to be rescued by the police.

Slamming me against the wall, he pushes me up.

My feet leave the floor.

Frantic, I kick him in the groin.

He doesn't seem to register my kick and keeps raising me higher until his gray face is even with my shoulder.

White blotches of oxygen deprivation invade my sight.

There's a scuffle in my peripheral vision, but I can't make out what it is. With my luck, it's probably Mr. Crown Vic joining his buddy.

The worst thing about the stress symptoms brought on by suffocation is that you can't do breathing exercises to calm down. After so many seconds without air, I'm approaching a point of no return.

Something inside me snaps, and the more primitive, lizard part of my brain takes over.

I squeeze my hand over the key so hard the sharp edges pierce my skin, and with zero hesitation, I stab at my attacker's face.

The key goes into my enemy's one remaining eye, like a spoon into Jell-O.

I yank the key out of the gory hole.

Unfathomably, he continues to squeeze my neck, unfazed.

I kick him again, but it's like kicking a wall. I flail

harder, my body wasting its remaining strength on useless convulsions.

My consciousness is fading faster.

It might be an artifact of all the white flecks messing up my vision, but I think I see white hands grab my tormentor by the neck.

With a sickening crunch, my attacker's head separates from his body, and I see Vlad—the owner of the white hands.

Though my enemy has no head anymore, his grip on my throat doesn't loosen.

Vlad grabs my attacker's wrist and elbow and violently pulls.

The arm that was holding me rips into two pieces, a bone sticking out where the elbow used to be. Only the detached hand is at my neck now, like Thing in *The Addams Family*.

Vlad rips the hand off my neck, throws it on the floor, and stomps on it with a viciousness arachnophobes reserve for spiders.

Gasping for air, I slide down the wall.

Vlad goes on a stomping rampage. His foot comes down hard on the glass sticking out of the detached head, pushing the shard all the way into the skull, and then more stomping follows, with bones crunching and body parts exploding all around us.

I scramble for my apartment door.

My savior might be more dangerous than my earlier attackers.

At the very least, he's more savage than they were.

Lunging for the door, I get the key ready for rapid insertion.

The sounds of bones breaking cease, which means Vlad must've found a reason to stop his grisly task.

I stick the key into the lock and turn it so hard I scape the skin off my fingers.

The door unlocks, and I shove it all the way open, but before I can enter, a powerful arm blocks my path.

"Who controlled them?" Vlad's face is a mask of such ugly fury that I can't believe I found him attractive only minutes prior.

"Let me go," I croak out, ducking under his arm.

He grabs for my shoulder but gets my shirt.

The material rips as he spins me around to face him.

His eyes are mirrors—like the eyes of the men who wore all black in my TV studio maybe-not-nightmare.

"Who controlled them?" he demands again, and this time, his voice seems to take over the universe.

"I don't know." I somehow find the strength to pull away, leaving a part of my shirt in his grip as I take a step back, nearly tripping over the threshold.

His nostrils flare, but he makes no move to come after me. "Invite me in," he commands through gritted teeth. My reflection in his mirrored eyes is so translucently pale you can almost see the living room through me.

His request is utterly unreasonable, yet something inside me makes me yearn to comply.

Dazedly, I fight the compulsion as a flurry of motion on the floor catches my attention.

Fluffster is standing between me and Vlad.

To my shock, the chinchilla makes a sound that resembles a hybrid between an angry bird's chirp and a snake's hiss.

Vlad looks down, his eyes widening as the mirror effect fades. "Domovoi?"

Fluffster stands on his back legs and chirp-hisses again.

I fully expect Vlad to kick my furry friend, and if he does, I'll stab him in the eye—apparently, I'm capable of that.

To my surprise, Vlad backs away from the door. Before he changes his mind, I slam the door shut and quickly lock it.

Apartment secured, I slide down the door, panting as I rub my aching throat.

Fluffster loses his aggressive stance and jumps onto my lap.

Stroking his heavenly fur instantly calms me, so I double down on relaxation and breathe for five seconds in and out, the way I learned earlier today.

Soon, I drop to just a fifteen out of ten on the freak-out scale. Weirdly, what bothers me the most is that I didn't faint during this whole incident, yet I did when speaking to a bunch of hedge fund guys this morning.

What's wrong with my danger priorities?

When I can approximate thinking again, I get my

phone out to dial 911, noticing as I do that my fingers are still trembling.

"Sasha," Ariel says from the middle of the living room. "Are you okay?"

Ariel's hair is wet, and she's covered in a bath towel, so in an epic effort of mental finagling, I realize she must've just come out of the shower.

"I'm so far from okay that 'okay' might as well be in Australia," is what I want to say, but all I manage to squeeze out of my dry lips is, "They tried to kill me."

"What?" Gripping her towel, Ariel rushes over to me and sits on her haunches. "What happened?"

"Body parts," I say, and the reminder makes my breathing go ragged once more. "Hallway. Vlad. Two guys crash into me with their cars."

"Slow down." She puts a hand on my shoulder. "You're in shock."

I stroke Fluffster once more, take a deep breath again, and hold it for five seconds before letting it out. A bit calmer, I tell Ariel a broken version of recent events, starting with the gray-skinned guy's attack at the TV studio and ending with the gray-skinned guys coming out of the elevator—and how Vlad turned them into a pile of gore.

Ariel listens with wide-eyed shock but without the appropriate disbelief. When I'm done, she says urgently, "Don't call the police."

"What are you talking about?" I look at her for any signs of this being a joke, but she looks as serious as liver cancer. "There are body parts in the hallway. How can I not call them?"

She gets up, takes Fluffster from me, and puts him on the floor. Then she pulls me up, tugging me away from the door.

"Wait," I say, but she's already stuck her head out into the hallway. "He might be lurking there," I finish lamely.

Ignoring my warning, Ariel leaves the safety of the apartment. I stumble after her on shaking legs, and as I touch the doorway, I hear her murmur to herself, "Wow. These bodies were embalmed at some point."

"What did you say?" I ask, but she just drags in a man's smashed torso from the hallway and drops it in the middle of our living room.

I gape at it, unable to believe there's a chunk of human meat just sitting there. The stench reaches my nostrils, and I gag.

Coughing hoarsely, I pull up my shirt to cover my nose and mouth. "Did you say these guys were already dead a while?"

"I wasn't thinking straight," she says, giving me a fake smile. "It was the shock of seeing that slaughter."

I'm not as good as Nero at lie detection, but when it comes to Ariel, I can easily tell when she's lying.

Before I can challenge her, she goes back into the hallway and returns with another limbless—and headless—stinky torso.

That I don't throw up is a symptom of shock—that, or some other stress-related altered state of consciousness. Through the shreds of this man's shirt, I can see the carvings that Beatrice—the woman in my dream—made on his skin.

Trying not to breathe in the foul air, I gingerly approach the body and move the shirt over with the tip of my shoe, so I can see the center of his chest.

There are indeed a number of embalming scars.

Checking the other torso, I find the carvings and the scars there too—plus the phone holder Beatrice had made with her knife.

If I wanted a logical explanation for how an embalmed corpse might move, I'd hypothesize a metal skeleton robot under all the dead flesh—something like a Terminator, only with a rotting outer shell. However, I don't see any metal gleaming from the rotting stubs where the arms, legs, and head used to be.

"Get away from them," Ariel says as she drags in two legs. "You could get an infection."

The idea of infection jolts me out of the numb bewilderment encasing me. My stomach violently turns over, and I nearly trip over Fluffster as I run to the bathroom, where I bend over the toilet and lose my second dinner of the day.

Throwing up makes me feel a tiny bit better—as though this is just a case of alcohol poisoning, not an impossible situation that I've found myself in. After I wash my hands and face and thoroughly brush my teeth, I feel almost human.

Back in the living room, the pile of body parts is

THE GIRL WHO SEES

now complete with heads and limbs—but both Fluffster and Ariel are missing.

Before I can freak out, Ariel appears from her room, having changed into jeans and a t-shirt.

She walks determinedly into the kitchen and comes back with a roll of garbage bags in her hand.

"What are you going to do?" I ask, even though it's obvious she plans to fill the garbage bags with human remains.

"We need to get rid of this before Felix gets home." She unrolls a bag and separates it from the others. "He'll freak out."

I hysterically chuckle at her understatement. Felix is so skittish about blood he once fainted at the sight of a used tampon in the bathroom, and we've been covering them with toilet paper ever since. He also forbade Ariel from sharing stories about her med school program because he nearly passed out after hearing one.

"If he sees this, he'll develop a speech impediment." I wave my hand to encompass the stinking mess in front of us. "I don't understand why I'm not fainting myself."

"Faint if you must. I've got this." Ariel bends down and picks up a small piece of flesh that might be the remnants of the hand that was around my neck.

"But what is your plan?" I ask, trying not to throw up yet again as I hold my shirt up to cover my nose. "You can't just put garbage bags with body parts into the trash chute. Or are you planning to dump them in the Hudson with all the tourists filming us? You can get a ticket for throwing regular garbage in there, you know. And what about the stench and all the stains in the hallway?"

I picture us getting caught by the cops with bags full of cadavers and shudder.

"I have no idea, but I'll figure it out." Ariel puts her grisly trophy into the bag and picks up the eyeless head of Mr. Charger.

Not for the first time, it strikes me that she's way too calm about this situation. I know she's seen some things in the Army, and she's a medical professional and all, but like me, she should be wondering what the hell is going on with embalmed corpses stalking me and Rose's boyfriend/nephew playing Jack the Ripper.

And why exactly are we not calling the cops?

"Ariel... you seem to know what's going on." I put my hands on my hips. "Spill it."

Without saying a word, she puts the head into the bag and picks up a leg.

"I'm serious. Ariel, if you know something, tell me. What's happening?"

The doorbell rings.

We exchange terrified glances.

"Maybe Felix lost his keys?" I suggest weakly.

Ariel puts the bag and the leg down, approaches the door, and looks into the peephole.

"It's not Felix," she says over her shoulder and, to my utter amazement, unlocks the door.

A short middle-aged man in a leather jacket is standing in the doorway. He looks familiar. I think I've seen him walk his dog in Battery Park, but I can't swear it in my current condition.

His gray eyes examine Ariel, then me, then settle hungrily on the pile of body parts in the middle of the room.

"Greetings," he says to Ariel. "Vlad called me. My name is Pada," he says to me—as though Ariel already knows that.

Fluffster runs out of my room and stops in front of me, as if defending me from the newcomer.

"Vlad mentioned the domovoi," Pada says, eyeing the chinchilla with concern. "Can you ask him to stand down?"

"Fluffster, sweetie, go to my room," I say, mainly to keep him away from any potential danger. To the stranger, I say, "What do you want?"

What I really want to know is why Ariel hasn't already smacked the door in the man's face—just another mystery on a fast-growing list.

"Vlad took care of any nosy neighbors, but you still have a disposal problem." His eyes dart all over the mound of gore. "Disposal is my specialty."

"Come inside." Ariel politely holds the door, as if the stranger has simply offered to fix our broken plumbing.

Pada walks in, wheeling two large suitcases in each hand. Stopping in front of the pile, he lays the suitcases flat and zips one open.

Inside are bone cutters of various sizes and instruments that would probably make Felix faint if he saw them. There are also cleaning products and garbage bags that look sturdier than ours.

"Would you like some tea?" Ariel asks Pada with a politeness I'd expect from British royalty.

"Yes, thanks," he says gruffly as he double-bags the garbage bag Ariel herself prepared earlier with his heavier-duty one. "Green if you have it."

Ariel looks at me and then pointedly at the kitchen. She then walks over there, presumably to make tea, and I follow on autopilot.

I sit down at the table, and she starts the blender without putting anything into the device—I think her goal is to cover any unpleasant noises that might arrive from the living room. If so, I'm grateful.

"What's going on?" I shout over the noise.

Ignoring me, Ariel pours water into the electric kettle and sets it to boil.

Reaching into the drawer next to the fridge, she takes out a pad and a pencil and sits at the table next to me.

"Tell me again what Beatrice—the woman in your dream—said to the mystery man on the phone," she says into my ear with obvious urgency.

Straining my memory, I tell her what I can recall, and she writes it down word for word on the pad. Whenever I mention a few really crazy things from the dream—like vampires and werewolves—Ariel seems to shudder, like I've slapped her with my words.

"Is this the part where you start explaining to me what you know?" I ask after she stops transcribing.

The kettle whistles. Ariel jumps to her feet and begins to fuss over three teacups.

"Here." She hands me a cup of chamomile tea—my evening favorite.

"How long do you think you can ignore my questions?" I blow at my tea with frustration, causing a bit to spill on the table. "What is happening?"

There's a knock on the wall, so Ariel stops the blender and picks up the cup with the green tea.

"I'm done." Pada walks in and gives Ariel a grumpy half-smile. "Vlad did most of my work for me."

Ariel hands him his tea.

He gulps it down like it's cold spring water on a hot day and not the boiling hot liquid that it is.

Ariel sidesteps the older man and goes into the living room. Curious, I follow.

The room smells like a Febreze factory after a terrorist act—but that's infinitely better than the horrific stench just minutes earlier. All signs of the body parts are gone.

"I can't believe it's the same room," Ariel says, summing up my feelings on the matter.

"I did the hallway outside too." Pada regretfully looks at his now-empty cup.

"How much do we owe you?" Ariel opens the window—presumably to air out the cloud of Febreze.

Pada sets the cup down on the coffee table. "Vlad took care of my compensation tonight."

"Then thank you, and good night." Ariel walks over

to the front door and holds it open in a polite but insistent gesture.

Pada ignores the door, reaches into his pocket, and takes out a business card. Handing it to me, he says, "In case you need my services in the future."

"She will not need your services," Ariel mutters as she watches him march toward the door. "Not if I can help it."

"Thanks." I examine the card. All I see is his name, Pada L'Shick, and a 212 phone number.

Ariel slams the door behind him so hard that some dust and plaster are knocked loose.

Taking out my phone, I enter the odd man's phone number and name into my Google contacts—just in case—and then walk back to the kitchen to throw away the actual paper card.

Joining me, Ariel sits down at the kitchen table, picks up her own tea, and cradles it in her hands, as though to warm them.

"You've got to tell me what you know." I grab an ice cube from the fridge and angrily drown it in my tea. "I won't stop asking, no matter how much you try to pretend you didn't hear me."

She puts down her tea, her forehead creasing as though she's straining to think of something to say.

"Do you think you're protecting me from something?" I stand up, looming over Ariel like *I'm* the one who's Army strong. Infusing my voice with as much authority as I can muster, I demand, "Tell me what's going on."

She looks the most miserable I've ever seen her— even worse than after her last breakup. I feel an illogical pang of guilt, but steel myself against it. Adding more ice into my voice, I say, "If our friendship means anything to you, talk. Now."

"I can't," Ariel says, and I watch in shock as her whole body begins to convulse.

The cup slips through her trembling fingers and shatters on the floor.

I gape in paralyzed horror as blood starts to trickle from Ariel's nose, ears, and eyes.

CHAPTER TWELVE

ARIEL GRABS her head as though she's trying to prevent it from exploding, and for all I know, maybe that's what's about to happen.

"I'm sorry," she mumbles. "I can't. I can't."

Panicked, I grab a paper towel and hand it to her. "What's going on? Are you hurt? Do you need me to call 911?"

She shakes her head, taking the towel from me and pressing it to the blood trickling down her face. "No, stop," she manages to say as I pull out my phone, about to call an ambulance regardless.

I stop, feeling utterly helpless. For the first time, I wish I had medical training, like Ariel, so I would know what to do.

Instead, all I can do is watch as Ariel pats at the blood, which fortunately seems to be slowing.

In a minute or two, but maybe an hour of silence

later, Ariel recovers enough to bend down and try to pick up the pieces of the cup she dropped.

"Leave that," I say, eagerly seizing the chance to do something. Grabbing a broom and a mop, I methodically take care of the mess, my mind racing at two hundred miles an hour but coming up with no explanations.

Watching me, Ariel sniffles.

Oh, crap, is she about to cry? That would be harder than hearing Mom cry when I was little. Mom was such a crybaby that everyone eventually got desensitized to her tantrums, while Ariel has never cried in all the years we've known each other. In fact, if someone asked me, I'd guess that Ariel would only cry during her parents' and my funeral—and I might be fooling myself about that last one. She might also shed a tiny tear at Felix's funeral, though that would probably depend on the nature of his demise.

Putting the mop away, I approach Ariel. "I think I get it," I say. "You *can't* talk about it. Whatever *it* actually is."

She nods and wipes at a fresh trickle of blood from her nose. Clearly, there is a correlation between the blood and her attempts to communicate with me about this subject.

"I'm sorry I pushed you," I say, feeling like I'm about to win the worst friend award—but also more confused than ever. What could prevent her from speaking? And in such a violent way, too? Can a mental illness manifest itself with blood out of the ears, nose, and eyes?

If Ariel were a magician, I'd suspect some illusion behind the blood, like the stigmata effect that I performed two Halloweens ago when I made Felix almost faint again. But she's not a magician, and if she were, then she's pulled off the best effect ever—convincing the world she isn't one.

Ariel stands up, grabs the entire roll of paper towels, and walks over to the sink to clean herself up. Returning, she sits down and looks at me, her eyes clear once more.

"I have what I need to help you," she says, her voice regaining its usual composure. She rips the top page with the transcript of my dream from the notebook and says, "You're still in shock. You're probably seeing things. I've witnessed this happening on the battlefield. You should finish your tea and go straight to bed."

I open my mouth to protest, but Ariel covers my hand with her palm. "Please?" she says softly. "Just go to sleep, Sasha. Really, it's the best thing for you right now."

I pick up my cup and gulp down the tea to give myself a moment to think. Now that the immediate danger is over, I *am* feeling like I'm about to pass out, the post-adrenaline crash combining with the many days' worth of sleep deprivation, courtesy of my TV performance.

"Okay," I say reluctantly. "Maybe things *will* seem clearer in the morning." What I don't say is that we'll have to find a way to talk about this without Ariel bleeding to death.

She stands up and grabs me in a tight hug. The modest release of oxytocin makes me feel a little bit better, though not closer to any answers.

"Good night," she says as we separate, and I nod at her.

"Good night." I stumble out of the kitchen on noodle-like legs, get a robe in my room, and head into the shower. As I run through my evening routine, theories, one crazier than another, swirl in my head, and despite the weariness, I worry I might not fall asleep once I get into bed.

My worries are unfounded. I'm out as soon as I cozy up with my blanket.

———

I'M A NAKED CONSCIOUSNESS, but with senses, floating again—just like that time in the morgue.

There's a smell of antiseptic in the air, and medical equipment is clustered around a nearby hospital bed.

An emaciated bald woman in her forties reclines in the bed, and according to the wristband on her thin wrist, her name is Amie Descanso. The bottom of the wristband reads "Room 4128, Maimonides Hospital"—which means that not only did I lose my body, I also somehow ended up in Brooklyn.

I guess it could've been worse. I could've lost my senses completely and ended up in Queens.

Attempting to look around, I find that I can—which is odd given that I don't possess a neck to turn my head, or a head with eyes for that matter.

The TV is showing the news, but I only pay attention to the date and time scrolling on the bottom: 10:19 a.m. on Tuesday, October 10th.

The door opens, and a familiar-looking woman comes in. The heart-shaped face belongs to Beatrice from the morgue incident. Only now she's wearing hospital scrubs, and her ID clip claims that her name is Bea T. Rice, RN.

Unlike before, Beatrice is smiling. She's also ceremoniously holding a tray covered by a shiny, dome-like metal lid. It makes her look like a fancy waiter, or a room service attendant in a five-star hotel.

"Hello, Amie," Beatrice says, her voice much kinder today than when she spoke to the mystery man on the phone.

"Hi," Amie says, her voice hoarse, as though she'd been screaming for days on end. "Haven't seen you around."

"How are you feeling?" Beatrice approaches the bed and examines Amie carefully, like an art critic trying to authenticate a priceless painting. "Your chart mentions a lot of pain."

"I've had a couple of very bad days, but I'm feeling surprisingly well today," Amie says and shakes the nearby IV. "Morphine drip notwithstanding."

Beatrice frowns as though she's disappointed at this news, but quickly recovers her composure. "I understand you haven't eaten breakfast yet today, am I right?"

"No, I haven't," Amie says. "In general, I've had a bad appetite for days now."

"I'm so sorry to hear that." Beatrice looks genuinely upset. "Hopefully, this can help."

Opening the special folding table attached to the bed, Beatrice places her tray on it and removes the big lid with a showy movement that makes her look even more like a waiter.

The tray is stuffed with delicacies like lobster, escargot, filet mignon, caviar, and a bunch of things I don't even recognize. If I had a mouth, it would be watering now, and if I had a belly, it would surely rumble.

For someone with a poor appetite, Amie attacks the morsels with surprising gusto, and Beatrice seems to take vicarious pleasure in watching her feast.

"That was amazing," Amie says, covering her mouth with her hand as she burps. "Sorry about that."

"That's fine," Beatrice says with mirth in her eyes. "I'm very glad you liked it."

She walks over to Amie's IV bag and fusses with it.

"What did you just do?" Amie asks curiously, her face relaxing in a blissful expression.

"I tweaked your morphine," Beatrice says. "You should feel even better soon."

Amie closes her eyes for a moment, then opens them. She looks as though she's trying to fight drowsiness and/or the ecstasy of the drug.

"I'm worried I'll get addicted to this stuff." Amie's pupils turn so small they're almost invisible. "I know it's a silly concern for someone in my situation, but—"

"Hush." Beatrice softly strokes Amie's head. "You don't need to worry about that anymore."

Soon, Amie slumps back, her eyes closing and her lips taking on a blueish tint.

The monitoring equipment complains about Amie's slowing heart rate, but Beatrice does something to it, and it goes silent. She then fiddles with the rest of the equipment, and uses the bed controls to put the now-unconscious Amie into a lying position.

"I'm sorry about this," Beatrice says, taking out her butterfly knife and opening it with the same flourish as in the morgue. "I needed a very fresh corpse, and I chose you because you only had a few agonizing days left."

Not surprisingly, Amie doesn't reply—if the morphine overdose hasn't killed her already, it probably will soon.

"That poem, 'Do not go gentle into that good night,' is complete bullshit," Beatrice continues, turning Amie onto her stomach to expose the hospital gown opening. "If I were in your shoes, I'd want someone to do for me what I did for you today." She unties the straps on the gown to expose the poor woman's skeletal back. "Maybe a part of you is going to be conscious, on some level, once I bring you back," she says soothingly as her knife cuts into Amie's back. "True, I'll be in control, but—"

I don't hear what she says next because blood wells up under the knife and darkness sucks me in.

———

I WAKE up in cold sweat.

"It was just a nightmare," I tell myself, trudging to the bathroom. "Just a stupid dream."

By the time I come back to bed, my breathing has slowed, and when I lie back down, I manage to doze off into unrestful sleep.

CHAPTER THIRTEEN

A SUN RAY hits my face, causing me to wake up angry at myself.

Like an idiot, I forgot to close the blinds last night.

What time is it? The sun implies morning, but then why do I feel like I've only gotten a couple of hours of sleep? Is someone using sleep deprivation as an interrogation technique on me? If so, I'm ready to spill national security secrets, so long as my tormentors close the stupid blinds and let me get back to sleep for just a little longer.

The sun doesn't go away, so I check my nightstand clock and groan.

The blinds were not the only thing I forgot. I also didn't set an alarm, which is why I've slept in until a whopping 9:07 a.m.—a luxury I rarely get even on the weekends.

In a half-daze, I drag myself to the laptop and email work, telling them I'm very sick. I wonder if I'm actually lying about that; the drowsiness and the sore muscles could be a sign of the flu. In any case, after yesterday's fainting, they should accept my excuse without any skepticism, especially since this is my first sick day of the year.

My butt feels glued to my chair, and somehow, knowing that I spent a respectable number of hours in bed only makes me angrier about the wretched sleep deprivation I feel. If this isn't the flu, then I must've been tossing and turning all those hours, without going into healing REM sleep. Now that I think about it, I even vaguely recall what kept me restless: the theories about what happened to me yesterday kept circling in my head. That, and I had a nightmare again.

Forcing myself to get up, I head to the bathroom.

A shower does almost nothing for my wakefulness, nor does brushing my teeth. The sight in the mirror actually worsens my mood because a huge fingerprint bruise on my neck reminds me of the sad domestic violence posters I sometimes see on the subway. I'll have to buy a turtleneck before I return to work; else my coworkers will think there's a guy I need to put in jail.

I pull on a robe and look for my roommates. Sadly, neither Ariel nor Felix are home.

Heading back to my room, I pick up my new phone and see that the battery is dead. Charging it is yet another thing I forgot to do yesterday.

I stick the phone on a charger, and when it boots up again, I call my friends, but get their voicemails.

This really blows because I have to talk to Ariel. I have some ideas on how she might be able to communicate with me without speaking, but I guess those will have to wait.

Since I have the phone on me, and because Fluffster finally deigns to greet me with a friendly chirp, I look up *domovoi*—a word that was mentioned twice yesterday, directed at him.

Apparently, a domovoi is a protective house spirit in Russian and other Slavic folklore. That sort of makes sense, if I assume Vlad is originally from Russia, which his knowledge of its history supports. He must've used that term poetically because it looked like Fluffster was trying to protect me in my home.

If chinchillas were anything supernatural, they would be part of Peruvian folklore, not Russian.

I feed Fluffster and make my way to the kitchen so that I can fix myself some oatmeal with bananas and almonds.

Eating my breakfast, I realize that Ariel was wrong. Sleeping did *not* aid me in making sense of my crazy new life. In fact, I would've slept better if I'd taken the time to sort out my thoughts last night.

I might as well do the thinking now. Hopefully, my subconscious mind worked out some good theories while it was messing up my sleep.

Fluffster jumps onto the chair next to me and looks longingly at the spoon I'm about to put into my mouth.

"Here." I let him eat a little piece of banana off the spoon. "Now let me think."

Something happened to me on that TV stage, and that's probably a good place to start. The weird events began when I felt that pleasurable flood of energy. If it weren't for the clean bill of health I got at the hospital yesterday, I'd think something broke in my brain. As is, ignoring the strong case for the insanity option, I have to entertain the possibility of a supernatural explanation—and I hate that.

I've always been fascinated with mysteries, but especially so when I was very young. As a little girl, I devoured anything that talked about alien abductions, ghosts, Bigfoot, the Bermuda triangle, ESP, and the like. As I grew up, though, a lot of these entities went the way of Santa Claus for me. To some degree, I got interested in magic because magicians have an air of mystique about them that sometimes seems real—but of course, when I learned all the methods behind those mysteries, every single effect had a rational explanation.

In a way, becoming an illusionist made me an even bigger skeptic, because I could see that miracles could be staged, and that powers such as ESP could be easily simulated.

If I've developed a supernatural power, I'm probably the worst person to be in this situation— aside from someone like James "The Amazing" Randi, who's made a career out of debunking the paranormal.

Fluffster jumps onto my lap, and I absentmindedly stroke his fur as I sip my orange juice and think further about this.

I had the first nightmare featuring a gray-skinned man on the TV stage—and then I was attacked exactly like that. I explained it all away with Valium side effects, but what if that really happened?

That would mean Gaius and his people have impossible strength—and now that I think about it, so does Vlad.

Unless embalmed corpses are easier to rip apart than I imagined. But then all of these super strong people also did that mirror trick with their eyes. Usually, I'd explain it by special contacts, but the eyes had an effect on me that can't be explained—unless it was a placebo.

My head is starting to hurt from all this, so I refocus on my own possible supernaturalness—specifically, on the fact that my second dream was of Beatrice raising two dead people. As crazy as it sounds, how could that be just a dream if I was then attacked by people who looked exactly like the ones she reanimated? People who had been embalmed, no less? My theory about subconscious warnings could explain some of it, but not all; I don't see how my subconscious could've known the details of the TV studio attack, nor the bit about the embalming.

So, I have to ask myself a simple question. It's a question that strangers have asked me a lot in my life, and I've always replied with a vehement "no."

Am I psychic?

CHAPTER FOURTEEN

FLUFFSTER JUMPS from my lap onto the table and steals a piece of almond from my bowl as I mull over that impossible idea.

In my philosophy class, we learned the technique of *reductio ad absurdum*—to prove something false, you first assume it's true, then use logic to carry that assumption to some ridiculous conclusion.

So what if I assume I can "dream" the future?

For one thing, it would create a small paradox right off the bat. When I see the future in my dream, I immediately gain the power to change it, so I'm not *really* seeing the future, just a possibility that can be thwarted. In fact, my very first "prophetic dream" was about getting strangled (they do like to do that to me) by that first cadaver on the stage. But when I came to my senses, I ran away from him—so I didn't dream the future in that case, not in the strictest sense of the word.

So then maybe I see *possibilities* of the future—a sort of forecast. This is better, because it deals with any pesky fate and/or free will problems—and since it makes predicting the future harder, I'll pretend that free will is *not* an illusion for this chain of logic.

So, if I assume that I can make these data-lacking but accurate forecasts, what ridiculous conclusions does that lead to?

Not many come to mind, but there is one elephant-sized thing. In the morgue dream, words like "vampire" and "werewolf" were thrown about. That puts me deeper into la la land, because mythical creatures are much more incredible than predicting the future. After all, most movies and books that feature precognition (like *Dune* and *Minority Report*) are considered science fiction, but stories featuring vampires (i.e. *Dracula* and *Twilight*) are firmly in the realm of fantasy.

And science fiction is more realistic than fantasy, right?

Unlike *Alice in Wonderland,* I have limits on the number of impossible things I can believe before breakfast (and during). So, for my own sanity, I focus on one impossibility for now—prophetic dreams. Assuming for a moment that this might be possible, it means that my last dream about Beatrice might've correctly predicted what's going to happen to a woman named Amie in a Brooklyn hospital later today.

The oatmeal suddenly tastes like sandpaper as I fully register the implications. It's 9:23 a.m. now, which means in forty-seven minutes, a woman will be killed, just so that she can become a fresh cadaver for Beatrice to raise (necromancy is another aspect of this whole thing that I won't dwell on at the moment).

I force myself to swallow the food in my mouth and push aside my bowl.

My course of action is crystal clear.

I must go to Maimonides Hospital and stop that murder from happening.

If I don't go, and I later learn that Amie does exist and that she died, it will be on my conscience forever. Going there is also my best chance to validate this forecast theory. If Amie is there and Beatrice arrives in her room at the same time as in my dream, I'll be that much closer to accepting my powers as fact.

It would also be possible to ask Beatrice some pointed questions.

Dumping the rest of my breakfast into the trash, I run to my closet. Since I'm in a rush, I grab the first thing I see—the outfit I usually wear at my restaurant gig: black leather pants, a shirt with breast pockets and a hidden inside pocket attached by a safety pin, plus a leather jacket. I also grab my phone from the charger.

It's only at seven percent, but it will have to do.

On the elevator ride down, I debate the fastest way to get to my destination. A car ride there can take anywhere from fifteen minutes to over an hour, depending on traffic. A subway ride is more reliable than a car, but that would involve transfers, so it would take forty to fifty minutes, which means I definitely wouldn't make it in time. My Vespa would be perfect for this, but it's toast.

Launching a ride-hailing app, I summon a car as soon as I exit the elevator, and three minutes later, I'm sitting in a nice Honda Civic, en route to the hospital.

I consider bribing my driver the way I did yesterday, but I didn't bring any of Nero's cash with me. Also, this driver doesn't look friendly, and our arrival time depends on traffic much more than on his driving skills.

Calling Ariel again, I get voice mail, so I leave a message asking her to call me back immediately. For good measure, I text her the same demand. The main thing I want to know is whether I can I call the cops about Amie's possible murder. When Ariel told me not to call them yesterday, was that a generic prohibition, or was it specific to the body-parts scenario?

Of course, if I did call 911 and told them the truth, they would think I'm crazy, but I'm a good enough illusionist to spin a false tale that would hopefully convince them to go check on Amie. For instance, I could claim that I heard gunfire from her hospital room, or cries for help.

"Watch it, retard!" my driver shouts with a heavy accent, hitting the brakes so hard I nearly fly off my seat. I'm pretty sure he just cut off a bus, rather than the other way around, but I decide against saying anything and make a mental note to leave him a bad review.

The adrenaline rush clears some of the lingering

fuzziness in my mind, and an obvious idea occurs to me.

I can call the hospital and see if they have a patient named Amie Descanso.

Before my mind can launch into a list of pros and cons, I look up the number for the hospital and dial it. While the phone rings, I force myself to recall everything I've ever heard about hospital privacy policies—the last thing I want is to get tangled up in red tape.

The phone connects, and a woman says, "Maimonides Hospital."

"Hi," I say, getting into an illusionist mindset—otherwise known as "preparing to lie my ass off."

"How can I help you?" the woman asks.

"I'm on my way to visit my sister," I say. "Her name is Amie Descanso. I think she's in the long-term care unit, or hospice. Can you please tell me what room she's in?"

I wait tensely as the woman starts typing away.

"Please tell me you don't have a patient by that name," is what I want to say, but I bite my tongue. I'm also a little worried that the lie I concocted isn't good enough and that the operator won't give me an answer by the time we enter the tunnel—a no-reception area—that we're swiftly approaching.

"She's in room 4128," the woman says to my shock and proceeds to tell me how to best navigate to the room.

"Thank you," I say as we drive into the tunnel. My

palms are damp, and my head is spinning from the implication, but I gather my thoughts enough to say, "Actually, there's something else I need help with—"

The call disconnects, my phone showing zero bars. What's worse, the battery is on one percent now.

Numbly, I stare at the tunnel wall lights flashing by. So the hospital *does* have a patient with that name, and she's in the exact same room as in my dream.

What are the odds of this being a coincidence? My analytical mind tells me that they're low—so low that when combined with everything else, my dream must not be just a dream.

Amie's life really is in danger, and I must do whatever I can to save her.

Frantically, I consider calling the police despite Ariel's admonition, or at the very least, trying the hospital again. I'll have to dance around the truth, but I'll come up with something plausible. Maybe I can claim that a nurse named Bea T. Rice molested my "sister," or that Amie told me she's feeling very sick or is being stalked—

My phone makes a death-throes sound as its battery dies—and we haven't even gotten out of the stupid tunnel.

"Excuse me," I say to Raj Harry, the name on the driver's prominently displayed ID. "Do you have a USB Micro B charger for my Android phone?"

"I'm sorry," Raj says, his heavily accented voice devoid of any hint of apology. "I use iPhone."

Indeed, there's an iPhone running a GPS app in the

front dashboard. The app has our route mapped out and estimates our arrival at 10:09 a.m. He sees me looking at his phone in the rearview mirror and tilts it toward himself so I can't see the screen anymore.

"Can I please use your phone then?" I say, ignoring the rude gesture. "After we exit the tunnel, I mean?"

"I'm sorry," he says and shrugs in the rearview mirror. "I have a T-Mobile data-only plan."

I find his statement hard to believe. Even if such a plan exists, I doubt you could get it with an iPhone.

"It should still allow 911 calls," I say, trying to call his bluff. "I need to call emergency services—my sister is in trouble."

"It can't call 911." For the first time, I see some emotion on his face. He looks very concerned.

Does he have some issue with the police? Is that where the reluctance is coming from?

Did a rider report him to the cops before?

Pushing that scary thought aside, I scramble for solutions. "What if I PayPal you a hundred dollars?" I catch his gaze in the rearview mirror. "Can I use your phone then? Maybe I can email the hospital?"

"I'm sorry," he says, his face impassive once again. "I need my phone to navigate. I cannot give it to you."

If this were a limo, I bet the guy would close the partition between us.

We finally exit the tunnel, and I debate asking him to let me out of the car. But we're on the highway, and I'd definitely be late to the hospital then. I also consider just leaning forward and boldly grabbing the phone, but this is even more likely to lead to a delay—plus, I could get beaten up or arrested.

The driver cuts off another car, honking furiously, and zooms by the toll booths.

"Is it the bruise on my neck that's making you uncomfortable?" I ask on a hunch.

"I'm sorry," he says again, turning his mirror in such a way that I can't see his face anymore. "My English is not so good."

"You're getting a bad review, I can tell you that," I say, crossing my arms over my chest.

"I'm sorry," he says again, reminding me of those customer service reps who sound like a broken record. "Let's not talk anymore. I need to focus on the road."

"Can you at least tell me what time it is?" I try to sound polite despite my anger. "Or tilt the phone my way?"

He must've really meant the whole no-talk thing because he doesn't reply to me.

We hit the first patch of traffic after a few minutes of sullen silence. I try asking for the time or the phone in light of the traffic, but he continues the mute act.

Sitting in traffic always feels like forever, but this time, I swear I see my nails grow before we leave the patch of congestion.

To stay sane, I practice the breathing techniques Lucretia taught me and fantasize about the evil pranks I can pull as payback to the unhelpful Raj Harry. Since I know his name, maybe Felix can hack into the DMV for me and get me his address. I could then take my revenge via snail mail with a postcard offering "Discount Adult Diapers," or with a bag of gummy penises I bookmarked online "just in case."

No, those are too mild. I'll instead mail him a box with Fluffster's poop, or a rotten fish accompanied by a dead flower arrangement.

The severity of the punishment will depend on whether I save Amie or not.

We leave the highway and wind our way through the Brooklyn streets.

The one nice thing I can say about Brooklyn, or at least this part of it, is that we pass numbered avenues, which makes it easier to follow our route without GPS. The hospital is on 10th Avenue and 48th Street, so when I see 47th Street, I get excited.

We reach 10th Avenue in a few moments and turn right. I already have my hand on the door handle.

He stops by the hospital entrance but doesn't break the uncomfortable silence.

"I sincerely hope you get replaced with a self-driving vehicle," I say as I leap out of the car and slam the door as hard as I can.

His tires screech as he drives away, and I hurry toward the entrance.

The key to making sure no one asks you dumb questions when you go into semi-restricted areas, such as a hospital, is to look confident.

So, looking confident, I go in and dash down the hallways connecting the buildings before I find the right one. From there, I take the elevator to the fourth floor. All the while, I try to look like I belong, and my haste is the most natural thing in the world.

My strategy works. Even the few nurses at the station on the fourth floor must assume I'm supposed to be here because no one blinks an eye.

I spot a big round clock above the nursing station, and a chill wraps around my spine.

It's 10:35 a.m., long past my target of 10:19.

Then I realize not all is lost. In my dream, Beatrice didn't kill Amie right away—she let her have a last meal first. I can still save the day, depending on how long that part took. I wish I'd checked the time periodically inside the dream, but I didn't.

I sprint for room 4128 so fast my boots skid on the recently washed floor.

Facing the door, I brace myself for a possible encounter with Beatrice. My breath is ragged from the recent run and the adrenaline pounding through me.

Hand quivering, I reach for the door handle.

CHAPTER FIFTEEN

AMIE IS LYING face up on the bed. She looks exactly like she did in my dream—which clearly wasn't just a dream.

Beatrice isn't here.

Am I too late?

The hospital equipment has been tampered with and doesn't help with proof of life.

I approach the bed and check Amie's pulse on her wrist.

It's gone.

As a mentalist, I know some methods to create an illusion of one's heart stopping. For instance, a ball under the armpit can make the pulse seem to slow and then stop. So I check Amie's neck.

No pulse here either.

I put my dead phone's screen under her mouth to see if she fogs up the glass with her breathing.

The screen remains clear.

My heart sinks.

I failed.

She's dead.

I consider running to the nursing station, so they can try to resuscitate her, but then I notice streaks of blood on the bed and recall Beatrice's carvings. In the morgue nightmare, their purpose was to delay the corpse's reanimation until Beatrice is gone.

And Beatrice is not here.

A potent sense of foreboding grips me.

"I better go get the nurses," I say out loud to no one in particular.

As I head for the door, a simple and terrifying idea swirls through my head. In my haste, the only possibility I didn't let myself fully dwell on was that Amie would not only die, but come back. And if everything until this moment has been confirmed as true, then logic (or the twisted sister that has replaced it) dictates that Amie is going to become a walking dead, and soon. She will also be in some way superior to the other cadavers, or so I assume based on Beatrice's comments about her "freshness."

I'm by the door when I hear the rustling of a hospital gown on the starched sheets behind me.

She's moving.

I grab the door handle, but it slips though my sweaty palm.

Naked feet slap against the gray vinyl tiles of the floor.

Wiping my hands on my shirt, I wrench open the door, rush out, and slam it behind me.

Leg muscles straining, I sprint toward the nursing station.

The door behind me opens and slams with a bang.

"Call security," I yell at the nurse at the station. "The patient behind me is having a breakdown."

Without waiting for the nurse's reply, I run up to the elevator and stab at the plastic button.

I inhale a dozen ragged breaths in the moment it takes me to decide that the elevator isn't going to cut it, and dash for the staircase.

I'm halfway to the third floor when the staircase door above me slams. I flinch at the noise, but keep running down the stairs.

The shuffling of bare feet on dusty cement follows, leaving no doubt about who's following me.

Leaping down two steps at a time, I nearly fall and almost twist my ankle twice, but I reach the first floor in mere seconds.

Running out of the main entrance, I have a new hope. Someone will stop a hospital-gown-wearing patient before she flashes her naked butt on the street, right?

When I reach the corner of 10th Ave and 48th Street, I chance a glance back at the hospital entrance.

Either the security didn't care, or they couldn't handle Amie—she's only a few yards behind me. I notice that she indeed moves much faster and smoother than the cadavers who came after me earlier.

She also looks less "dead," and now that I think about it, she didn't smell at all.

Turning the corner, I pick up the pace because I see the brownish-green of the aboveground subway tracks in the distance—a noisy eyesore from another era.

The weather-beaten pavement squares blur under my feet, and the red stone buildings seem to merge together. The few pedestrians I pass give me questioning looks, but I ignore them, running with all my might.

When I reach the street with the subway overhead, I turn right at random, figuring a stop will be forthcoming either way I turn.

Some of the businesses I pass are still closed, and graffiti adorns their ugly gray security gates. Their awnings haven't been changed in all the history of Brooklyn, and each one has those hazardous basement street entrances via a cellar with double hatches. I make sure to stay clear of the cellars as I sprint; the last thing I want is to fall into one, like Samantha did in *Sex and the City*.

I see the subway entrance a block and a half away, and there's a train in the distance.

Finding new strength, I race for the stairs leading up to the 50th Street D-train station. If my Stuyvesant High track coach could see my performance today, he'd regret not letting me on the varsity team.

I catch a flicker of motion in the reflective window of a laundromat I run past, and in the next business window, I confirm it.

Despite my speed, Amie is right behind me.

My heart gallops madly in my chest and my lungs feel like they're about to burst as I reach the station. Wheezing for breath, I zoom up the stairs in double- and triple-step leaps.

When I encounter a turnstile, I don't bother reaching for my wallet with the MetroCard. I just jump over the obstacle like a steeplechaser. It would be great if a cop saw me and decided to give me a ticket for cheating the MTA, but Murphy's Law makes sure there isn't one around.

I head for the Manhattan side of the station, my feet tingling as they detect the vibration of the arriving train.

Amie is still right on my tail.

Like a human torpedo, I jet all the way up to the station and see the train approaching.

I feel pressure on my shoulder and glance back.

Amie's hand is gripping my jacket, her eyes scarily blank.

My stomach clenches over the undigested oatmeal.

As fast as the train is moving, it might as well be a slug for all the good it'll do me.

I spin out of her grip, leaving my jacket in her hand, and sprint toward the arriving train.

My new idea is pure madness.

If I time this wrong, there will be two corpses at the station—and mine will be much less spry than Amie's.

The train is a dozen yards from entering the station

when I reach the end of the platform, Amie on my heels.

Sucking in a breath, I jump down in front of the train.

CHAPTER SIXTEEN

MY KNEES SCREAM in complaint when I land, but I manage to hit the ground running. Jumping over rail after rail, I make it to the Brooklyn-bound train track.

Looking back, I see Amie land in the spot I just vacated.

Crap. My plan was to leave Amie behind the approaching train.

The train's brakes screech like a metallic dragon. The conductor must be attempting to stop.

He fails.

Just as Amie gets to the second railing, the train smashes into her, and she's dragged under.

Bile rushes up my throat as crunching sounds reach my ears. I know my pursuer was already dead, but it's still sickening to imagine her body being mangled like that.

With effort, I swallow and force myself to vault up the train track wall on the other side. I don't want to be around to answer the inevitable questions about the accident or about my own suicidal, and possibly illegal, maneuver.

My arms shake with exhaustion by the time I climb out, and I send mental thanks to Ariel for all the pull-ups she makes me do at the gym.

The train has fully stopped by now, and morbid curiosity makes me look back again.

To my shock, Amie's body is not under the train anymore. Instead, it's between the two train tracks—and moving.

At first, my brain has trouble parsing what it's seeing.

Amie's left leg is missing below the knee, and her right leg is broken at the ankle, with jagged bone sticking out of it. The gruesomeness of these injuries would make a seasoned World War I medic cringe.

The worst part is *how* she's moving—on all fours, like a cheetah from hell.

I blink, as though that can change what I'm seeing, but that doesn't help. Amie leaps over the rail in her path, her blank eyes zooming in on me like self-guided missiles.

I'm too shocked to move. All I can do is stare at her missing right hand, the reason she's using a meaty stump like a hoof.

She leaps up, her stump scraping over the wall as she attempts to climb out with inhuman agility, and a fresh flood of adrenaline cuts through my paralysis.

I break into a run.

In a haze of horror, I dash out of the station. Every muscle in my body is trembling with exhaustion, my lungs working like bellows as I burst out onto the street.

Behind me, I hear the sound of bone clanking on hard pavement.

I pick up my pace, my mind frantically scrambling for a solution.

Half a block in front of me, I see a store's basement cellar hatches propped open with a stick.

On autopilot, I sprint for it, a half-formed idea appearing in my mind.

Reaching the open hatches, I stop and glance over my shoulder, panting.

Amie is a dozen yards behind me, galloping on all fours.

I steal a quick glance down.

The metal door on the bottom of the twelve-foot shaft is locked from the street side—a common practice when store owners expect a delivery over an indefinite range of time.

Steeling myself, I spin on my heels and meet my pursuer's blank gaze.

CHAPTER SEVENTEEN

AMIE'S unnatural gallop speeds up, her eyes never leaving my face.

I stare her down, as though I'm not afraid—the biggest acting challenge of my life.

When Amie is within leaping distance, she opens her mouth, exposing her teeth.

I understand her plan immediately.

She's about to chomp at my throat.

She leaps up.

At the last second, just as I can almost reach out and smack her, I jump sideways instead.

She plummets down the open cellar, landing with a hard plop.

I grab the stick that keeps the metal hatches open, and the doors slam closed.

There's a lock and chain to my right. I use them to secure the hatches and then reach into my shirt.

With unsteady fingers, I unhook the safety pin that

keeps my hidden pocket attached to the cloth and pull the pin out. Sticking it into the lock, I twist and break the metal apart. This way, even someone with a key will have trouble opening the hatches.

Straightening, I scan the street for witnesses and thank the stars there are none. I'm dripping with sweat and out of breath, but I can't afford to rest yet.

Spotting a 99 Cents store half a block away, I make my way there and purchase a charger for my phone for almost ten bucks. (So much for that 99 Cent claim.) I then find an electrical outlet in the store and plug in my phone.

As it reboots, I ponder how to deal with Amie before someone clips that lock. 911 is out. Not only did Ariel say not to call the cops the last time I was in a similar situation, but I'm also too tired to come up with a story to explain what amounts to a zombie in the basement cellar.

Thinking of last night gives me an idea. Once the home screen reappears, I locate Pada L'Shick—the body disposal expert—in my contacts.

"Greetings," a man's voice drawls.

"Pada, this is Sasha. You gave me your card last night."

"Sasha. I didn't expect to hear from you. Especially so soon."

I look around the store to make sure no one is eavesdropping. "I'm afraid I could use your help again."

"Assistance similar to what I provided last night?"

Pada sounds almost giddy with the prospect of that horrific cleanup.

"What I need is similar, but there's going to be more work on your end." I again look around furtively. "You'll have to finalize the transaction when you get here, if you catch my drift."

"I think I do." Pada's creepy excitement seems to rise a notch. "You want me to do what Vlad did last night, is that correct?"

"Yes," I say, wondering how implicating this whole exchange could be in the court of law if the NSA is spying on our cell conversation (and aren't they always?). "Though you don't need to be quite as viciously thorough as he was."

"What's the location?"

I give him the Brooklyn address of the store and explain that he should look for "the mess" in the cellar.

"Brooklyn." His excitement wanes. "I usually stick to Manhattan, but I like you, so I'll do it. It will cost extra, however."

Somehow, having to pay for this makes me feel that much dirtier. "What do I owe you?"

"With the first-time customer discount, this will be eight thousand," Pada says, his earlier excitement gone. I guess money is the boring part for him. "Would you like to pay by check or credit card? If you have gold coins, I can knock off ten percent, but I don't take paper cash."

"That's a lot," I blurt, then catch myself. How much would someone have to pay *me* to open those hatches and deal with Amie? Probably more than a hundred times what Pada just quoted. Even then, I'd only agree if I had a shotgun, a chainsaw, a barrel of gasoline, and some big dudes to assist me. Also, like him, I'd charge extra to schlep to any of the boroughs.

"So you don't need my help?" Pada's tone is dry.

"Can I pay in two months?" I ask, already calculating the impact on my "Quit Nero's Fund" savings account. At the current rate of expenditures, I'll be stuck in that soul-crushing job for an extra few months. Now my only hope is a lucrative TV deal suddenly coming my way, which could happen, thanks to my TV performance on—

"There will be a five-hundred-dollar fee in two months," Pada says. "Oh, and I don't like people who owe me money to leave town without notice."

"Forget it," I say. "The credit card interest rate will be less than that."

"If you say so."

Pulling out my credit card, I ask, "Can I give you the number over the phone?"

He takes my card number, and when he asks for the expiration date, the transaction takes on a surreal quality.

Hiding a mangled, still-alive body shouldn't be so reminiscent of ordering pizza.

"Leave it to me from here," Pada says after I provide the security number on the back of my card. "Go home."

"Thanks. Bye." I hang up before he remembers some other fee or changes his mind.

Unplugging my phone, I take the charger and escape the dollar store.

There's an apple-green taxi across the street, so I drag myself toward it, the post-adrenaline crash hitting me hard. Though the subway right above me is a small fraction of the cost, I dare not go to the station so soon after jumping on the rails.

Climbing into the car, I state my destination.

"Hey," the cabbie says with a cute Spanish accent. "Aren't you that girl on TV?"

Despite my exhaustion, I feel a jolt of excitement at being recognized. It's so nice that I don't even bother pointing out that "a girl on TV" could mean anyone from Cinderella to Miley Cyrus. "Yes," I say, smiling modestly. "I was on *Evening with Kacie*."

"That's right." He smacks his forehead. "You predicted the earthquake. That was very impressive."

"Thank you," I reply, my tiredness returning. Leaning back, I try to exude a default New Yorker attitude that says, "Please stop being friendly. I just want to be left alone."

"Were you trying to charge your phone?" The guy looks at the charger I'm clutching in my hands. "You can use my charger, if you want."

"Thank you." I squeeze out a weak smile, hand him my phone to charge, and make a mental note to tip more than I originally planned.

I pointedly stay silent after that, and the cabbie

leaves me be, further increasing his tip. Exhaustion presses down on me, dragging my lids closed, but my mind is undergoing a paradigm shift.

My natural skepticism and reluctance to believe in the paranormal are cracking like thin ice under the tank-like pressure of my recent experiences.

So, here are the facts: I have prophetic dreams, and the dead can be raised by a necromancer named Beatrice who shoots multi-colored bolts of energy at corpses.

A necromancer.

If Occam were in my shoes, he'd slit his wrists with his razor.

I also have to open my mind to the possibility that vampires and werewolves—the other creatures mentioned in the phone conversation in my dream—are as real as necromancers and the walking dead. Come to think of it, according to myths, vampires are a type of walking dead, so it's not that big of a leap.

There were other things mentioned in that conversation, words like "Cognizant" and "the Mandate." What does it all mean? And how is my roommate involved? What does Ariel know and why can't she tell me? The whole "bleeding from her orifices" thing was beyond creepy and is yet another weird thing to put on an ever-growing list.

I'll have to locate her and try to extract some information—without making her hemorrhage, of course. And I also need to visit Rose, to see if she can explain her gorgeous, Jack the Ripper nephew/boyfriend.

Leaning back in my seat, I close my eyes, put one hand on my chest and one on my belly, and fiercely practice the five-in/five-out breathing to cope with the anxiety squeezing my stomach.

To my surprise, the relaxation spreads through my body like warm water, and the exhaustion wins out.

———

I'M STANDING on a circular platform in the dark as the scent of sage incense tickles my nose.

Before I can even think about escaping, a bunch of candles light up all around me, temporarily blinding my dark-adjusted eyes.

When my vision and pulse even out, I notice that each of the candles looks to be floating, creating a Hogwarts Great Hall vibe.

As I examine my strange surroundings, I get progressively more concerned and confused.

With its gray circular walls and seats around the circumference, this place reminds me of a miniature indoor Colosseum.

I'm in the middle, where the gladiator would traditionally stand, which must be why I feel like I'm about to be pitted against lions, suicidal berserkers, chariots with swords sticking out of their wheels, or worse.

There are a few dozen people in the seats around

me, all wearing differently colored ceremonial robes with hoods on their heads, their faces barely discernible in the gloomy light. Is this a secret meeting of the Illuminati or a cosplay convention? Whoever they are, I'm grateful they skipped the creepy Venetian masks today, and I hope they'll continue to abstain from *Eyes Wide Shut*-inspired orgies as well, or at least not force me into one.

The nape of my neck breaks out in gooseflesh as I realize everyone is staring at something behind me.

My muscles prepare to leap, but a hand touches my back and a vaguely familiar voice whispers, "I need to put this around your neck."

I almost jump out of my skin at the touch, but the voice calms me for some reason.

Turning, I spot a man whose face is hidden deep inside his cowl. In his ceremoniously extended right hand, he holds a necklace that reminds me of a BDSM collar with a ring in the front. Embedded in the ring is a big, blue, shiny stone, a dead ringer for the diamond from *Titanic*—only round instead of heart shaped.

"What is that? Who are you? What is this place? What's going on?" I whisper so that only this guy can hear.

Instead of an answer, he touches my back in a familiar, and strangely reassuring, way. He then uses my momentary confusion to wrap the collar around my neck, locking it into place.

I reach back and try to unclasp the necklace, but I

can't feel any locking mechanism. It's as if it were welded shut.

"Take this off," I hiss at the guy, but he doesn't respond.

Everyone around us shifts to the edge of their chairs and stares hungrily, to the point where worries about orgies reenter my mind, and I swallow so loudly the sound echoes.

Channeling *E.T.*, the man extends his index finger toward my face. I prepare to bite it off, but he doesn't actually touch me. Instead, he points at the stone in the middle of my neck.

Curiosity mixes with panic as he mumbles something to himself and a flow of bright blue energy pours from his finger and into the stone on my neck.

"How are you doing that?" I whisper in awestruck fascination.

I'd do anything to master an awesome effect like that for my future magic show.

The energy flow intensifies, reminding me of the Force lightning from *Star Wars* or the thing Beatrice did at the morgue. Yet I feel no pain; the stone on my neck absorbs every ounce of power, leaving my body unscathed.

My list of impossibilities already includes necromancers, and tentatively vampires and werewolves, but now I reluctantly have to add magic spells to it as well—because what else should I call this amazing special-effects display?

"This will not hurt you," the guy murmurs, and his

identity is on the tip of my tongue when he suddenly steps back.

I turn and see him make his way toward his seat in the first row.

The glow from my odd jewelry illuminates my surroundings with ocean-blue light.

A woman clears her throat behind me, so I spin around.

In the third row, at my one o'clock, a slender figure in a magenta robe is on her feet, pulling down her hood. She's Asian, with cherub-like round cheeks and wavy peroxide-blond hair. A tear-shaped diamond necklace adorns her robe, matching her flower-shaped earrings.

"I'm Councilor Kit," the woman says in a little-girl voice that reminds me of anime. "I'm the designated neutral party in tonight's proceedings. Please state your name for the record."

"Sasha." My throat is so dry the reply is barely louder than a whisper. Speaking in front of all these people is activating my worst fear, and the weird ambience amplifies it. My heart pounds violently, and I half expect it to rip out of my ribcage, *Alien* style.

At my reply, the blue light around me turns green, and though I can't see it below my chin, I'm certain the stone on my collar is the source of this new hue.

Kit covers her head with the hood again and sits down. Immediately, a man in a baby-chick yellow robe stands up in the second row at my three o'clock. He removes his hood, revealing a contagious smirk that showcases his cheek dimples. His pointy chin also has a dimple, which combines with the goatee-shaped stubble on his tan skin to make him look like a mischievous satyr.

"I'm Councilor Chester, the Plaintiff in today's proceedings," he says in a vaguely familiar voice, looking straight at me. His black lashes are so thick it looks like he's wearing eyeliner. "I'll cut to the chase. What did you do at eight p.m. on Sunday, October 8th?"

The circular room spins around me like a carousel, but I fight the sudden bout of nausea. Puking in front of a large crowd would be the epitome of humiliation.

"I was on TV," I croak out. "It's on YouTube."

My necklace shines green again.

Chester looks at the crowd around him theatrically and says, "She admits it. Case closed."

"A fact any idiot with an internet connection can verify," says yet another familiar voice, this one with a British accent.

It's Darian, the TV executive who got me the gig.

"Please wait your turn," Chester tells him.

Slowly, and strangely mockingly, Chester sits down, and Darian stands up and removes his hood.

"I'm Councilor Darian, the Defense in today's proceedings," he says, looking at me. "Are you familiar with the term Cognizant?"

My hands tingle in the most unpleasant fashion, and my breathing approaches hypersonic speeds.

"Answer the question, love," Darian says soothingly.

"Are you familiar with the term Cognizant—not the dictionary definition?"

"I had a dream where the term was mentioned. I have no idea what it means," is what I want to say, but my tongue is refusing to move with all this attention on me. So I just stutter out, "N-no. I… no."

The stone around my neck glows red, and the room erupts in hushed whispers.

"A lie," Chester says loudly without getting up.

"Who are your parents?" asks yet another familiar voice (the fourth one if I'm counting them correctly). Is the fear damaging some voice recognition center in my brain? Is that why everyone in this room sounds familiar?

A black-robed man stands up and pulls down his hood—and I know him too because adrenaline has etched his perfect pale face into my mind.

"I am Councilor Vlad, Leader of the Enforcers," Rose's boyfriend/nephew states, and I yet again wonder if I'm losing my mind.

"Answer," Chester demands.

I jump at the intensity in his voice, my stomach twisting. "M-Makenzie Ballard and Braxton Urban."

The stone around my neck glows red again, and the people in the room exchange meaningful glances.

"He meant your biological parents," Darian clarifies.

The weight of the stares boring into me seems to double Earth's gravity, and my nausea intensifies as my hypersonic breathing impossibly speeds up. The room seems to shrink around me, the walls closing in.

"I was adopted," I hear myself gasp out, as though from a distance. "I don't know my biological parents."

My vision blurs, the green light in front of me permeated by white blotches of unconsciousness, and to my horror, I realize I'm about to pass out, like at the One Alpha presentation.

"Did you know that you're a Cognizant that evening?" someone asks in the distance. I don't know who it is, nor do I get a chance to answer because my public speaking anxiety finally defeats me.

I faint.

Except I'm not unconscious.

I'm looking at my body slumped on the floor.

CHAPTER EIGHTEEN

WITHOUT ADRENAL GLANDS, all signs of the panic attack that knocked me out are blissfully gone, and I become a pure observer, just like I was at the morgue and at the hospital.

"What the hell?" Chester says, the mockery in his tone giving way to confusion.

"It's the fear of public speaking," says the unidentified familiar voice behind me. "She had a panic attack."

"This is unprecedented," Kit says, tugging on a blond strand of hair. "Do we wait for her to come to? Can someone soothe her once she does?" She looks pointedly at Vlad.

"I think we've heard enough," Chester says.

"I concur." Darian stands up and removes his hood. "There's no way she knew she was a Cognizant."

"That's not obvious at all." Chester also stands up. "Nor am I convinced if it matters what she knew."

They both look at Kit, who grudgingly rises to her feet.

"Let's tackle Chester's second statement." She waves her hand in front of her face, and it changes into Chester's, right down to his devilish grin. If not for Kit's jewelry and robe on the faux Chester, I'd have thought they'd somehow switched places. "We agreed that it *will* matter if Sasha intentionally broke the Mandate—"

"But she's not under the Mandate," Darian says.

Kit waves her hand over her face again, and now she looks like Darian. "I meant, 'broke the spirit of the Mandate.'"

"It's her actions that matter, not the intent," Chester says. "She violated one of the biggest taboos of our kind."

"But intent does matter—we all agreed on that." Darian's British accent deepens. "She didn't know she was one of us, which means she didn't know the taboo —which means this meeting is adjourned."

"Not knowing a rule is not an excuse to break it." Chester isn't looking at Darian but is speaking for the benefit of the surrounding crowd. "It would be like a human eating another human and being pardoned by the courts because he didn't know that cannibalism is against the law."

"As you so often like to point out, 'we're much better than the humans,'" Darian says, his British accent gone when he quotes Chester. It makes me wonder if he could speak without any accent if he wanted to, and just affects one to sound sexy.

"I'm not convinced she didn't know, and in any case, I still strongly feel that she should be neutralized," Chester says, the smile replaced by an earnestness that looks foreign on his face.

Darian raises his hand, palm out. "I think we need another seer—"

"Like we need a hole in our heads," Chester interrupts, glaring at him.

"Gentlemen," Kit says, her face back to her own. "If I may. There is a difference between grabbing power intentionally—which is punishable by death—and accidentally stumbling upon it."

"But doesn't the severity of her transgression matter?" Chester asks. "Millions of humans think she's an oracle. That hasn't happened since antiquity—and we all know what manipulating faith can lead to." He looks around and in a lower voice adds, "Can you all even imagine how powerful she is now?"

"Fear-mongering isn't becoming of you," Darian says dismissively. "She's but a pup, untrained and innocent of our ways. Besides, if we were to neutralize all Cognizants with too much power, all of us in this room would have to slit our wrists, wouldn't we?"

"Your kind invented sophistry," Chester says in frustration.

"And yours perfected bollocks," Darian says, his tone even.

"Vlad, what do the Enforcers think?" Kit waves her

hand over her face, and her features morph into Vlad's marble-cut, brooding countenance.

"We either kill her, or she goes under the Mandate and is forbidden from performing her tricks ever again, under penalty of death," Vlad says ceremoniously.

"Right, that is the decision in a nutshell," Kit says, her face now turning into mine. "I was hoping you'd lean one way or another, not enumerate our choices."

"Seers are useful to us, and powerful seers are doubly useful," Vlad says after a moment of consideration. "But this could set an unfortunate precedent."

"I see that, as usual, Vlad will not commit to a choice, especially if it seems to favor one kind of Cognizant over another," Kit says, her face fluctuating between that of Chester and Darian.

"I don't approve of frivolity," Vlad says, looking at Kit sternly.

"I say we vote then," she says, her face back to her normal round-cheeked visage.

"I don't see why," Darian says.

"See, something we can finally agree on," Chester says. "Why vote if we can just kill her right here, right now." He looks eager to jump down and personally slit the throat of my unconscious body.

"If Kit says 'vote,' we vote," says the man who put the stone around my neck. There's a steely undertone in his voice, and the crowd goes silent and still.

"We vote then." Chester visibly forces himself to relax.

"Even if that's a waste of our precious time," Darian says, his mouth tight.

"Everyone in favor of leniency, stand up," Kit says.

Vlad, Darian, Kit, the stone giver, and a couple more people stand, but the vast majority remain seated.

They just voted to kill me.

The stone giver steps forward. "Councilors—"

———

I WAKE up to the roar of the cab's motor. Opening my eyes, I see we're already in the city.

Was that another one of my vision-dreams? It seemed to combine the two types I experienced before. The first half of this dream was like what happened on TV. I was fully present and experienced everything with my own senses—and just like that time, it was horrifying. The second half, the one that began after I fainted, was like the morgue and the hospital episodes. I guess if my future self is not at the location of the forecast, or is there but unconscious, I float like a disembodied ghost—which makes some kind of warped sense.

So was it a vision? Or could it have been a weird nightmare that has nothing to do with the future?

I strongly hope the latter to be the case because this Council, or whatever they are, voted to kill me.

One piece of evidence that this was just my brain

randomly misfiring during a regular REM sleep cycle
is that Vlad and Darian were in this dream. And there
were way too many familiar voices. That happens
when you're dreaming sometimes; your brain
regurgitates your waking experiences and puts a weird
spin on them.

"Can you please hand me my phone?" I ask the
cabbie, my voice scratchy from my impromptu nap.

"Here you go." He unhooks the phone from the
charger and hands it to me over his shoulder without
turning.

I take the phone and dial Darian, though I don't
know what I'll ask him when he picks up.

"We are sorry," a robotic female voice says after a
doo-dee-doo sound. "You have reached a number that
has been disconnected or is no longer in service. If you
feel you have reached this recording in error, please
check the number and try your call again."

Since his number is recorded in my contacts and
has worked before, there is nothing to check. They
should really update those disconnect auto-messages
for the cellphone era.

I log in to my email, find Darian's most recent
message (the one with the video of me), and write back,
"We need to talk."

An auto-reply comes almost right away, informing
me that my email has gone into the internet equivalent
of a black hole.

Darian deleted his email profile and disconnected
his number—but why?

I call the studio and ask for Darian, only to be told that no one by that name works there.

Desperate, I call Kacie—the show host—but I get her voicemail. And something tells me that if she did pick up the phone, she wouldn't know who Darian is anymore.

This is bad. Darian disappearing supports the dream, because why would you disappear if you're just a normal guy?

Vlad was never normal to start with. I have to talk to Rose about him; if nothing else, she should know about his violent tendencies.

I dial Rose's number, but her phone just rings until her voicemail picks up.

"We're here," the Spanish-accented voice of the driver intrudes into my thoughts.

He's right. We're standing right by my building.

"Can you autograph one of the bills for me?" he asks sheepishly.

"Sure." I sign a dollar for him and pay for the rest of the ride, making sure to tip him extra generously.

This is the first time someone's recognized me, and it would've felt really good if I weren't dealing with all this other crap. Lost in thought, I trudge into my building and catch the elevator. If that dream was a vision, they—whoever they are—will kill me. I have to prevent that. But how?

So far, I get the feeling that the future doesn't like to change. Case in point: I couldn't save Amie. Maybe the change I made on that TV stage was a rare event.

Maybe, going forward, I'll be cursed with seeing unfortunate events without being able to do anything about them—assuming I don't get killed, that is.

The elevator dings, and I beeline for Rose's apartment door.

I ring once and wait.

Nothing.

I ring a second time, then a third for good measure.

Still nothing.

I look left and right to make sure no neighbors are watching, then unscrew the top and bottom balls that hold together the two pieces of the stud in my tongue. I take the whole thing out and unfold it into a set of lock picks. The guy who made this gimmick for me builds illusions for the biggest names in Vegas, and this thing cost a small fortune.

Making short work of the lock, I open the door and step in, unsure how I'll explain the breaking and entering to Rose if she comes out to greet me.

Rose isn't home. Neither is the cat.

A lot of Rose's things are missing, and all cat accessories as well.

Maybe Vlad took Rose on a vacation? Perhaps he didn't like her proximity to the zombies he dispatched the other night?

Locking the door behind me, I head for my own apartment.

As I open the door, I dial Ariel again.

A phone rings in her room.

I wait to see if she picks up, but my call goes to voicemail.

Did she forget her phone?

I pad softly toward Ariel's room, unsure why I'm being stealthy. When I'm by the door, I hear faint shuffling sounds coming from inside.

Without a knock or a warning, I barge into the room.

The cold barrel of a gun presses against my forehead, halting me in my tracks.

CHAPTER NINETEEN

"ARIEL!" I shriek. "Why are you pointing a gun at me?"

"Sasha." She lowers her weapon. "Where did you come from? Why didn't you knock? You almost made me shoot you."

In a break from hyperventilating, I take a good look at my friend. Dressed in a standard-issue Army Combat Uniform, Ariel looks ready for a black ops mission.

"Where are you going dressed like that?" I ask, realizing I didn't even know Ariel kept a gun in our apartment.

Random thoughts flit through my adrenaline-oversaturated brain as I stare at the weapon. What if she or I got pregnant and the hypothetical offspring shot one of its friends with this gun? Or, perhaps slightly more realistically, what if Felix found the gun? It's all too easy to picture him roleplaying Neo and shooting his foot off. Oh, and I thought it was hard to get a gun in NYC—I toyed with the idea of performing the famous bullet catch effect, as well as the fake Russian Roulette act, but I put those ideas on the back-burner, thanks to the city's restrictive gun laws and, to a larger degree, my overdeveloped sense of self-preservation.

"I'm sorry." Ariel slides the weapon into a holster at her side. "I don't have time for twenty questions."

"This is about Beatrice, isn't it?" I say on a hunch. "You found out where she is."

"I really have to go. I only have a small window of opportunity," Ariel says without meeting my gaze, and I don't need Nero's truth-discerning abilities to know I hit the bullseye. This *does* have something to do with Beatrice.

"Fine." I put my hands on my hips. "Wherever you're going, I'm coming with you."

Ariel glares at me, then strides to her closet and takes out a coil of rope. She hangs it on her shoulder cowboy style and heads for the door.

I move to follow her.

With inhuman speed, Ariel closes the distance between us and grabs my elbows. By the time I have a chance to blink, she's twisted my arms behind my back. "Please don't move," she says. "I don't want to hurt you."

"You're already hurting me," I complain as I futilely try to break free but only manage to hurt my shoulder blades and yelp in pain.

"I'm sorry." Ariel drags me to a chair and forces me to sit. "I'll make it up to you, I promise."

"I can't have you fight this for me," I say, suppressing another yelp of pain as she brings my wrists together. "If something happens to you—"

"I'm trained; you're not." Ariel starts to tie my wrists with the rope.

I go silent, all my concentration on feeling the rope against my skin. My struggles become very calculated now—but to Ariel, they probably look like the last-ditch efforts of a trapped woman.

Done with my wrists, she wraps some rope across my chest and torso.

"Ariel, please think about what you're doing," I say. "You might need me. What if I get a useful vision? I haven't even told you about the thing at the hospital. Beatrice is dangerous."

Ariel doesn't reply to my pleading. Still avoiding my gaze, she comes around to examine me from the front. After studying her handiwork, she walks over to her nightstand and takes out a pair of handcuffs.

Despite the seriousness of the situation, I can't help but ask, "You just happen to keep those in your nightstand?"

Ariel blushes but remains silent as she drags me in the chair to the window and cuffs my ankle to the radiator.

"I'll be back soon," she says. She straps her M9 knife to her outfit, grabs her cellphone from the table, and leaves, ignoring my last-minute pleading.

As soon as she's out of the room, I start working on the rope.

Escapes are classic fare for illusionists, so I've included them in my preparations for my future show. I mastered rope escapes early on, because I had tons of rope after adding a cut-and-restore rope illusion to my restaurant repertoire. More recently, I've been practicing getting out of straitjackets and handcuffs, and have even experimented with a combination of them all.

If I ever get a kinky boyfriend, he'd have to be a master of his craft to properly tie me up.

Having said that, if I had my choice, I'd rather not be tied up with rope because it's the restraint that takes me the longest to escape. In this case, though, Ariel either never learned how to tie someone up, or she was in too much of a hurry to do it correctly. Furthermore, as she was tying my wrists, I'd managed to wiggle just enough to give myself an edge.

It takes me only a few seconds to free my hands, and the rest of the rope comes off after some further wiggling, like a too-tight sweater.

The picks in my tongue defeat the handcuffs in another few seconds.

Free, I leap to my feet and barge into my room, taking care not to trample Fluffster.

Grabbing Nero's cash, a windbreaker, and my favorite scarf (which I also use as a blindfold at my restaurant gig), I sprint after Ariel, nearly knocking over the coffee table in the living room.

Just as I slam the apartment door behind me, I spot the elevator doors closing.

Ignoring my poor legs' protests, I dash for the staircase and zoom down, leaping over multiple steps at a time.

The last time I used this staircase was when we lost power after a brutal winter storm, and the heavy layer of dust on the cement steps makes me suspect my neighbors also haven't used it since.

By the time I get to the first floor, my calf muscles burn as though someone branded me, and I'm panting like an overheated dog. I really hope my legs get toned as a result of all this running; it would be nice to make lemonade out of my life's torrent of zombie lemons.

Staying firmly in the cardio zone, I head for the building's exit. Running out, I see Ariel getting into a green Hyundai Sonata with an Uber sticker on the back.

I sprint toward the road, pulling out a hundred-dollar bill from the stack of Nero's cash in my pocket.

The Sonata signals a left turn. It's about to depart.

I wave my hundred at a passing yellow cab and make eye contact with the Sikh cabbie.

He pulls over next to me with a screech of brakes.

I immediately jump in. "Follow that green Hyundai Sonata," I tell him after I exhale the cloud of burned rubber out of my lungs. "If you don't lose them, I'll give you the meter plus this hundred."

"You got it," the guy says, and the cab jerks forward so fast it gives me minor whiplash.

We get on the Sonata's tail right away. Say what you will about Uber, but yellow cab drivers still have the edge when it comes to aggressive maneuvering.

I slide behind the cabbie, hoping his turban will hide me in case Ariel glances back. Unless she spots me, I doubt she'll realize she's being followed. Yellow cabs are so common they're practically invisible.

As we swerve in and out of traffic, I let my mind drift back to my last prediction dream and try to incorporate what I've heard into my new paradigm.

The word "Cognizant" featured prominently. Based on context, it seems the people in that room referred to themselves as such. Also, the way they said the word "human" implies that a Cognizant isn't human, though I could've misunderstood that part. Most interestingly, I seem to be one of these Cognizant, and my TV performance broke some big rule of theirs—a rule that has something to do with faith, if I remember correctly.

Could it be that I started seeing the future in my dreams simply because a lot of people in the world falsely believe me to be a psychic? The timing seems to coincide—plus, I felt that first warm flow of energy just as the largest chunk of people saw me perform.

But no. Going on TV can't give you powers, or else all the fake psychics would also become real. Then again, the Council made it sound that being a Cognizant was a key factor here. Specifically, that Cognizant are forbidden from doing exactly what I did. Could it be that when enough people believe a

Cognizant to be capable of something, the Cognizant in question gains that power? If so, I sure wish I did something else that evening, like one of my telekinesis effects (I have several methods for seemingly moving objects with my mind).

This faith business, if true, could also explain something: why Darian insisted I don't openly deny being a psychic on TV. He knew he couldn't get me to make that claim, but leaving the question ambiguous was enough to get tons of people to assume that I *am* for real—and thus, according to this theory, make me so. As to his motivation, it sounded like he wanted another seer, something that Chester guy opposed—

"They seem to be going to JFK," my driver says, bringing my attention back to the chase.

"Why do you think that?" Looking out the window, I realize I'm in Brooklyn for the second time today.

"Professional hunch," the cabbie says. "If that's where they're going, do you still want to follow?"

"Yes," I say, though my heart is sinking. If Ariel plans to fly someplace, it will be very hard to inconspicuously follow her.

To deal with the nervous anticipation, I take out a deck of cards (every item of clothing I own has at least one) and practice a few moves that I'm still rusty on. And sure enough, before long, Ariel's car takes the JFK airport exit, and we follow it all the way to Terminal 5.

"Thank you," I say to the cabbie. I pocket the cards and thrust two hundred-dollar bills at him.

Since I don't have time to wait for change, I leave the ecstatic driver behind me and hurry after Ariel.

As usual, the drop-off area is teeming with people, which is useful because Ariel is less likely to spot me if she turns around.

She doesn't turn around, though. Instead, she goes through the rotating glass doors without pausing.

I follow her, staying a dozen feet behind her and making sure to keep at least a few people between us.

As always, whenever I enter an airport, especially JFK, I get unpleasant flashbacks from the incident I shared with Lucretia. A knot forms in my throat at the old memories, so I push them away. The last thing I want is to lose focus and let Ariel get away—not that I know how I'd follow her onto a plane without a ticket or any clue about her destination.

Still, I have to try.

I follow Ariel through the crowds for a couple of minutes, and whenever I get a chance, I glance at the upcoming flights. According to the tableau, it's 12:37 p.m., so Ariel could be heading to Houston, Texas, on the 1:15 p.m. flight, or she could be getting on any of the dozens of later flights to other destinations.

Then I recall Ariel's gun, and the flying theory becomes less solid. TSA won't let you bring a gun onto a plane, even if you're going to a gun haven like Texas. Even I—an expert at hiding stuff on my person— wouldn't risk trying to smuggle something as big as a gun. Ariel stands no chance.

In another few minutes, it becomes clear she isn't

heading toward security anyway. Instead, she makes her way to the back of the terminal and unlocks a nondescript door before going through it.

I sprint like a zombie is on my tail and catch the door with my foot before it closes.

Then I wait for a couple of breaths to make sure Ariel gets sufficiently far before opening the door and stepping in.

For the second time today, I find myself with a gun to my forehead.

"Sasha!" If it weren't for the deadly weapon in her hand, Ariel's wide eyes would seem comical. "How did you get here?"

"Can you stop pointing that thing at me?" I raise my hands palms out. "Pretty sure you could get arrested for bringing a weapon to an airport."

Ariel lowers the gun and steps back, rubbing her forehead with one hand.

"I'm not letting you go without me," I say, crossing my arms over my chest.

Ariel stuffs the gun into her holster. "Yes, you are."

I put my hand on the door handle. I could probably escape before she grabs me, but I'm not certain. "If you so much as touch me again, this is it." I'm so frustrated I can't help but play dirty. "I promise you, we'll be through. I'll get my own apartment and never speak to you again. Friends don't treat friends like—"

"I'm trying to protect you," Ariel says through gritted teeth, and I feel a pang of guilt.

"I can take care of myself," I retort, wishing I felt as

confident as I sound. "Besides, you didn't give me a chance to tell you everything. I had more visions. There was this Council—"

At the mention of the word "Council," Ariel looks like someone's slapped her across the face. It's clear she wants to ask me for details, but she doesn't say anything.

Maybe it has to do with the bleeding incident?

"I understand you can't tell me anything, but you can listen," I say on another hunch. "I *know* I'm one of the Cognizant."

Ariel's eyes threaten to pop out of their sockets.

"In my vision, I was alive when I talked to this Council, so unless that's where you're headed now, I'm going to survive wherever we go."

I don't mention that I might have trouble surviving the Council itself.

Ariel frowns, then shakes her head. "I don't understand, but there isn't time to discuss."

"So take me with you, and I'll explain on the way," I say, watching her intently for any sudden movements.

"Fine, but you have to be blindfolded until we get to our destination." She points at my scarf.

"Deal," I say, taking it off. I'm extremely glad I've never shown Ariel any effects featuring this particular item of clothing.

Ariel extends her hand for the scarf and steps toward me.

"Wait," I say, grabbing the door handle again. "First, you have to swear you're actually going to take me with you. For all I know, you'll put that blindfold on me and knock me out or tie me up—or do something else I'd never expect my best friend to do to me."

"I swear," she says solemnly. "And I'm sorry about twisting your arms at the apartment. I was trying—"

"To protect me. I understand and resent it." I hang the scarf over my shoulder and turn my back to Ariel. "It's all forgiven and forgotten—if you take me with you."

Until now, I've never had to rely on Ariel's word, so I still half expect to get knocked out instead of blindfolded. If our roles were reversed—if I truly thought Ariel was in danger and breaking a promise would save her—I'd probably do so. Then again, being a magician makes me comfortable with deceit.

Fortunately, it soon becomes clear that Ariel is more honorable than I am. Instead of knocking me out, she puts the scarf over my eyes, and the only sign of her displeasure is how tightly she ties it around my head—I might've just heard my skull creak at the pressure. What Ariel doesn't realize, though, is that the tighter this blindfold is on me, the easier it will be to peek from it. When I use it at the restaurant, I always emphasize how tight I want it around my head.

Blindfold work is a staple of mentalism because something about seeing without eyes really resonates with the audience. There are dozens of methods for seeing once "blindfolded," and my scarf is perfect for the oldest of the classic methods—peeking down your nose. Anything below my navel is crystal clear, as though I'm not blindfolded at all, and—and this is why my scarf is extra nice—the fabric isn't as thick as it appears, which allows me to see vague shadows in well-lit rooms.

"Hold my hand," Ariel says, grabbing me like a mom who's walking her five-year-old over Broadway.

I do as I'm told, and we start our speed walk down the hallways.

"Tell me everything." Ariel's hand is cold—a sure sign of stress.

I tell her about the dreams and my confrontation with Amie.

As expected, she doesn't clarify anything.

"I had an idea," I say. Pretending to be blind (and maybe vindictively), I step on the heel of her right army boot. "I know you can't tell me things, but can you sing the explanations to me?"

"No." Ariel drags me through yet another door.

"How about texting, or tapping it out on my palm in Morse code?"

"No," Ariel says, turning the corner.

"How about Pig Latin?"

"No."

"I notice you can say 'no' when I say something dumb, so maybe that can be a way for you to confirm something for me. For example, are we currently in the Pentagon?" My question isn't just a joke—the labyrinthian corridors we pass through belong there more than under JFK.

"No," Ariel says.

"I'm a Cognizant," I say, and Ariel doesn't reply.

I take it as a confirmation.

"Felix has a girlfriend," I say next.

"No." Ariel chuckles humorlessly.

"You're a Cognizant also," I say.

No response confirms my suspicion.

"From here, we'll need to stay silent," Ariel says and opens a door.

We enter a room with a floor made of some slippery chrome material that gives the impression of standing on a mirror. From the echoing of our footsteps, I estimate that the room must be huge, and the reflection of the ceiling in the shiny floor material confirms my supposition.

A glow of multi-colored light surrounds us, though I can't be sure what the source of the light is without bending my head back—which I dare not do so as not to give away my nose-peek secret to Ariel.

Her grip tightens, and she pulls me in the direction of a purple light.

When we're a couple of feet away, in my down-the-nose-view, I see the lower half of the light source—and it takes all of my self-control not to squeeze Ariel's palm in shock.

Back in college, in my *Intro to Physics* class, we learned about plasma—the fourth state of matter, the others being liquid, solid, and gas. If someone were to make a 3D flattened sphere out of plasma, and make it glow purple, it would probably look like the thing in front of me. It's as though someone has taken lightning (which is plasma), compressed it into a circle, and colored it purple. It vaguely reminds me of the magic energy I saw come out of Beatrice's hands—only much bigger and more impressive.

"We're about to step outside again," Ariel lies—or at least I assume she does because she actually drags me toward the giant circle of purple light.

When her right leg crosses the threshold of the plasma, her leg disappears.

I suppress an awed gasp. This must be the hardest bit of acting any magician in history has had to do to maintain the secret of the blindfold.

Given that Ariel is not screaming about her missing limb, I assume that its disappearance is just a visual illusion.

The rest of Ariel's body follows her foot into the light. Only her hand is visible now—the hand I can't help but grip a little firmer as I follow her in.

My leg also disappears, and I feel no pain. I feel nothing unusual, in fact.

Fully crossing the plasma's threshold, I fight the overwhelming temptation to rip the stupid scarf from my face.

The mirror floor below my feet looks exactly like the floor in the room we just left, but what I see reflected in that mirror isn't the same at all.

We're no longer in JFK, or even on planet Earth.

We've just stepped into a completely alien world.

CHAPTER TWENTY

THE SKY above us is a fluorescent purple—the kind used in psychedelic black light paintings. The clouds are pink and look like blobs of heavenly cotton candy.

When I was a kid, I had the worst case of what Mom later called "whyism"—I asked the question "why" about once every half hour. I recall being specifically curious about four big questions: Why is sitting still so boring? Why is sugar sweet? Why is water wet? And (relevant to the current situation) why is the sky blue?

I later learned why my parents had so much trouble explaining that last question to a five-year-old; the answer is so complex that I only vaguely understand it now, as an adult. The short version is that light coming from the sun has every color in it (colors being light of different wavelengths), but the atmosphere (oxygen and nitrogen) scatters this light in a way that causes the shorter wavelengths to hit our eyes. Shorter wavelengths are blue and violet, but due to the way our eyes work, we only perceive the blue.

Also, though I didn't care about cloud color as a kid, I now know that they appear white because water molecules aren't as picky as oxygen and nitrogen are in the way they scatter light. So, when the cacophony of all the colors hits our eyes, we perceive white.

Not pink, like the clouds above.

My breathing speeds up, and this is when I realize that the air is unusually thick and sweet as I gulp it down. Could this place have a different atmosphere as well, and if so, is it safe to breathe?

Thinking about air quality makes me lightheaded. Of course, that could also be because I'm not getting enough oxygen. And now that I'm paranoid, I could also swear that my steps are lighter than usual. Is the gravity slightly off as well?

If Ariel hadn't forbidden me from speaking, I'd be asking all of these questions now, but I can't—especially since I'm not supposed to be able to see any of this.

Ariel keeps dragging me away from the gateway, and she's clearly unimpressed with everything. It's as though we're just taking a hike through some forest upstate.

I get a half-baked idea. What if the reflective flooring somehow creates this sky-color illusion? Since Ariel's back is to me, I risk tilting my head back and raising the blindfold slightly to look directly at the sky.

The sky stays purple and the clouds pink.

The only difference is that in my wider view, I spot more impossible things, like two moons—one slightly smaller than the one I'm used to seeing, and one twice the size. There also seems to be a Saturn-like ring orbiting us—maybe remnants of a third moon?

It takes an enormous effort of will to stop gawking at the sky and look back down—and as I do, I glimpse our immediate surroundings. We're standing on a large mirrored surface the size of Madison Square Garden, and around its circumference are multi-colored plasma warp gates. Each gate repeatedly gets hit by lightning from the pink clouds above, but no thunder reaches our ears.

Un-freaking-believable.

The emotion magic tries to evoke in spectators is awe. As a magician, I'm sadly limited in how often I can feel this emotion because I know too many secrets. What I just saw, however, opens the constipated gates of my awe, and I feel like I might drown in it.

Sliding the blindfold back down with trembling fingers, I try to update my world paradigm with this new development as I keep walking. Unless I'm sleeping, I must be on another planet, or maybe in a different universe... or realm, or dimension, or plane, or a parallel world, or whatever. And I've gotten here by way of something like Stargate, a wormhole-like magical teleportation artifact.

Of course, as Ariel drags me deeper, a part of me screams out rational explanations. For example, someone could feasibly create a giant dome and depict the strange sky and clouds on it, like in *The Truman Show*. Yes, there's no reason for someone to bother doing that to me, but isn't that explanation easier to swallow than "another world?" Then again, another world is still not as weird as necromancy. After all, it's a fact that countless other planets do exist, and wormholes/other universes are covered by some legitimate scientific theories.

Is this where the Cognizant are from? A place like this? That would explain why the Council didn't consider themselves human—but it also raises a million follow-up questions. Why do we (it's so strange to include myself in this) look so human? Could the Cognizant be from a parallel world/universe where evolution—or design—led to beings that look just like humans, but have slight oddities, like the tendency to manifest powers that regular humans believe them to have?

If I don't find a way to get some answers soon, my brain will implode from curiosity.

On a whim, I sneak the hand Ariel is not holding into my pocket and palm my phone.

As the name implies, "palming" is the magician's technique of hiding objects, usually cards, in the palm of one's hand. Being a girl, my hands are small, a disadvantage in this area, which is why I try to make up for it with practice. I often sleep, eat, and commute to work with a card (or coin, or sometimes a phone) palmed using a variety of methods, some of which were invented by me.

So, for example, I'm now holding a phone in such a way that the back of my hand hides the phone from Ariel's view, even if she were to turn and look at me.

It's now 12:41 p.m. That means we've been walking through these secret tunnels for a little less than eighteen minutes. Unsurprisingly, the phone has no reception, and the GPS doesn't work when I bring up the Maps app. The strangest part is how the compass feature behaves—the digital arrow spins around nonstop, like a spin top inside of a dream in *Inception*. Phones don't have a traditional compass (a tiny magnet spinning on its axis) built into them, but they do have a magnetometer which allows for the same functionality.

Is something in this world messing with the magnetometer, or is the spinning somehow due to the lack of a GPS signal?

Slipping the phone back into my pocket, I follow Ariel for about ten more minutes until I finally see our destination—a blue gate. Aside from its color, it looks just like the gate we walked through to get here. Ariel's pace speeds up as we approach it, and I jog to keep up with her despite the violent complaints of my leg muscles.

Just like before, Ariel disappears into the gate, her outstretched arm hovering in the air for a few seconds before it pulls me in.

This time, I follow eagerly, wondering if I missed any odd sensations when crossing that first boundary.

The feeling of crossing is very brief and subtle, but —and this could be my already overstimulated imagination—I think I do feel *something:* a momentary weightlessness and a hint of an ozone smell. Perhaps this is what it feels like to be taken apart, molecule by molecule, in one spot, and instantly reassembled at the destination (assuming that's how these gates work).

A crazy thought occurs to me. If some molecules got lost in transit, would I look thinner?

We end up in a room with a roof, where the ceiling reflection looks identical to the one I saw at JFK. I catch glimpses of the warp gates here too.

When we exit the gate room, we end up in a hallway with a floor that also looks similar to the one at JFK.

Did we go back?

No.

That would be pointless.

There has to be a better explanation.

I palm my phone again and sneak a peek at it.

The time is 12:43 p.m.—which doesn't make sense. We walked for over ten minutes in that alien place and for about three more minutes after we came out. Could those missing ten minutes have been a fluke due to the lack of cell reception? Or—a more intriguing possibility—does the time spent in that purple sky place not count here on Earth? Maybe time passes much more slowly there?

Frustrated by the lack of answers yet again, I launch the Maps app and see that the GPS signal is back.

According to the phone, we're still in an airport, but not JFK. Instead, we're at LAS—the McCarran International Airport in Las Vegas, Nevada. As in, twenty-five hundred miles away—a distance we seemingly walked, even though, according to my phone, such a stroll would normally take over a month (or thirty-seven hours driving, or five hours on a plane).

Obviously, the gate we just used can save its users—the Cognizant—a ton of time.

Hiding my phone again, I follow Ariel out of the LAS version of the labyrinths into the terminal.

The crowds here are not as bad as at JFK, but they're large enough for me to wonder why no one is confronting the girl leading her blindfolded friend around like a walking dog. I guess they all assume it's something kinky and take the whole "what happens in Vegas stays in Vegas" motto very seriously.

As we make our way out of the terminal, Ariel takes out a phone from her pocket and does something with it.

A car is waiting for us when we exit, so I assume Ariel summoned a ride.

She guides me inside, and we start driving. To my disappointment, Ariel doesn't discuss the destination with the driver or talk to him at all; he just follows the directions in the app.

Since my body is blocking my right pocket from Ariel's view, I sneak out my phone yet again. The battery is running low, which makes sense as it only charged for forty minutes in the cab. Oh well, I might as well squeeze all the remaining usefulness out of it by keeping an eye on our progress.

It doesn't take long before I see that we're headed to the famous Las Vegas Strip.

Given that Ariel didn't say it was okay to speak again, I do not utter a word until the car stops.

According to the GPS, we are next to the Luxor Hotel—a place I've dreamed of visiting for years because this is where Criss Angel regularly performs his *MindFreak* show.

A half-formed thought flits through my mind. Could I be taking part in the most elaborate prank ever created? Did Ariel somehow get in touch with Criss Angel and tell him how much of a fangirl I am? Maybe he offered to involve me in a *Punk'd*-type TV show with a huge budget. Derren Brown, a British mentalist, once convinced a guy that a meteor had hit the Earth, resulting in a zombie apocalypse. Could something like that be behind all of the crazy things I've gone through?

If that were the case, this would be a great place to finally reveal it all.

The problem with this idea is the nagging question of "how." The only way what I've seen is even remotely plausible is via hallucinogens as strong as the ones the *Scarecrow* weaponized in *Batman Begins*. Come to think of it, it *is* Ariel's favorite film, so it could be the inspiration for all of this. But how can someone direct hallucinations to cause dreams that come true? This theory completely breaks down upon examination, no matter how much I wish I were being fooled (especially by Criss Angel).

We leave the car and walk into the hotel. My resentment of my blindfold grows.

I'd like to get a real look at the Egyptian theme of this place.

The Luxor is such a huge place I soon lose track of where Ariel is taking me, and my phone finally dies, so it can't help me.

Eventually, we stop by some door, and Ariel clears her throat. "It's okay to take the scarf off now."

I rip the thing off my face and pretend that my eyes need to adjust to the bright light.

Posters everywhere inform me that we're next to Luxor's less-interesting-for-me attraction, *Bodies... The Exhibition.* A big sign on the door in front of us states that the show is closed for renovations and will reopen tomorrow.

Ariel once took me to a version of this exhibit at the South Street Seaport. I was both impressed and grossed out. In a nutshell, the creators of *Bodies* took a bunch of dead people, skinned them (in some cases, taking the meat off the bones), and arranged them in different poses. Sometimes, they'd drive the gruesomeness home by exposing a cadaver's brain; other times, they'd have the muscle-encased skeleton hold its own skin or exposed organs, or they'd just put the tree-like circulatory system on display. If Hannibal Lecter, Leatherface, Freddy, and Jason all decided to get artsy, their masterpieces would fit right in with those exhibits. What made that trip worse was that Ariel—who, as part of her studies, works with cadavers

—kept adding juicy details, such as how magnificent the vivisection work was.

"She's there." Ariel tugs at the door, but it appears to be locked. "Are you sure you want to be part of this?"

I finally connect all the dots.

Beatrice, a necromancer, would naturally be in a morbid place like *The Bodies* exhibit. She's probably doing the renovations in question—and having a blast playing with all the dehydrated, mutilated corpses.

"Isn't this a dangerous place to deal with someone like her?" I examine the lock on the door and twist the handle a couple of times.

Ariel doesn't reply but pulls out a gun, which is an answer in itself. She must've correctly figured that Beatrice was going to send more corpses my way—and that I wouldn't survive the next wave. Somehow, she learned where Beatrice is, assessed the risks, and decided to arm herself to the teeth.

Sometimes I think Ariel follows only one motto in life: "What would Batman do?"

"I guess she always hangs out around corpses anyway," I say, not sure who I'm trying to psych up. "And besides, she can make corpses at any time by killing innocent people. Oh, and I think the older the corpses, the worse—"

"I really think you should stay here," Ariel says tersely.

"No." I take out my lock picks and unlock the door in front of us. "Let's go."

Sighing deeply, Ariel takes the lead and walks into the exhibition.

The people (assuming it *was* people) behind the Luxor exhibit clearly decided to take the morbidness of the New York expo and ratchet it up a few grisly notches.

There's a skeletal corpse on a bicycle, and another riding a skinless horse. In general, there are a lot of sports depicted—because everyone knows the dead love their sports. There's a cadaver throwing a baseball, one holding a basketball, one playing football, one playing chess (hey, it's a mind sport), one throwing a spear, and even one with a golf club. Other corpses are playing cards (if the game is poker, that's another mind sport), and one with a hollow skull is conducting a symphony with a baton. And if that weren't enough to make you ponder your mortality, there's also a pregnant woman's corpse, with her insides and a pale dead fetus exposed.

We find Beatrice next to a cadaver who's been sawed into two halves that are high-fiving each other. She's behind the two halves, working on one of them with some kind of metal instrument.

"I'm sorry," she says when she sees Ariel. "We're closed for maintenance today. Please come back tomorrow." Then her gaze falls on me, and her eyes widen before narrowing into slits.

Ariel raises her gun and switches off the safety. "We need to talk, Beatrice."

The necromancer raises her hands, and the tool she was holding clanks against the floor.

"As you can see, I found you," Ariel says, and though not directed at me, the malice in her voice gives me the chills. "If you don't leave my friend alone, I will find you again—or I'll make sure *others* find you."

"I understand," Beatrice says, her voice shaking. "I don't want any—"

Before she finishes speaking, electricity arcs from her hands into the two halves of the cadaver in front of her.

They come alive instantly, their high-fiving hands gripping each other as the two halves hop forward on one leg, as though to become one whole corpse.

Ariel fires, but the corpse reaches Beatrice in time, shielding her from the bullet.

In horror, I watch as more necromancer lightning arcs through the exhibit.

CHAPTER TWENTY-ONE

ARIEL JUMPS to the side so fast my eyes have a hard time following her.

She aims the gun again.

"Behind you!" I yell and leap to help.

I'm too late.

A golf club crashes into Ariel's back, and her shot goes into the ceiling.

Spinning faster than humanly possible, Ariel pistol-whips the golf-club-wielding cadaver. His head flies across the room like a hollowed-out melon and lands with a crunchy splat.

I spot a flicker of movement, but before I can cry out, a baseball slams into Ariel's temple.

She staggers but doesn't fall. In the meantime, more cadavers—probably the ones playing cards earlier—surround us, and Beatrice dashes away.

"Go after her." Ariel takes out her knife and half

slices, half punches off two cadaver heads. "I'll take care of them."

I sprint after the necromancer, but a corpse crosses my way.

It's the orchestra conductor holding a baton, with ninety percent of his skull bones cut out, leaving his head looking like two suitcase handles crisscrossed.

I skid to a halt.

The conductor throws the sharp wooden stick at my face in a gesture reminiscent of demanding a crescendo from the percussion section of some infernal orchestra.

I duck.

Instead of plunging into my right eye, the wooden stick grazes my forehead, leaving a splinter embedded inside.

The pain fuels my rage. I close the distance between us, grab at the conductor's hollowed-out skull, and yank.

The sharp bone cuts my hands, but the conductor's spine severs, leaving his head in my hands.

These corpses are even more fragile than the guys who attacked me in the hallway—hopefully, that gives us a chance.

Tossing the head at the nearest approaching corpse, I resume my sprint after Beatrice.

A gunshot rings out from Ariel's location, but I don't have time to look back.

In a glass display to my right, I see a shadow

approach. I dodge it, and a football-carrying corpse crashes into the display.

If there had been a girls' football team in school, I could've been a running back.

As if to curb my athletic ambitions, a football slams into my back.

My shoulder blades scream in pain. Fine. Maybe football is not for me, after all.

Emboldened by the ever-shrinking distance between me and Beatrice, I grit my teeth until my jaws ache and keep running.

Spotting a movement to my right, I halt.

A bicycling corpse whooshes by where my body would've been had I not stopped.

I kick the bike's back tire, causing both the corpse and the vehicle to tumble into a naked circulatory system under a glass display. Shards of glass, bits of capillaries, and pieces of bone crunch under my boots as I resume my pursuit.

Ariel grunts somewhere closer to me, then fires another round of bullets at whoever she's fighting. All this is followed by thuds of cadaver bits hitting the floor.

Beatrice glances over her shoulder, her face pale and sweaty.

When she spots me so close, her gaze shifts to the pregnant woman cadaver, and two arcs of energy spring from her fingers.

The exhibit animates and stands between me and Beatrice—who resumes her escape.

Deciding it will be faster to run around this obstacle than to fight it, I make a wide circle around the preggers corpse, keeping her firmly in my peripheral vision.

The corpse reaches into her exposed innards and pulls out a writhing cadaver-fetus from her womb. The underdeveloped zombie-kid hangs by a pale umbilical cord, and the mom zombie starts to twirl it, like a cowgirl from hell.

My stomach churns at the sight of this abomination. Speeding up, I half expect the fetus to yo-yo back at its dead mother, but the cord must've been cut because the projectile takes flight, spinning through the air like a macabre bolas.

I stop to try to dodge it, but the gruesome lasso gets me where I stand. The umbilical cord wraps around my throat, and the fetus smacks into the side of my head. Before the full horror of it can penetrate my brain, I feel tiny fingers and toes firmly gripping my hair.

Squealing like Felix at a butcher shop, I grab the little offender by the torso and yank it away with all my might.

I get it off, but sacrifice some hair—a totally worthwhile exchange.

The umbilical cord around my neck seems to turn into an anaconda as it tries to strangle me, so I violently rip it off of me, leaving burn marks on my already-bruised neck.

As soon as I'm free, the overdose of adrenaline

helps me bolt away from the crawling little horror and its snake-like appendage.

A single thought circles though my mind, over and over. *I'm not supposed to die here*. Otherwise, how could I have seen that vision of myself at the Council meeting?

I'm meant to die *after* that meeting, not before.

Unfortunately, this mantra does little to calm the insane beating of my heart, probably because I don't entirely believe it. What if seeing that future created a type of butterfly effect that leads to me dying here? I did change the future on the TV stage, so maybe I've done it again. If I hadn't told Ariel about my vision to convince her to bring me along, I wouldn't be here— and now that I am, all bets are off.

Putting those thoughts out of my mind before they become a self-fulfilling prophecy by getting me killed, I sprint until I see Beatrice again.

A bullet shatters a display to Beatrice's right, and I take sadistic pleasure in her startled jump. The necromancer recovers quickly, though, and responds by throwing her energy mojo at the skinless horse and its skeletal rider.

Do her powers only affect former humans?

No such luck.

Both the steed and its rider come to un-life and charge right at me.

I dash behind the exhibit of a corpse that has been sliced into thin pieces, each of which has been enclosed in glass to create the illusion of a see-through body. My hope is that all this glass will unnerve the horse—with the reanimated cross-sections wriggling inside the glass, I'm certainly disquieted.

The horse doesn't care where I stand. It rears up on its hind legs, and I see that I'm moments away from getting trampled by its stone-like hooves and cut up by the glass.

I scramble out of the way just as the right hoof connects with the display and shatters it. Bits of glass fly at me, slicing at my forearms as I try to shield my face.

A flat slice of the see-through cadaver slithers out of its broken glass prison and onto the ground toward me, but it's quickly squashed by a hoof.

The horse rears again.

A gunshot rings out behind the animal. Its rider's head flies off, but his legs and torso hold on, turning the exhibit into the headless horseman from *Sleepy Hollow*.

Clearly annoyed, the monstrosity turns toward Ariel.

I lower my arms, ignoring the stinging and the blood from the cuts, and stomp on the still-moving slice of dead flesh before me.

Ariel elbows the horse smack in the snout.

It sounds like all thirty-four bones in that equine skull break as one, and the horse stumbles.

Doubling down on her success, Ariel kicks at the horse's two front legs. The animal's legs fold at the knees, and Ariel jumps around to the thing's midsection. Throwing her leg back like a soccer player, she kicks the horse with devastating force.

The broken horse monster flies at the wall, taking a couple of glass displays with it.

"Flank her from the right!" Ariel shouts and rushes for Beatrice, staying to the left herself.

With all my remaining energy, I do as Ariel says.

Beatrice must know by now who's the bigger threat, so almost all of the remaining corpses attack Ariel.

In the corner of my vision, I see Ariel rip a feminine dancer-corpse in half. Meanwhile, I vault over a barely crawling, quadriplegic zombie whose earlier job must've been to expose his organs for display.

Ariel yanks the exaggerated lungs out of the open chest of a singer-cadaver and smacks him on the head with them. She then shoots in Beatrice's general direction, but a moving skeleton takes the bullet for his mistress.

I can see we'll have Beatrice cornered in a few moments.

Unfortunately, Beatrice realizes this too, so like a cornered rat, she summons all her minions with renewed vigor. The energy waves she's shooting from her hands could power the Apple Store for a week.

I glance at Ariel and see her focus on something behind me. "On your right!" she screams.

I turn my head and catch a glimpse of a basketball right before it smacks into my face.

The bridge of my nose explodes in pain as horrid memories of playing dodgeball at summer camp flit through my mind.

My legs falter, and my mind goes blank.

CHAPTER TWENTY-TWO

I COME to my senses on the floor.

Ariel is extending her hand to me, so I grasp it and get back on my wobbly feet.

A dozen of the walking dead have begun forming a wide circle around us. Some of the corpses look like pasta drainers with all the bullet holes Ariel put in them. She must've gotten some target practice in as she made her way to me.

"Let's flank her again. I'll thin this herd and you follow," Ariel whispers and takes a few steps away from me.

The corpses—or Beatrice—do not like the idea of Ariel moving, so they begin to slowly constrict the circle.

Ariel stops, reaches into her inner pocket, and takes out a clip. She must need to reload that gun.

Still dazed, I glance around. The floor is littered

with body parts Ariel must've ripped off with her bare hands.

There's a flutter of movement in my peripheral vision. I turn and see a cadaver who looks like the one that used to hold a spear—or was it a disk?

Whatever the weapon, he's not holding it anymore.

There's a loud scream from Ariel's direction.

I look back.

A spear is sticking out of my best friend's chest.

The shock hits me like another basketball to the head.

The clip and the gun drop out of Ariel's hands as she grasps at the spear lodged in her chest. She tries to pull it out but screams in pain.

Her eyes roll back, and like a cut tree, she starts to topple over.

I reach Ariel in one leap—just in time to slightly soften her fall by catching her shoulders. Numb, I kneel over her to take a closer look at her wound.

It's bad.

The whole spearhead is inside her chest.

Ariel's breathing is extremely labored, and blood is oozing from her mouth.

"No," I whisper. "Please, Ariel. No."

"I'm sorry." She opens her bloodshot eyes, her beautiful face contorted in pain. "Here," she says, with blood gushing from her mouth. She takes my hand in hers and puts it on the bloodied knife strapped to her belt. "You have to—"

"Hush. Don't talk like—"

She grabs me by the collar, shakes me for a moment, then gurgles, "You have to get away from me—"

Her body slackens, and her breathing stops.

I stare into her eyes uncomprehendingly, watching them turn lifeless.

No.

This can't be happening.

If I could rip out Beatrice's throat with my teeth right now, I would. I've never felt this kind of bloodthirst before, but I don't reject it—I let it fuel my revenge.

Grasping the knife, I leap to my feet.

An arc of energy shoots from Beatrice's fingers into Ariel's dead body.

I now understand why Ariel told me to get away from her, even as a part of me rejects that conclusion. Surely the universe wouldn't allow—

Ariel's body stirs.

Now I'm ready to torture Beatrice before I kill her. First, though, I have to run.

Ariel jumps to her feet with supernatural speed.

Somewhere far in my brain, I recall that fresh corpses make superior killing machines for Beatrice. I don't want to believe that Ariel—even a dead, reanimated one—would hurt me, but I'm not sticking around to find out.

Turning, I start to run, but a vise-like grip on my left elbow yanks me to a halt.

It's Ariel.

She got me.

Her neck muscles strain, and something in my arm breaks with a horrible crunching sound.

The agony hitting my brain is all-encompassing and pure.

I must be in shock because my mouth is screaming, yet my mind is observing my surroundings with a strange detachment.

How am I not fainting?

Three cadavers grab the knife from me, toss it aside, and grab hold of my right hand, leaving me stretched out between them and Ariel like I'm being crucified.

My scream devolves into a hoarse hiss as I lose my voice.

Beatrice approaches, unfolding her butterfly knife.

"It was a valiant effort," the necromancer says, her tone almost sympathetic. "This wasn't personal. I hope you understand that."

"Wait," I try to scream, but my vocal cords fail me.

With a practiced thrust, Beatrice buries her knife in my chest.

I look down and see blood spreading over my shirt pocket.

"I wasn't supposed to die here," I futilely try to say, but my heart stops and I die.

CHAPTER TWENTY-THREE

I HANG bodiless and stare as Beatrice reanimates my corpse and says, "This was a close call, but you two will make great bodyguards for what's to come. So there's a silver lining. For me."

She walks up to my corpse and pulls out the knife.

She then rips the spear out of Ariel's chest.

———

I COME to my senses on the floor.

Ariel is extending her hand to me.

She is alive.

I am alive.

But how?

Of course. That was another psychic vision.

The ball knocked me out, and just like at the TV studio, I saw the near future.

I was correct to worry about butterfly effects. The

vision of that Council meeting did change my future, and I *can* be killed. The only bit of silver lining here is that if we survive the next few minutes, there's a chance that the future could be changed enough that I won't have to face the Council at all.

I grasp Ariel's hand and get to my unsteady feet—though the adrenaline helps me recover quicker than in my vision.

Just as I've foreseen, we're surrounded.

"Let's flank her again. I'll thin this herd and you follow," Ariel whispers, and before I can grab her hand, she takes a few steps away from me.

As before, the corpses—or Beatrice—don't like the idea of Ariel moving, so they begin to constrict their circle.

"Duck," I shout at Ariel. "Drop to the ground! Now!"

She doesn't seem to hear, focusing on getting the gun and clip from her inner pocket.

There's no more time for talking.

I have to undo everything I saw in that vision, right this moment.

There's a principle in magic that I often use in my restaurant act: a large movement will cover a small movement. Since Beatrice is looking at me closely, I decide to utilize that principle now.

Reaching into my pocket, I prepare for the small-movement portion of my plan. Then I spin toward Ariel, preparing my legs for the much larger movement.

Though I'm not looking in that direction, I detect

the flicker of movement from the cadaver throwing his spear.

I leap for Ariel, bodyguard style.

In the air, I complete the smaller movement. I probably won't even need this precaution, but if the future decides to be stubborn, this can help.

My larger movement is also a huge success. I tackle Ariel. Her gun and clip drop to the ground, and we fall onto them in a two-person heap.

The spear grazes my neck and clanks on the floor a few feet away.

Ariel's gaze falls on the spear, then darts to me.

"My gun," she says. "I have to grab it—"

She sees something over my shoulder and violently pushes me away. I fly almost a foot into the air and land on the ground, rolling. My breath vacates my lungs, and as I wheeze for air, my ribs scream in protest.

Catching my breath, I see the reason for Ariel's action. As soon as that spear had taken flight, the dead circling us must've started running toward us. Ariel had gotten me away just as they'd closed in, and now they're piled on top of her like a bunch of demon kindergarteners.

I rush to excavate Ariel from all the dead, but a skeletal arm grabs my left elbow.

I twist, kicking the corpse in the shin, but then I spot a movement to my right.

Spinning, I see that this corpse is missing the top of its skull, so I reach in and yank out the exposed brain.

Necromancy clearly doesn't require the corpse to have a brain of its own, because my attacker doesn't slow in his effort to grab my right arm.

Yet again, I'm caught in a crucifixion position. I struggle, trying to get free, but nearly dislocate my shoulders to no avail.

Damn it. The future does like its patterns. That, or this is the worst case of déjà vu I've ever had because I again have a corpse holding me on each side—almost exactly like in my earlier vision, except (and this is huge) Ariel is alive.

To complete the picture, Beatrice comes toward me.

She takes out her butterfly knife and readies the blade—just as before.

In my periphery, I see the mound of corpses on top of Ariel shake, as if it's about to erupt like a volcano. But even if my friend frees herself, she won't get to me in time to stop Beatrice.

"It was a valiant effort," Beatrice says in that oddly sympathetic tone. "This wasn't personal. I hope you understand that."

With a practiced thrust, she buries the knife in my chest.

CHAPTER TWENTY-FOUR

I SLACKEN and feel the cadaver hands on my arms loosen. Beatrice probably needs them to help keep the almost-escaped Ariel in check.

I look down, but this time, there's no blood spread over my shirt pocket.

Beatrice clearly didn't catch the small movement that was covered by my leap.

This is what I did: I palmed my trusty deck of cards and hid it in my shirt pocket, just in case the future tried to be stubborn, which it did. The knife couldn't get through the barrier I created—even Ariel isn't strong enough to pierce more than half of the cards in a deck.

I'm not sure how different stabbing a deck is to stabbing a ribcage, but it looks like Beatrice isn't experienced enough with stabbing to tell the difference —she must usually use the knife for carving fleshy parts.

Ripping my arms from the loosened grip of the corpses, I grab Beatrice's wrist and attempt to wrestle her knife away.

I'm not sure if it's the element of surprise, or if I'm just stronger than the necromancer, but I rip the knife away, cutting her palm as a bonus.

Without thought or hesitation, I slice at her.

The knife cuts through something soft.

Beatrice screams, and her hands clasp her face.

The scalpel-like knife has cleaved open her cheek, and blood is gushing out of it.

Despite her screaming, she has enough sense to back away from me.

I come after her, readying for a stab.

Something—probably a corpse—grabs my shirt from the back, so I spin on my heel and slice at it.

The knife enters the mummified meat in the creature's neck and cuts through the vertebrae. My attacker's head falls to the ground.

This knife is *sharp*.

Unfortunately, two more corpses are running straight at me.

I pivot back toward Beatrice.

Knife throwing is something else I've always wanted to add to a future show, but I haven't yet mastered this skill as much as I'd like—mostly for safety reasons.

Aiming fast, I hurl the butterfly knife at Beatrice's back.

The formerly chess-playing cadaver jumps up and takes the knife for his mistress.

He then runs for Ariel's pile.

The two cadavers from earlier grab me by the shoulders. I try to wriggle free, without much success.

Ariel's pile finally erupts, leaving her in the middle with someone's detached leg in her hands. Ariel then uses the leg as a club to clear a path toward Beatrice.

I jerk away from the corpses holding me, but they grab me again.

Ariel's head is bleeding; one of the cadavers must've hit her with a blunt weapon. But she doesn't seem to notice her wound, and as soon as she catches sight of Beatrice, she rushes toward her.

The dead—or more likely, Beatrice—don't like that. A bunch of corpses desperately clutch at Ariel's boots and clothing, but she keeps moving. If a corpse can't get a grip on Ariel, they grab on to one of the corpses who've managed to get a grip on her. Soon, Ariel ends up dragging a literal dead weight behind her, like a morbid bridal train.

The blood trail she leaves behind worries me, so I again try to rip out of the arms that hold me, but only succeed in hurting my shoulders.

More dead attempt to stop Ariel from proceeding forward, but they only slow her down. Despite the trickle of blood, she looks so determined I doubt anything short of decapitation would stop her.

When Ariel is only a leap away from Beatrice, the cadavers holding me decide they might be more useful at the battlefront. The restraining hands let me go, and I torpedo forward.

Ariel must've saved some strength all this time, because despite the corpses anchoring her, she leaps like an Olympic jumper and is instantly free of them.

Landing next to Beatrice, she strikes the necromancer in the chest.

Beatrice flies several feet and lands on her back with a satisfying smack.

I jump over several corpses as I rush to help Ariel.

Ariel leaps again. This time, she lands on Beatrice in some sort of wrestling maneuver. Grabbing the necromancer by her shoulders, Ariel lifts Beatrice's body off the ground for a moment, then slams it back down.

I'm almost there when the corpses pile on top of Ariel once more, trying to pry her away from their mistress.

I grab the nearest cadaver by the leg and pull him off my friend, dragging him face down.

The cadaver's head does an *Exorcist*-style one-eighty, and he yanks his leg so hard I'm left holding just his foot.

Hopping up onto his remaining good leg, he faces me. I throw the foot at him. He bitch-slaps me across the face, then clasps my head between his bony palms, as though to force me into a staring contest.

I try to jerk away, my hands grabbing at his wrists to pull them away, but my head is stuck in a literal death grip.

The cadaver's thumbs reach for my eyes.

I squeeze them shut and desperately kick out, ramming my boot into a bony shin. It cracks with a dry crunch, but the thumbs are on my eyelids, pressing.

My stomach rolls, my heartbeat supersonic as I claw at the corpse's hands. The pressure on my eyeballs is the most frightening thing I've ever felt.

In a few moments, I'll be blind at best—but more likely dead.

There's a thud and a crack from Ariel's direction.

The pressure on my eyes disappears.

Through the white blotches in my vision, I see my attacker collapse where he stands.

Then I stare, dumbfounded, as the corpses begin to fall in a second death all around the exhibit.

The pile on top of Ariel stops their fidgeting.

Ignoring the pain of my injuries, I drag the nearest corpse from the pile, then another, then another.

By the time I finally expose Ariel and Beatrice, my arm and back muscles ache almost as much as my legs.

Now I see why the corpses re-died. While Ariel is lying with her face pillowed on Beatrice's chest, the necromancer's head is unnaturally flat on the floor. That, and bits of her brain matter amidst a big puddle of blood, tells me that Beatrice is dead—a fact I have very mixed feelings about. The most selfish thing that crosses my mind is the relief that the necromancer won't walk around with what would've been a horrible facial scar from my knife-slice... as in, I don't have to feel guilty now that she's dead.

Doors open in the distance. Has someone come to check on us? How long has it been since Ariel first fired her gun?

Ariel lifts her head and turns toward me, her hair matted with blood that covers most of her face.

"It's over," she gasps and lays her head back on Beatrice's chest, as though it were a nice memory foam pillow.

"We have to get out of here," I say, kneeling next to her.

No response.

I wipe the blood from her cheek and notice how extremely pale she is. Panicked, I press my finger to her pulse.

It's there, but weak. This must be due to blood loss from that head wound.

She needs a hospital, pronto.

I take out my phone, but the stupid battery is dead.

Unwilling to needlessly jostle Ariel in her fragile state, I check Beatrice's pockets and locate her phone, which is eighty-something percent charged.

Without a second of hesitation, I dial 911.

"911. What's the address of the emergency?" a female voice says.

"Put the phone down," says a hypnotic male voice that I recognize.

Looking up, I confirm my suspicions. Crinkling his too-pretty-for-a-guy nose at the carnage around him stands Gaius—the man in black who saved me at the TV studio and escorted me home. His entire black-suited team is with him, and they all stare at Ariel's and Beatrice's blood like starved children at marshmallows.

"She needs help," I say without hanging up the phone.

"I can see that," Gaius says and lifts his sunglasses to expose those mirrored eyes.

Before I can look away, the eyes grasp my attention and don't let go.

"Hang up now," Gaius says, enunciating every word.

I fight the urge to let his voice become the center of my universe.

"Ariel," I say, unable to look away.

"Oh, I'll save your friend," he says without blinking.

"What is your location?" the 911 dispatcher asks urgently, but I hang up on her. Not because he took over my mind, but because I believe he'll help Ariel. Plus, I just had an idea that might not work out if I don't hang up.

My mind is hazy as I pocket the phone, but I channel all my willpower to say, "Help her. What are you waiting for?"

"Right," Gaius says and approaches Ariel. "Just one very important thing before I proceed." He looks at me as intently as before, but his eyes are back to their Siberian ice color. "You'll soon have a chat with some important people, and they will ask you about that TV incident when we first met. If you mention me, Darian, or my team, she'll die."

A chat with some important people.

My thoughts are jumbled by the lingering haze, but I'm beginning to understand why Gaius is here.

He must be how I get in front of the Council I saw in my vision.

He was always going to find me using some magical vampire means.

The stupid future sure likes to be stubborn.

"I can't lie with the polygraph stone they'll put around my neck," I say, staying alert with a huge effort.

Gaius looks shocked, then mumbles under his breath, "Of course. Damn seers." Louder, he says, "Just don't bring it up, and you should be fine. No one would insult a Council member or the Enforcers by making open accusations."

"Deal," I say and repeat to myself what I'm supposed to do a few times, just in case this haze messes with my long-term memory.

Then again, maybe I shouldn't worry. I didn't expose Darian in my vision. Unless it was *because* I got this same threat before the events in the dream? No. Even if I didn't get the threat in that timeline, I was too terrified of speaking in front of all those people to come up with such creative ideas. And history is about to repeat itself.

"Good," Gaius replies. "Now let me help your delectable friend."

He leans over Ariel and—as though it's the most normal thing in the world—licks up all the blood covering her face. He then pulls away, and fangs glint in the air before he sinks them into his own wrist.

Blood starts gushing from the wound, and he brings it to Ariel's mouth—undoing his earlier work by covering the lower portion of her face with blood again.

Though I don't have Ariel's medical background, I'm pretty sure this is *not* how blood transfusion works.

Yet what he's doing seems to do *something* good, because color returns to Ariel's face. She grabs Gaius's forearm and keeps drinking his blood with way too much enthusiasm.

The word "vampire" penetrates my dazed consciousness, but I mentally swat it away like an annoying mosquito.

As she gulps down the blood, Ariel starts making the most disturbing sounds—orgasmic-type moans that leave no doubt about her health but major doubts about her sanity.

As my worry about Ariel abates, it becomes harder to resist the haze. I should probably run, but I can't get my body to move.

Besides, I can't leave Ariel here, with this man who threatened her.

In the middle of the feeding, Gaius lifts his head and looks at me again, his eyes mirrored, and the haze intensifies, taking over my mind. Just like after the show, time seems to move in jolts, my memory short-circuiting intermittently.

One moment, I'm watching the strange blood transference, and the next, I'm being led away.

Gaius is holding a blissed-out Ariel in his arms, and

some of his black-clad colleagues are tidying up the exhibit.

Next, I register walking through the Luxor hotel. Here and there, figures in black are staring down cops and security personnel with their mirrored eyes.

"No one will know what happened here," Gaius says when he catches my unfocused gaze. "I'm glad you got rid of the necro. If we'd arrived while she was still alive—"

I must've spazzed out in the middle of his monologue because I next come to my senses in front of two limos.

"Here," Gaius says, handing me a small plastic bag with a single hair in it. "This belongs to you."

He looks at Ariel, who's draped over his shoulder, and adds, "Your friend insisted you get this back."

I blink, taking the bag from him. Is this how he found us? By somehow tracking me through my hair?

I hope I'll remember this after the haze is gone, so I can shave my head as a preventative measure.

The ecstasy on her face receding momentarily, Ariel half grunts, half moans something in approval—she's clearly doing a million times better than before.

"Sorry about this." Gaius takes out a canvas sack and puts it over Ariel's head before handing her off to one of the men in black, who takes her to the farther limo. "Security precaution," he explains. "I'm sure you understand."

"Wait," I say, but a sack goes over my head as well—

and despite all my experience with blindfolds, I don't have a way to peek out of this one.

The mind fog intensifies without visual input to keep my brain busy. One minute, I'm sitting in a driving car, and then almost instantly, I'm being led somewhere.

"You have to heal her quickly," Gaius says to someone. "She can't face the Council with those horrible bruises, and I've been explicitly forbidden from healing her my way."

I'm still in the dark, but my guess is that someone shoots magic at me, because it feels like all my cuts and bruises are being erased with a warm energy that spreads through my whole body, leaving pleasurable relaxation behind. The splinter in my forehead falls out, and my neck bruises become but a distant memory. It's as though I've gotten a massage, used a steam room, and then slept for fifteen hours, all in a few seconds. I sigh in pleasure and hear Gaius chuckle approvingly.

"That's enough," he says and leads me away from wherever we are.

I must be in the car again because I feel the engine revving.

After an indeterminate amount of time, we stop and someone leads me through a tangle of corridors to some place that's cold and smells like an ancient castle.

Eventually, we make our way to what feels like a large room.

Someone guides me to the center of the room and yanks the hood from my head.

The room is dimly lit, so my eyes don't need to adjust. I meet Gaius's mirrored gaze again, and the haze in my mind dissipates.

"You should be back to normal in a moment," he says and walks away.

When my mind is completely clear, I recognize the scent of sage incense in the air and instantly know where I am.

I was right. The future *does* have a preference for how events play out.

Since I survived Beatrice, I get to die here.

I'm standing in front of the Council in the circular room from my dream.

They're about to interrogate me and then take a vote to kill me.

CHAPTER TWENTY-FIVE

FRANTICALLY, I try to recall what happened in my dream to help me scheme better. In the magic parlance, this is called "being ahead of the audience."

If memory serves, the Hogwarts-like candles will light up, and I'll find myself in a mini Colosseum. The Council will all be dressed in their *Eyes Wide Shut* sex-orgy best.

As I expected, or predicted, or whatever the correct term is, the candles come to life.

I stare at the Council members in the circle around me and try to not freak out at the upcoming public speaking. If I have a panic attack and faint as I did in my dream, my fate as a dead woman will be sealed.

They're all staring, but I know there's going to be a guy behind me with that BDSM collar, so I spin around.

As expected, the guy is just a few feet away from me, his hand already extended.

He didn't expect me to turn, so he didn't hide his face deep inside his hood—which is why my eyes want to jump out of my head from shock.

I now understand why this man's voice was so familiar in the dream.

I know him.

Know him very well.

The reason I hadn't attached his very distinct voice to his identity—other than my battling a panic attack—must be because it was so out of context. The man standing in front of me is the last person I'd expect to be supernatural, which I assume is a prerequisite for being on this Council.

It's the owner of the hedge fund I work at.

My boss, Nero Gorin.

He's also kind of a bad-luck charm for me, as far as panic attacks go. He's now witnessed two of them (unless the one in my dream doesn't count).

"I need to put this around your neck," Nero murmurs like before.

"Okay, boss," I whisper back conspiratorially.

He pauses as though to register my recognition, then removes his hood, erasing any remaining doubts as to his identity.

As he puts the necklace around my neck, his fingers gently brush my skin, and my breathing quickens as gooseflesh rises on my arms.

Am I dreaming about kissing him again?

But no. *That* dream never involved an audience.

In any case, there's some warped logic to his

presence here. Nero has always been eerily good at seeing through lies. Some even said his skill is "almost supernatural." Turns out, they were spot on. During my dream, the stone in this necklace worked as a lie detector: it lit up green when I told the truth and red when I inadvertently lied—something I'd better avoid this time around. Under my new world paradigm, it seems feasible that Nero has transferred some of his lie detection ability into this stone on my neck.

Using special-effects-like moves.

Nero Gorin.

Sure.

Leaning closer to my boss's ear, I whisper, "Please don't let them kill me."

Just like in my dream, he reassuringly touches my back—and I recall he did the same thing at the Alpha One conference, right before I fainted.

Well, I can't faint this time, so I pull away from his touch and preemptively breathe five in, five out, just as Lucretia—the shrink at *his* hedge fund—taught me. My anxiety abates enough for me to spot other symptoms of an incipient panic attack, and I do my best to convince myself I have this all under control.

Slightly calmer, I let Nero lock the necklace into place. Knowing how it would go, I don't bother trying to get it off me this time.

Especially since I hope the right truth will set me free.

Everyone around us looks eager to watch Nero do his lightning thing. I just keep my breathing exercise going because I know how close I am to having to speak.

"This will not hurt you," Nero says softly, and I remember he was standing during that vote.

"Don't let them kill me," I want to beg him again, but he's already halfway to his seat.

As the ocean-blue glow illuminates my surroundings, I face the location where Kit—the magenta-robed, face-shifting Asian woman—is about to stand.

"I'm Councilor Kit," she says just as expected, in the anime-sounding voice. "I'm the designated neutral party in tonight's proceedings. Please state your name for the record."

Because everything thus far has transpired as expected, and thanks to my breathing exercise, the prospect of saying my name doesn't terrify me nearly as much as it did in my dream.

It does terrify me more than anything from the *Bodies* exhibit, though—and that set a new bar for horror.

Clearing my throat, I say, "My first name is Sasha." I enunciate everything slowly and deliberately, like I'm trying to impersonate President Obama. "My last name is Urban—I got it from my adoptive father, but I might soon change it to my adoptive mother's maiden name, Ballard. I don't know my biological parents, or else I'd use their last name."

The lie detection stone lights up green to all of that, and that's good; I need to keep it that way.

Chester, the guy in the yellow robe, stands up again and reveals his mischievous satyr face, now noticeably less smug than in my dream. He must not appreciate all the truthful information I packed into that one answer.

"I'm Councilor Chester, the Plaintiff in today's proceedings," he says, and this time, I think I know where I've heard his voice. I don't dwell on it now, though, since I have to focus all my energy on not fainting, which is getting harder and harder to do. "I'll cut right to the chase," he continues. "What did you do at eight p.m. on Sunday, October 8th?"

Even though I'd expected the question, the room still spins around me. Fortunately, the deep breathing staves off any nausea, so my voice is semi-normal as I enunciate every syllable again. "I was performing on a show called *Evening with Kacie.*" I inhale deeply and wish I had a bottle of water that I could slowly uncap and sip to let myself relax more. "I didn't realize that mentalism was a crime that required proceedings such as this one, but I'm very sorry if I broke some rule I didn't know about. Or are you asking about that event because it was the first time a corpse raised by a necromancer named Beatrice attacked me?"

The necklace shines green, and I enjoy the gaping look of incomprehension on Chester's face. He definitely didn't expect me to say all that.

Everyone in the room flouts decorum to discuss what I've just said.

When the noise level reaches high-school-cafeteria

decibels, the black-hooded figure of Vlad stands up and clears his throat.

Everyone shuts up.

Vlad clearly has clout.

"The Enforcers have recovered the corpse of the necromancer she mentions." He gives me a strangely approving look, then turns to face the Council. "I was going to bring this up after we'd settled Sasha's fate."

The stress might be playing tricks with my vision, but does Chester look relieved at learning of Beatrice's fate?

"If Sasha rid us of a necromancer, you should've told us," Darian says, this time without an introduction.

Vlad's forehead reaches a new level of broodiness as he stares at Darian. "She wasn't the one who dealt the death blow, and besides, you know how my people feel about necromancers. I'm more grateful to the defendant than the rest of you are. However, as Leader of the Enforcers, I don't think my gratitude is relevant to these proceedings."

"It's relevant," Darian says without much confidence. "It speaks to her character."

"Can we resume the proceedings?" Chester says. "Or let's just neutralize her and be done with it." He seems to have regained some of his good humor.

"I don't see much point in the proceedings anymore," Darian says and looks at Vlad, who seems to nod, though almost imperceptibly. "We know she didn't think the performance was against the rules—

and we know she was adopted, meaning no one could've taught her the rules."

"Are you familiar with the term 'Cognizant?'" Chester asks me instead of acknowledging Darian's iron-clad arguments. "You must answer. Now."

Fighting my fear of public speaking with all my might, I inhale deeply, count to five, and exhale. "Yes. I first came across this term the night after the TV appearance, when I eavesdropped on the late necromancer Beatrice during her conversation with her employer."

The stone on my neck shines green, and I gulp in another breath. I was worried it would reject the word "eavesdrop" in lieu of "heard it in a psychic dream," but it seems the stone is flexible enough to consider my prediction a form of eavesdropping.

The reaction in the room is priceless. If I'd planted poisonous snakes in the robes of everyone here, I don't think it would've created as big of a commotion.

"Ladies and gentlemen, please," Kit yells eventually. "The proceedings are not complete."

"Who was her employer?" Vlad is on his feet, ignoring Kit's call to order. "That's more important than—"

"I think he's in this very room," I say, and the green of the stone confirms my statement.

The room falls into a dead silence, and I take another slow breath. This is when the stone could've shown me to be a liar, but it did not. The truth is, I have a theory as to who Beatrice's employer is—but I'm obviously not sure, which is why I used the strategic word "think" in my statement. Luckily, it seems to have worked.

Of course, if my theory *is* wrong, it will undo the advantage I've gained.

I palm Beatrice's phone in my pocket and take it out, making sure my suspect doesn't realize I have the phone in my hand. The other Council members might see it, but they wouldn't know how it's relevant.

"Who is he?" It's amazing how scary Vlad's gorgeous face can be. If I hadn't seen it, I wouldn't have thought it possible.

"How is this relevant anyway?" Chester asks, and I detect worry in his question.

I surreptitiously scan Beatrice's recent calls and zero in on a contact named "Jester." It sounds close enough to be a nickname; my suspect does like speaking mockingly and in general looks like a guy who's into making jokes at other people's expense.

Crossing my fingers, I dial the number.

As Beatrice's phone connects to cell towers, I realize that a million things could go awry even if I'm right. The Council could have a "no cell phones during proceedings" rule. Or my suspect could've forgotten his cell—or not charged it.

The theme song from *The Walking Dead* rings out in the room.

It's coming from Chester's direction.

I theatrically raise the phone above my head. "In my hand, I have Beatrice's phone," I quickly rattle out, and the stone shines green, confirming my words. "I just dialed her employer, and Chester's phone started ringing."

The stone shines green again.

I was worried the stone wouldn't come through. After all, this could be the phone of at least seven Councilors who sit next to Chester. But the stone knows I believe Chester was giving Beatrice orders, and it must know I finally recognized his voice, so it confirmed my words.

"How dare you!" Chester puffs up with outrage, but quickly deflates when Vlad glares his way. If a look could unman someone, Chester would already be squeaking falsetto.

Darian stands up and reveals his face. He looks radiant in his victory. "Ladies and gentlemen. The Plaintiff Chester's hypocrisy seems to know no bounds. He isn't a Herald, so if he spoke the word 'Cognizant' to this Beatrice, a person outside the Mandate, he was in effect abusing the exception to the Mandate that the Council enjoys. And an argument can be made that he broke the Mandate altogether—"

"Beatrice was a Cognizant," Chester says. "Speaking to her about us doesn't break the Mandate."

"If you weren't on the Council, you wouldn't have survived such a conversation," Vlad says. He sounds like he'd be very happy if Chester died by hemorrhaging blood from every orifice—like what almost happened to Ariel when I was questioning her.

"I think we should dismiss the charges against

Sasha and have another set of proceedings," Darian says gleefully. "This time, we should discuss Chester's actions."

"What I did or didn't do doesn't have any bearing on these proceedings," Chester grits through his teeth.

Vlad regards Chester with disgust but says, "He's right. Why don't we all vote."

"Please, everyone," Chester says. "Think about what you're—"

"We've heard enough from you." Vlad's voice booms throughout the room with such malice that Chester and half the attendants, myself included, whiten.

Kit clears her throat uncomfortably.

"I apologize for my outburst," Vlad says to her. "Please speak."

"Everyone in favor of leniency, stand up," Kit says solemnly, and I hold my breath.

The last time they took this vote, I was sentenced to death.

CHAPTER TWENTY-SIX

IN MY VISION, only a few of these people stood up to save my life.

Now, however, as though preparing for a standing ovation at my great oratory skills (and lack of fainting), everyone but Chester stands up.

I can't believe it.

I beat the stubborn future after all.

I'm safe.

"Leniency it is," Kit says ceremoniously. "Vlad, can your Enforcers protect her until she undergoes the Mandate Rite?"

As though in answer, Gaius walks into the room with a dozen black-clad figures. They must be Vlad's Enforcers. Did he summon them telepathically, or can he text in secret better than a teenage girl?

"The Rite should commence right after the next proceedings," Darian says after everyone sits back down.

The hooded figures around the room nod approvingly.

"Wait," Chester shouts, increasingly desperate. "How did you get on that TV show? Was Councilor Darian involved with it in any way?"

The room falls silent again.

Gaius said this type of accusation wouldn't happen today, but I guess Chester has nothing left to lose, and since he doesn't seem to like Darian, he wants to drag him down too.

I wouldn't mind ratting out Darian—he clearly set me up for something that could've ended my life—but Gaius raises his sunglasses and looks at me. In his eyes, I read a reminder of the earlier threat to Ariel, should I blab about his and Darian's involvement.

"Answer." Chester's voice is hoarse now.

A strong hand touches my back reassuringly, and then there are fingers on the back of my neck, sending hot chills down my spine. In the next moment, the polygraph-exam jewelry comes off.

I guess I'm officially off the hook, and whatever Chester is demanding from me is not part of my proceedings.

"Thanks, Nero," I think to myself. Out loud, I answer, "I got that TV show based on my merit as an illusionist. I met Darian for the first time during these proceedings."

Since the stone isn't around my neck, no red glow highlights my lies.

"You may go," Kit says and waves her hand over her

face the way she did during my vision. Instantly, her face changes to mine—which I take as a compliment, especially since *this* Sasha looks much more confident than I feel.

"Just one second," I say, trying to be as brave as Kit's version of my face.

Everyone looks at me with renewed interest.

"I've puzzled out a few things based on the context of these conversations," I say slowly. All this attention is peaking my adrenaline once more. "Am I right to think that after I fall under this Mandate, I'll be unable to speak about certain subjects?"

"You'll learn all the details later," Kit says in my own voice.

"What about my magic?" I ask.

"The Mandate will forbid you from displaying your powers to the public, if that's what you mean," Vlad says, and for the first time, I hear something like empathy in his voice—an emotion that seems foreign to those vocal cords.

"She means her tricks," Darian says, and for a guy who should owe me big, he doesn't sound supportive enough at all.

"Yes. I do mean my *effects*," I say. "I understand that going on TV is a no-no, though not fully why that's so, but what about other situations? I have a job where I perform at a restaurant. I may wish to have a show in Vegas one day—"

"Anything that can be perceived as supernatural

powers will be forbidden," Vlad says, the earlier hint of kindness expunged from his voice.

"Even if it's fake?" I can't help asking.

"The Mandate is as much about people's reactions as your intentions or methods," Darian says. "I'm sorry. You'll have to find yourself another hobby."

A hobby.

Did he just call my life's dream a hobby?

Nero's hand touches my back again. He and I had a big fight once, after he insulted me by calling my mentalism a hobby, so he probably knows I was about to give this room a piece of my mind.

His touch reminds me where I am, and I realize speaking back would be a very bad idea. I just got away with my life, and now I'm basically telling them Chester was right about me.

I inhale, trying to calm myself. I know I should be grateful for keeping my life, but I feel like someone just told me that Fluffster died. And a bunch of kittens. And a bunch of puppies. And maybe Felix too.

"I just wanted to clarify, that's all," I say as placatingly as I can. "I don't plan to disobey. Now that everything is clear, I'm ready for my Mandate Rites, or whatever."

Gaius takes this as his cue to walk up to get me.

As soon as we leave the room, he says, "You're either the bravest or the dumbest person who's ever faced the Council. I can't believe you kept speaking after being dismissed—and risking your hide over stupid tricks."

"It's an art form." I stare at the ancient corridor around us. It could easily belong to a medieval castle. "Illusionism was my future."

"You don't need parlor tricks," he says. "You're a real seer."

His words actually make me feel worse about my fate. My new powers would've been a huge boon to my career as a mentalist. I could've pretended to be fake when I'm actually real. Then again, this is what many of my spectators already suspect to be the case, no matter how much I deny being psychic, so maybe it's not such a clever idea after all.

Still, as we walk, I fantasize about a show I'll never get to do. A show where I could've combined real psychic powers with all the methods of deception at my disposal.

People's heads would've exploded in wonder.

Then another performance-related fact hits me.

I've just faced a group of hostile strangers without having a panic attack. That means I could probably do a show for a friendly group of strangers, except now I'll be forbidden to do so—

"This is where the Rite will take place," Gaius says, and I see we've reached the end of the dungeon-like corridor.

The room in question looks like a medieval torture chamber, only with the Rack and the Iron Maiden devices removed to keep up with the times. There is a big stone slab in the front of the room that looks like it has been recently used for human sacrifices. Behind the slab is a set of organ pipes—because it's the perfect instrument to play when you're ripping out people's organs. Facing the slab are rows of stone benches, and it's easy to picture a horde of excited sadists sitting there, enthralled by watching the agony of the hapless victims.

"Take a seat." Gaius gestures at the nearest bench.

I sit down. The bench is cold and unyielding. Maybe it was also designed as a mild form of torture.

"What happens now?" I ask. "What's going to happen to me?"

"That depends." Gaius places his foot on another bench and adjusts his sunglasses. "If you don't piss someone off so they call off the Rite altogether, you should be protected afterward, and have a Mentor to boot. Your survival chances will be even better if Chester gets kicked off the Council."

"Do you think he will get kicked off?" I ask, and make a pact with myself to be on my best behavior, at least until the Rite is over. "And if they forgive him, what is the risk?"

"He's a politician—slimier than a cross between a slug and an eel. All of them, but Chester in particular, would make that guy on *House of Cards* seem like a saint." He says this admiringly, and I get the sense he himself would love to be on the Council if he could—and that he'd fit right in. "If I were you, I'd hope Chester loses Council privileges," Gaius continues. "Then he'd be harmless to you."

I frown at him. "What is Chester's beef with me, anyway?"

Gaius shrugs. "Chester is a probability manipulator. His kind don't like seers in general, but he hates them on a personal level—especially Darian, the seer he holds responsible for his wife's suicide. So he was likely trying to get at him through you."

I blink uncomprehendingly.

"Darian prophesized that Chester's werewolf wife would be the cause of their daughter's death," Gaius explains, "so the mom took a drastic precautionary measure."

"Okay..." I can't even wrap my mind around that, so I focus on the more relevant topic. "But why would killing me hurt Darian?"

"I believe Darian has big plans for you, plans that must be part of some future he wants to bring about," Gaius says as his phone dings a text message alert. He looks at it, smiles, and replies impressively quickly. His thumbs move with supernatural speed— something that doesn't surprise me after everything I've seen.

"Whatever that plan is," he continues, putting away his phone, "Darian clearly needed your powers supersized, so he set up that TV performance for you. Chester must've figured this out and tried to thwart Darian's ambitions."

"I see." I bite the inside of my cheek. "Do you think Chester will get kicked off the Council?"

"Boss will be gunning for him, that's for sure," Gaius

says. "He'll want to make an example for anyone else who'd make a deal with the necros."

I nod. Vlad sure seemed really pissed in that meeting.

Pissed because he hates necromancers.

And I vaguely recall that *vampires* hate necromancers.

Between the blood licking and this bit of info, I can't help but draw the only possible conclusion. "Are you and Vlad vampires? Or is it impolite to ask?"

Gaius chuckles—so hopefully he isn't mad. "It would be impolite to ask someone under the Mandate before your Rite, as they'd risk death if they answered. But, lucky for you, I'm one of the Heralds and can thus educate an uninitiated Cognizant like yourself."

"Okay." I fold my legs under my butt in the hope of getting more comfortable on the stone bench. "So are you, or aren't you?"

"It's not a big secret," he says. "Yes. All of us Enforcers are vampires. We have useful skills when it comes to covering up messes, persuading humans, subduing errant Cognizant, and the like. But I fear you might have preconceived notions about what a vampire actually is, based on your human upbringing and all."

"Oh? So you *don't* drink blood? You're not the undead?" More sarcasm seeps into my voice. "You're not a creature with pale skin and fangs, with a fetish for black clothing?"

"Well, no, we're those things." He takes off his

glasses, exposing his icy eyes. "We just don't care about garlic and silver, and we care even less about religious symbols. And we sure as hell don't sparkle."

"Great. You've got all the good parts and none of the weaknesses of the vampires of myth. Are you impervious to stakes too?"

"Now this line of questioning *is* impolite. It sounds adversarial, like you want to know how to hurt us." He grins at me, exposing his fangs—which tells me he can bring them out at will. "We're just members of the Cognizant, like everyone else. We start off alive and turn into vampires when we die."

He'd probably consider a question about whether they require an invitation to enter a home impolite as well, so I don't ask. Besides, I got the distinct impression that he and Vlad do need my permission to enter my apartment.

Analyzing vampires like this makes my head spin. Though I've already accepted them into my paradigm, a part of me had denied it until this moment. Actually, I think a part of me will deny it until someone dies and turns into a vampire in front of my face, then drinks my blood, and maybe does something else vampy—like turn into a bat, assuming that they can.

"I suggest we talk about something else," Gaius says as though he read my mind—another power the vampires might have.

"Sure," I say. "I was wondering... Why did you help Darian during my TV debacle? Given your earlier threat, I assume you didn't act in the official Enforcer capacity."

Gaius's forehead creases. Is he trying to compete with Vlad in broodiness, or is glowering something they teach you in Vampire 101?

"When you really want something to happen in the future," he reluctantly says, "it's useful to have a powerful seer owe you a favor."

Before I can question him further, there's a sound of footsteps, and Ariel enters the chamber. In her hands are a bottle and a phone.

"You're okay," she says, and the relief in her voice reminds me of how big of a danger I managed to dodge. Or *possibly* dodge, pending Chester's fate and this Rite business. "Your injuries—"

"I took her to one of our healers," Gaius interjects. "Can't say who, though—Council secrecy and all that."

Ariel and I drove in different cars on the way here, and I guess she didn't get a healing treatment like I did. Yet she looks completely fine. More than fine, in fact. She's glowing. If our periods weren't synced, I'd wonder if she's pregnant. Is it Gaius's vampire blood? If so, how the hell does that work? Nanotech?

"Thank you," Ariel says to Gaius with genuine gratitude.

She comes up to me and hands over the bottle. It's vanilla-flavored Ensure—a meal replacement drink. My stomach rumbles, so I uncap the Ensure and take a swig. I must really be ravenous because the drink tastes more like a delicious milkshake than a bland mix of corn maltodextrin and lecithin.

"Why am I on a liquid diet?" I ask after swallowing another sip.

"If I were you, I wouldn't eat before the Rite at all," Gaius says, and Ariel gives him a narrow-eyed stare.

"Why?" I take another gulp and give each of them a worried look. "Does it hurt?"

"She can't comment on that." He points at Ariel. "But I can."

He stands there looking smug, clearly determined to make me sweat.

I take another sip in order to show that I don't care either way, but my heart rate is increasing. There's only so much I can withstand in one day, and I went over my limit back in Vegas.

Ariel types something on her phone, and Gaius's phone chirps a text message again.

I eye the two of them speculatively. They have each other's digits?

"Your friend wants me to tell you how impressed she is with my candor and good looks," Gaius says, and Ariel rolls her eyes but still says nothing. "She also wants me to tell you that the Rite is something every adult Cognizant goes through. That even Felix—"

"Wait." I nearly choke on my drink. "Felix is also a Cognizant?"

Ariel approaches Gaius, leans in, and whispers something in his ear for a few long seconds.

"Yes," Gaius says after she's done.

Ariel punches him in the shoulder, so he adds, "Oh, she also wanted you to know that Felix isn't as useless as all common sense would dictate." She punches him harder, but he must be unbelievably strong, because he takes it without a blink. As he looks at Ariel with faux naiveté, his pretty face reminds me of a cat playing with its prey.

Ariel texts him again, her fingers dancing angrily over her phone.

He reads the text and says, "Fine. It was Felix who helped locate Beatrice. You told Ariel the details of the conversation between Beatrice and her employer, so Felix hacked into the NSA and used those details to find a recording of the phone call you mentioned. From there, he triangulated Beatrice's side of the conversation and determined she was in Vegas, at the Luxor hotel—though what he should've done was figure out it was Chester on the other side of the conversation."

Ariel whispers something in his ear again, and though I can't hear, I'm sure she's defending Felix.

"Yes, but his only usefulness is to figure out such things," he says to her. "Chester's probability manipulations can only—"

It's odd to watch them argue like this. When Gaius brought me home after the performance, I got the sense that they'd just met for the first time and she hated him. Now, however, they sound like a bickering couple. She and I will have to discuss this when she can talk to me freely—after this Rite I'm dreading more and more.

"How is it that so many people in my life are Cognizant?" I ask. "For that matter, how many Cognizant are there in the world? And"—I look at Ariel —"did you and Felix know that I was one? If so, why did you let me go on TV?"

Ariel begins typing, but before he gets the text, Gaius says, "I can answer many of these questions; I'm used to them in my role as a Herald. A lot of this is what all Cognizant younglings want to know too—that and whether they still have to go to human schools, which I guess isn't your concern, being so old and all."

"Wait," I say, ignoring the dig at my age. "Parents can't even talk to their kids about any of this?"

"Correct," he says. "The Mandate forbids it. Proper dissemination of this type of information is key to everyone's security—and the reason for Heralds."

"Okay, fine," I say. "But can you please do your Heraldy thing now?"

"There are very few Cognizant in this world, less than a percent of one percent, but we attract each other." He winks at Ariel. "It's a power we all have, though those who can manipulate probabilities, like Chester, have it in spades. That's why we cluster together so much. We prefer to lose ourselves in the anonymity of big cities, and the attraction leads us all to the same neighborhoods, often the same buildings— a bit like some other minorities in New York."

He stops talking until Ariel, who texted him again, elbows him to proceed. "Ariel didn't know you were

Cognizant," he says. "Then, when you began predicting the market"—he looks at his phone—"and predicted the election results and major geopolitical events in multiple countries, along with the Mexican earthquake—"

"Half of that was luck," I say. "The other half was just analyzing facts and using logic. As for the Mexican earthquake"—I give Ariel an exasperated look—"that was a mentalism effect. That's all. I told you that."

"You didn't tell me how it was done," Ariel speaks for the first time, and even her voice is more vigorous somehow. "How did you do that? Did you seduce someone at the show and ask him to switch that envelope for you?"

"You're warmer now, but I resent the slutty image of me in your mind," I say. "I didn't even flirt with anyone for that effect."

"A better question is: why are you so fascinated with predicting the future in the first place?" Gaius says. He's probably seen Darian's damning video of my method, so he doesn't sympathize with Ariel's curiosity.

"I'm not fascinated by it," I say, but a hollow feeling forms in the pit of my stomach. "The headline prediction is a classic—something mentalists have been doing since the dawn of time. And all the magic books say your effects should be personal, so I went with the prediction because forecasting—albeit of the financial kind—is part of my job. I also participate in the Good Judgment Project, and—"

"Do you know anyone else as good as you at prognostications?" Gaius asks.

I consider it before answering. I'm not the best forecaster in the Good Judgment Project, nor am I the best (or luckiest) financial analyst in the world. But I am in the top percentile of both, and I'm not sure if anyone else can say that. Also, there's my ability to see story twists, and my ability to anticipate road accidents—

"Didn't think so," he says triumphantly.

Ariel writes another text, and Gaius's phone dings again.

He looks at it and says, "Ariel wants me to tell you that she didn't want you to go on TV, but didn't know how to stop you."

Ariel hurriedly types more text, and he adds, "She didn't know you're a Cognizant for sure, in any case."

I recall how unsupportive my roommates were when it came to my TV career—a fact that had bothered me more than I care to admit. Now I see that they were actually trying their best to be good friends—

Ariel kicks Gaius's ankle.

He looks at his phone, rolls his eyes, and in his best imitation of Ariel's voice says, "She is very sorry she didn't prevent that TV appearance." He switches to his normal voice. "If you ask me, there's nothing to be sorry for. Ariel should be glad she didn't stop you. That TV performance gave you loads of power—and you got away with it."

THE GIRL WHO SEES

"About that…" I look at each of them, unsure who's the best person to ask. "How does that work? Would I have gotten Magneto-like powers if I had done spoon bending on the show?"

Ariel looks at Gaius for help, so he sighs and says, "No one has done what you have and lived to tell the tale. I suspect you'd get no power over metal at all. Not unless one of your ancestors had such ability, and even in that case, double powers are exceedingly rare. No. Given how powerful your precognition was without any training, I bet your parents must've been seers. So it was very fortuitous for you to pretend to predict the future—almost as though a part of you foresaw that by doing so, you'd greatly enhance your powers."

"If a part of me made me do this to myself, I must secretly be suicidal," I say. "In any case, are you saying I was already a seer, but people's belief in me made me stronger?" I recall the rush of energy on the stage that supports this theory. "Does that mean beliefs can somehow alter reality if a Cognizant is involved?"

"Not exactly, but I'm not great at metaphysics, so I'll give you the dumbed-down spiel I give the younglings —the rest you'll learn later." He clears his throat, and his face takes on a professorial expression. "Back in the old days, when superstition reigned supreme, the Cognizant were worshipped as gods—and that made their power grow."

Ariel rolls her eyes, but Gaius gives her a narrow-eyed glare and continues. "Some of your Cognizant ancestors accumulated a lot of power thanks to that worship. They then had children with similar power, though sometimes diluted. Generations later, that same power still runs in you."

My head hurts, and not just because his "explanation" raises more questions than it answers.

"Around the Middle Ages, it was time for the Cognizant to stop gaining power by using human faith; else we'd face the wrath of humans, who by that point had perfected the technology of war, outbred us, and started to suspect that creatures of our kind might be meddling in their affairs—which, of course, we were." He looks thoughtful, and I wonder if he's old enough to have been there in the Middle Ages. I'll have to ask him about that, but first, I focus on what he's telling me.

"The Mandate is the standard solution used by our kind at that stage of human development," he continues. "The Mandate limits how a Cognizant can get power—and, indirectly, how much power anyone can have. More importantly, though, it makes certain that even torture can't make one of us reveal our secrets." He looks around the room meaningfully— maybe I was right to think this was a torture chamber in the past.

Mindlessly swallowing another gulp of Ensure, I try to even out my breathing. It will take me a long time to digest all this. Latching on to the question that bothers me most, I say, "If belief leads to power, wouldn't that mean the most powerful of all would be the gods of the modern religions?"

He grimaces. "I pity whoever ends up as your

Mentor. Let me try to answer that." He looks at Ariel for help, but she just shrugs. "When humans believe in the power of a Cognizant, they transfer some of their energy—for lack of a better term—to the source of their belief." He scratches his head. Clearly, his usual Cognizant youngsters don't ask difficult questions. "Such 'faith energy,' or whatever we want to call it, can only be utilized by a living Cognizant. So, for example, for Vishnu to have gained power from his believers, he would've had to have been one of us—something that may or may not have been the case. And even if Vishnu had been a Cognizant, his followers would've needed to believe just the right things about him during his lifetime."

"Interesting." I finish my Ensure and put the empty bottle on the bench next to me. "Given what you said, don't you, as a vampire, benefit from belief in vampires?"

"Few truly believe we exist, but yes, we all share the energy from the few who do believe the right things about us," he says. "But we didn't coerce humans to love us so much—we just happen to be irresistible."

A dozen monk-like figures in gray robes walk into the room, their faces obscured by hoods. One is sweeping the ancient floor, and his brethren are setting up black candles around the room. All are pretending we don't exist—and maybe they've been compelled to think so.

"The preparations for your Rite have begun," Gaius

says, rubbing his hands together like a supervillain. "Are you excited?"

"Thrilled," I say, the Ensure turning into antifreeze in my stomach.

"Any update from the proceedings?" Ariel asks out loud. I guess that statement is vague and neutral enough for the Mandate to allow it.

My ears perk up; Chester's fate could impact my own.

Gaius looks distant for a moment, then frowns. "I have bad news. Brace yourselves."

Ariel and I stare at him, petrified.

He bursts out laughing.

Ariel's hands turn into fists, but I just stare at him uncomprehendingly.

"You should've seen the looks on your faces," he says during a lull in his merriment. "I was just messing with you. Chester is off the Council."

Ariel uppercuts him in the jaw—which makes him burst out laughing again.

I breathe deeply to recover from the near heart attack.

"Sorry about that," he says after a few moments. "Chester isn't a threat to you anymore. So, provided you survive the Rite with your life and mind intact, you're golden."

"What does he mean, 'my life and mind intact?'" I ask Ariel, but she either refuses to respond or can't because of the Mandate.

"Seriously"—I give Gaius a pleading look—"what happens during the Rite?"

A dark and gloomy music vibrates through the room, silencing Gaius's reply. Scanning for the source of the sound, I spot one of the hooded figures sitting at the organ keyboard, playing up a storm. After a couple of extremely familiar melancholy chords, I recognize the piece as Bach's *Toccata and Fugue in D Minor*. My music professor at Columbia would've peed herself in pride at my recollection.

The smell of incense wafts through the room, and gray-robed figures walk around, waving pendulum-like censers similar to the ones you'd see at Mass, but with sinister symbols written on them. The symbols remind me of the marks Beatrice made on the corpses.

I get up so I can yell into Gaius's ear, but one of the robed figures grabs my arm and leads me away.

I glance over my shoulder at Ariel. She looks worried, confirming that the Rite must be as dangerous as Gaius implied.

Still, I don't struggle with the monk-like figure; I want to be on my best behavior. Ariel follows us at a distance, and that gives me a modicum of relief. As we walk, I accidentally peek inside my guide's hood and instantly regret it. His face looks like someone burned it and then put the fire out with acid.

Detecting my discomfort, he pulls the hood forward to obscure my view, but the gesture exposes his scarred hands.

We come to an alcove in the back, and the robed man gently pushes me in.

Inside is a robe—one of the front-open types—and a mask hanging on a golden hook.

This must be my outfit for the Rite.

The mask is of a serene feminine face made from marble. There's a smoothness where the eyes should be and an eyeball in the middle of the forehead that stares into infinity and beyond.

I press the cold mask to my face. To my surprise and relief, I can see through it. Someone has drilled tiny holes around the eye area—an interesting method for peeking that I file away for my mental encyclopedia of blindfold construction.

Ariel steps into the alcove as I'm wrapping the robe around my shoulders.

Looking at me, she shakes her head.

The music is even louder now, so I have to scream in her ear. "Did I put it on backwards?"

"You're not supposed to wear anything underneath," she yells back.

"What?" I examine the robe again. If I wear nothing underneath the rough, sandpaper-like cloth, I will be extremely uncomfortable. Also, I'm not sure how much of my body it would cover.

"It's tradition," Ariel yells again. "You have to strip."

She leaves before I can argue. I remind myself about my 'best behavior pact' and gingerly undress. The cold draft under the robe gives my gooseflesh a bad case of gooseflesh.

Ariel isn't around to tell me if I have to be barefoot, so I put my boots back on. I can always take them off later. I then place the weird mask on my face, tying the lace around my head.

Exiting my impromptu fitting room, I find the candles in the torture chamber already lit, and the Council members sitting on the stone benches. All of them are still wearing their multicolored robes, but now, they're also holding masks made of marble, each spooky in its own way. I guess they intend to put them on soon.

A colossal person in Councilor robes stands next to the sacrificial slab. He (though it could be a "she") must have an overactive pituitary gland—or is on stilts. Almost eight feet tall, with unbelievably wide shoulders, the figure is wearing a scowling mask that looks like a gargoyle but with a tentacle for a nose. In his or her hand is a giant staff that looks to have been carved from a whole tree trunk.

"I present Sasha," he—now I'm almost certain it's a "he"—says in a deep voice that would make Barry White sound like a chipmunk in comparison. He has no trouble screaming over the organ music, but as soon as his voice rings out, the music halts.

"Sasha," everyone chants.

"Hello," I force myself to say, my heartbeat skyrocketing. I really, really, really hope I'm not expected to make a big speech under these circumstances.

"Before the Rite can commence, a Mentor must step

forward," the giant says and slams the bottom of his staff on the ground with a loud bang, causing the podium and the slab to noticeably vibrate.

I look through the crowd and realize there are people here besides the Council members. I guess that makes sense. I shouldn't expect a Councilor to be a Mentor to a lowly newbie like me.

Everyone looks tense, and after a few moments, I start to feel anxious. Will this be like that time when no one wanted me on their soccer team? That would be as embarrassing as messing up a speech.

Chester stands up. From his fingers dangles a mask with a psychotic grin reminiscent of the Joker, or the monster clown from *It*.

"Chester," the giant says. "Anyone want to Challenge him?"

What?

Chester as my Mentor?

He wanted me dead. Doesn't that seem like a conflict of interest to them?

With effort, I stay silent, still focusing on my best behavior project.

Darian stands up. The mask hanging from his hand is blind, with an eye on the forehead like mine, only with more masculine features.

I exhale a sigh of relief. Darian has gotten me into this mess, but I don't think he wants me dead. If Gaius is right and Darian does have some plans for me, they clearly involve me as a powerful seer—and now his Mentee.

"Councilman Darian," the giant says, and I notice Chester wince. When *he* was announced, the Councilman honorific was omitted, probably for the first time in a long time.

"I yield," Chester grits through his teeth and sits back down, putting on his mask.

I hide a smile. Darian must outrank him now.

"Anyone else?" the giant asks.

The room is quiet.

I start thinking up questions I'll ask Darian when another figure stands up.

The room erupts into excited whispers, and even the giant on the stage appears shaken as he says, "Councilman Nero?"

"I yield," Darian says right away. "I yield," he repeats for good measure, his British accent stronger than usual. He plops down so fast his robes flutter in the air like a parachute.

Before he puts on his mask, I glimpse anxious confusion on his face.

Did he not see this coming with his psychic powers? In my vision, Chester did say seers weren't omniscient. Or is he afraid of Nero?

Maybe both?

Nobody asks for my preference, which is unfortunate. I'd much rather be Darian's Mentee. I don't need super powers to know that if Nero is my Mentor, I'm chained to my hedge fund job for good.

Before I can debate the wisdom of speaking up,

good behavior pledge or not, the Council members put on their masks and the organ music resumes.

The Mentor part of the Rite seems to be over, and I'm stuck with Nero.

How much worse can this get?

The giant gestures toward the slab.

I look at him, then at the cold stone, and mouth, "You've got to be kidding me."

"Get on," he says, his voice reverberating in my belly. "Try to relax."

"Try to relax," is what doctors, especially gynecologists, like to say right before they do something unspeakably unpleasant.

Cursing under my breath, I lie down on the slab.

The candles dim and from the bottom of the giant's staff grows a large circle of magical energy—a red plasma-like thing that must be a distant relative of the gate Ariel and I entered at JFK.

The candles go out completely.

The giant rips my robe open.

My chest heaves in shallow breaths, making my exposed breasts bounce up and down in the chilly air.

I cover myself with my hands.

Is there going to be an orgy after all? I hope not. My good behavior policy does have its limits—limits we've already passed with this public undressing.

The giant man raises his staff ceremoniously in the air.

I can't help but notice how much the red glowing circle looks like an iron brand.

Am I about to be branded like cattle?

"Try to relax," my foot. I move to skedaddle, ready to tell the Council to shove that thing someplace where it will have a better chance to shine, but the giant must see my intention and has a plan of his own.

His movements too fast for someone of such huge size, he lowers the glowing staff onto my stomach before I can dodge it.

I inhale so deeply I worry my lungs might burst.

My skin doesn't sizzle where the brand touches it, but if it did, the burning would've been preferable to the internal agony I'm experiencing.

It feels like my very essence is being branded. Like something that makes me who I am is getting violently rearranged.

I convulse spasmodically on the slab and scream out something inhuman. It's as though someone recorded the wails of all the pigs ever slaughtered and is playing this recording through my vocal cords.

As if in the distance, I hear the giant boom, "Her power might be too great for the Mandate to contain."

"There's no choice," someone says authoritatively, but I lose track of the rest of the conversation because, impossibly, the agony intensifies.

An ocean of foam, Ensure-vomit, and blood spews out of my mouth, and there might be more embarrassing body fluids coming out of other places.

The magical energy seeps into every one of my nerve endings, firing each one like a note in an infernal symphony. When this music of pain reaches a particularly unbearable crescendo, something inside me breaks.

I feel as though I'm falling, plummeting through the slab, the crust of the Earth, the tar-like mantle, and the liquid iron, and then slamming into the solid inner core that's as hot as the surface of the Sun.

With another inhuman scream that tears through my throat like a shot of hydrofluoric acid, I black out.

CHAPTER TWENTY-SEVEN

I WAKE up with a scream on my lips.

Opening my eyes, I'm relieved to find myself in my cozy bed, with no sacrificial slab in sight.

According to my nightstand clock, it's 9:37 a.m. The shades have kept the room dark enough to let me sleep well past sunrise.

I throw off the blanket. Someone dressed me in my favorite poker-themed PJs. I lift the pajama top and examine my stomach. There's no hideous burn where the brand touched me, which makes sense since I've never seen one on Ariel's flesh, and she must've lived through the same horrific Rite.

The door opens.

"Speak of the devil," I say, surprised my voice isn't hoarse from all the screaming and vomiting during the Rite.

"How are you feeling?" Ariel approaches and sits carefully on the edge of my bed.

"Surprisingly well," I say, mentally scanning my whole body and coming up with no problems to report. "They must've taken me to that healer again."

"They had to." Ariel grabs my hand and gives it a squeeze. "It was so horrible. I didn't think you'd make it."

I sit up and frown at her. "You said the Rite is something every Cognizant goes through."

"The nature of the Rite is to interweave the Mandate with your power," she says, releasing my hand. "When you have more power, the process is harder."

"Oh, hey." I slide my feet into the slippers someone left for me. "Now we can talk about all the Cognizant secrets without you bleeding."

"Well, yeah." Ariel stands up and reaches over to pull open the blinds, letting warm sun rays into the room. "You're now under the Mandate. Congrats. Now you too will bleed and/or die if you try to explain anything to someone not under the Mandate."

"I don't know enough to explain anything to anyone anyway," I say, stretching. "Speaking of which, what was that place we passed by on the way to Vegas? The one with purple sky and pink clouds?"

"That's one of the Otherlands," she says over her shoulder, then turns back to face me. "Wait a minute. How did you see the sky with your blindfold on?"

"Never mind that." I hide my evil grin from her by tiding up my bed. "Is that where all the Cognizant are from? From one of these Otherlands?"

"Yes," Ariel says. "That's what I've been taught."

"And where are the Otherlands?" I straighten my blanket. "Are they in some other galaxy? Or are they in a different universe altogether?"

"What difference does that make?"

"A huge difference." I walk to the closet and look for something warm. "Different universes can have different laws of physics."

"How do we know that the laws of physics aren't different in distant parts of our own universe?" Ariel asks.

"I'm not sure." I take out my fuzziest sweater and put it on. "I just know that visiting another universe is cooler than another planet."

"The Otherlands are worlds parallel to this one, so I guess they exist in another dimension or universe—whichever way that's supposed to work."

I turn around and start nodding, then freeze, my mouth falling open. For the first time today, I truly look at Ariel, and I can't believe what I'm seeing.

A red, aura-like field surrounds my roommate, with a big, glowing design at the center. The design looks exactly like the brand I was marked with during the Rite—a memory that makes me shudder.

I rub my eyes, but the visual artifact doesn't go away. I can't believe I didn't notice it earlier.

"What is that?" I wave my hand in the air around Ariel. "What is that glow around you?"

"That's the Mandate," Ariel says. "This is how you

can detect other people who are under it. How else are you supposed to know who's one of us?"

I shrug. "I never gave it much thought."

"That's a first." She winks at me. "This is like a new sense we all get after the Rite. You'll get used to it in time. I've stopped noticing it now, unless I need it."

"A new sense," I mutter under my breath and look around the room for Fluffster.

"I already fed the little guy," Ariel says, for some reason avoiding my gaze. "And gave him water. And put his dust bath in Felix's room. He's enjoying himself there for the moment. You have a lot of new stuff to take in, and I didn't want you distracted by anything before breakfast."

"Breakfast?" My stomach rumbles loudly.

"I made oatmeal," Ariel says, heading toward the kitchen.

I follow her, salivating like a Pavlov's dog.

"Sit," Ariel orders, and I gladly obey.

"You have to run to work soon." She ladles a cup of oatmeal into a bowl and sprinkles it with nuts and dried fruit. "Your new Mentor insisted you go back to your normal routine—and you don't want to piss him off, trust me."

"Of course that slave driver wants me back at work," I say, irritably swirling my spoon in the oatmeal. "I'm surprised he let me sleep in."

"You might want to cut the guy some slack." Ariel serves herself double my amount of oatmeal and triple the nuts. "He's hosting your Jubilee tonight, and he didn't have to do that. It's usually the family, not your Mentor, who foots that bill."

"My what?" My spoon hovers next to my mouth. "Please don't tell me there are more ceremonies. I don't think I can survive another Rite, even one with a perky name."

"No, silly, the Jubilee isn't like that," she says. "It's fun. It's where you're formally recognized as a Cognizant by our society. Everyone you know comes to it, and there's dancing, alcohol, food—"

"So it's some sort of a debutante ball?" I finally shovel some oatmeal into my mouth.

"Guys do it too," she says, blowing on a spoonful of her own oatmeal. "It's more like a bar mitzvah."

"Where is this going to take place?" I ask through the food in my mouth. "And when will it happen?"

"It's at the ballroom at your fund," Ariel says and beams excitedly. "It starts tonight, at six p.m."

So Nero is going to let me get off work early for this. He's clearly pulling out all the stops.

I focus on my food for a moment, digesting the information. I want to have a party as much as I want a leech on my forehead, but as long as it's not another Rite, I'd rather mingle with a drink in my hands than research stocks. Plus, Ariel will have a blast. She'd enjoy a trip to the DMV if there were dancing involved.

Remembering something unpleasant that I wanted to talk to her about, I swallow my spoonful and cautiously ask, "Do you think Gaius will be there?"

"Any Cognizant who wants to attend will have that option," she says, her face turning unreadable at the mention of Gaius.

Subtlety failing, I go for a more direct approach. "Is something going on between the two of you?"

"What would give you such an insane idea?" She adds more nuts to her oatmeal and looks at me so earnestly I almost wonder if I misread the situation.

Almost.

"Well, that's good to hear," I say after I lose our staring contest. "He threatened to kill you if I told the Council about his and Darian's involvement in the TV performance."

"Ah." She waves her hand dismissively, like death threats are a small nuisance—something along the lines of walking a chihuahua in the park without a leash. "That's just BS politics. I'm actually surprised Gaius was working with Darian at all—and that Vlad approved it, assuming that he did."

"Giaus said he wants a favor from Darian—a vision, I think." I go to the fridge, get a box of orange juice and two glasses, and bring them back to the table.

"He must really want to know his future. *I* wouldn't deal with a seer, even if I was about to be sent to Iraq again," she says and nods in thanks for the OJ I pour for her. "No offense, of course."

"I don't see myself as a seer, so none taken. But why don't you want to deal with one?"

"Because when you do, you can be certain you've become a pawn that the seer will use, and sacrifice, if needed." Ariel guzzles down her juice. "Again, I'm sure you won't be like that when *you* master your powers—or at least, you won't be like that when it comes to me. Hopefully."

An unpleasant feeling forms in the pit of my stomach at the idea of being Darian's pawn. It's a glove that seems to fit pretty well, except for the part where he didn't become my Mentor. Does that make me Nero's pawn?

"Is Nero a seer too?" I ask. "Everyone seems afraid of him for some reason."

Ariel chokes on her juice and coughs a few times before saying, "I'm not sure what he is; some Cognizant like to keep the specifics of their power secret. All everyone knows is that he's dangerous and not someone you want to mess with. But if you ever find out what he is, please tell me. I'm dying of curiosity."

"What about you?" I ask, realizing this should've been my first question. "What kind of a Cognizant are you? What are your powers? Unless that's a secret too?"

"Oh, that." Ariel swallows another small spoonful of her food. "I'm a pretty useless kind of Cognizant. All I have is strength and speed, nothing else."

"If you ask me, those are pretty useful powers. I'd gladly swap with you." I add some more dried fruit to my bowl, figuring I deserve a little extra sweetness after last night's ordeal. "So is your type of Cognizant a creature from legend, too? Like a werewolf?"

"It's a little embarrassing," she says.

I grin. "It can't be more embarrassing than my lack of sex life—and I told you about that. And you mentioned it in front of Felix yesterday, by the way. So you owe me."

"Fine." She shovels in a big spoonful of oatmeal and maliciously makes me wait until she's done chewing it. "Have you ever heard of Heracles?"

This time, *I* nearly choke on my juice. "You mean Hercules? As in, the Twelve Labours? As in, the Disney cartoon? As in, that movie with The Rock? As in—"

"Yes, that one," she says, rolling her eyes. "I was told my great-great-grandpa hated that the Romans renamed him. He was born Heracles, not Hercules. But yes, that was my ancestor."

Given my recent acceptance of the existence of necromancers and vampires, I'm not sure why this new shift in my paradigm is so jarring, but it is. There's just something so odd about—

"I've never told this to anyone," Ariel says. "Promise you'll keep it between us. If Felix teases me about my heritage, I might inadvertently twist off his head—and I'd never forgive myself if I did that."

"Sure." I chuckle. "I'll let Felix keep his head. What is *he*, by the way? Please say he's a leprechaun and his family secretly founded the Lucky Charms cereal. Or maybe—"

"Do you know how different Uzbekistan is from Ireland?" Ariel gestures with her spoon. "I can't tell you the human myth equivalent for his type of Cognizant. He either doesn't know or hasn't shared that with me.

What I do know is that his father can make sand and glass do his bidding, and Felix inherited a variation of that power."

"Let me guess," I say with mock triumph. "He can command a glass dildo to—"

"Gross." Ariel covers her mouth with her hand. "Too many horrible images in my head now."

"But seriously." I gather the remains of my oatmeal into my spoon. "What can he do?"

"I don't want to rob him of the pleasure of telling you all about it," Ariel says mischievously. "In all the gloriously boring little details."

"Fine," I say, finishing my food. "Be like that."

"I'll trade you," Ariel says. "Tell me how you did the TV prediction, and I'll tell you what Felix's power is."

"You're not going to leave me alone about that one, I see. Fine. Given that I've lost my mentalism forever, I don't see the harm in showing you how I did what I did. Be right back."

I grab my laptop from my room and come back.

Sitting down at the table, I navigate to my email. I'm about to locate Darian's email with the video when I notice that my inbox is overflowing with emails from every one of my acquaintances. Half are talking about my prediction, but the other half have more sinister-looking subject lines, linking to a YouTube video.

I follow the link from one of the messages to a YouTube video titled "Fake Psychic Exposed."

Without turning the laptop toward Ariel, I play the first few seconds of the video.

It's the one I was about to show her. Only now it's been seen by millions of people—people who think I'm a fraud.

Ariel must see my face whiten, because she frowns and asks, "What's wrong?"

I turn the laptop so she can see, and press play.

The video starts playing a security recording of what happened that Sunday afternoon, many hours before I came to the studio. Specifically, it shows me wearing a brown UPS uniform that's still hidden in the back of my closet. In the video, I pretend to have a package for Kacie's assistant, the guy who will later swear he never took his eyes off the envelope I mailed to the studio weeks in advance. Of course, as soon as they let me through, I swap my mailed-in prediction for the envelope in my hands—and the security camera zooms in on my face when I'm doing the dirty work, getting a great mugshot.

The comments under this video are brutal, and I quit reading them for fear of throwing the laptop at the wall—something I really feel like doing.

Ariel's disappointment is palpable. "So you just bought the Sunday paper, copied the earthquake headline—which could've been any other headline— put it in an envelope that looks the same as the one you mailed to the studio before, and then pretended to be UPS and swapped the original 'prediction.'"

I sigh. "This is why I don't explain these things. Wasn't it much more fun to wonder how it was done?"

"I guess so," Ariel says and types something into the

YouTube search bar. "That's odd," she says after a moment. "I can't find your original performance."

I slide the laptop toward me and look for the video in question, but I also find nothing.

"The Council must not want me to get any more power from people thinking I'm legitimate," I say, my own disappointment hitting me hard. "Darian must've been the one to post the debunking video."

"Even if people stop believing you're legit, you won't lose your powers," Ariel says, misunderstanding my source of distress. "Once you have the power, it's yours forever."

"I don't care about these stupid powers," I say, shutting the laptop with too much force. "No one will invite me to a TV show ever again. Or come see any show of mine. I'll forever be 'that faker.'"

"It doesn't matter anyway." Ariel lays a comforting hand on my shoulder. "The Council would kill you if you went on TV again. Doesn't that make this a moot point?"

"It's my reputation." Elbows on the table, I cover my eyes with my palms. "They made me into what I've always despised."

"But you're a *real* psychic," she says. "You couldn't be more different from those frauds you've always complained about if you tried. You *are* the real deal. Besides, since when do you care about what people think?"

"You're right." I lower my hands. "No more moping. I've got to get to work. Quickly, tell me about Felix."

"Fine," she says. "Felix can control those." She gestures at the laptop. "Silicone is related to silica—which is sand, his dad's domain—and Felix can magically make silicone turn zeroes into ones and vice versa, which helps with his hacking. Or at least that's what he said—though I'll admit, I tuned out a lot of the details."

"Controlling computers? That's actually really cool. A useful power for the modern age."

"Please pretend to be surprised when he tells you this," Ariel says, putting her hands in a praying position. "Or at least don't tell him I was the one who told you."

"I can keep a secret." I get up to put my plate into the dishwasher.

"I've got to study," Ariel says and stretches like a mountain lion. "I'll see you at the Jubilee."

"Later," I say, and prepare to head out.

———

WHEN I GET TO WORK, an email from Nero awaits me. He wants me to research a pharmaceutical company before the end of the day. No hint of the Jubilee, and no hint of our new Mentor/Mentee relationship.

Why am I not surprised?

Since I'm scheduled for my restaurant gig tonight, I give the manager a call, but I can't bring myself to tell him the truth—that I'm done with performing forever.

Instead, I say that I have a month-long work trip and that they should give my spot to another magician. I even recommend a guy.

The whole thing hurts almost physically, and I feel even worse once I start researching the company Nero requested. I see my whole life becoming a constant stream of stock research, without the glimmer of hope that the restaurant gig had always given me.

By lunch, I have my recommendation ready: the stock is a buy. I schedule my reply to go out at 5:59 p.m.

If I send it now, Nero will just give me another stock to analyze.

I'm on my way to lunch when Venessa, one of Nero's assistants, catches me by the elevator.

"Mr. Gorin wants you to stop by the Oscar de la Renta store on the Upper East Side," she says, her face unreadable. "Here is the card for the salesperson you need to speak with."

Confused into silence, I take the card and watch Venessa leave.

Using my phone, I look up the store, which turns out to be a high-end clothing boutique. Is Nero looking to diversify by investing in couture?

I go to a sushi restaurant for lunch, and as I sit there, I spot a couple of people with Mandate auras around them. Is it my imagination, or do they nod to me? It could be. It must be a treat for one Cognizant to spot another in these crowds.

"Excuse me," the waiter says when he brings my bill. "Are you that fake psychic?"

This is what I was afraid of. People will recognize me as the fake now. Hopefully, they won't remember it for long because I don't want to feel this crummy every time.

"I have a counter question for you," I say to the waiter. "Are you that waiter who was going to get a good tip but is doing his best not to?"

The guy puts the bill on the table and escapes my withering glare.

I still tip him the twenty percent I intended, then leave the sushi place and make my way to the Upper East Side, where the boutique is located.

Entering the store, I examine the impressive dresses on display and gawk at the even more impressive prices. If people actually pay this for prettily shaped fabric, we might indeed want a piece of this action.

"Sasha?" a saleswoman says, addressing me with a thoroughly rehearsed smile. "Mr. Gorin emailed me your picture, but you're even prettier in person."

She doesn't have a Mandate aura, so I choose my words carefully. "Thanks. What's this about? I need to go back to work soon, so..."

A theory forms in my mind as I speak, but I dismiss it. I mean, he couldn't have, could he?

"It's about the dress for your special occasion," the saleswoman says, her smile unwavering. "It's ready."

She leads me deeper into the store, and we pass a shoe display that looks like a catwalk. When Ariel learns I did this without her, there's going to be major pouting.

"This is it," the saleswoman says, pointing to a little black dress that was clearly inspired by Audrey Hepburn's iconic look in *Breakfast at Tiffany's*. "Please, try it on."

Feeling as though I'm inside one of my weirder vision-dreams, I make my way to the dressing room. Before I enter, the saleswoman also thrusts a Christian Louboutin box into my hands and plops a jewelry box on top of it.

I close the door and try on the dress.

It looks amazing and fits me down to a millimeter. Did someone secretly take a cast of my body and design the dress around it, or did I sleepwalk into this place and get measured at some point? The alternative —that Nero has looked at me closely enough to know my measurements so precisely—is too disturbing to think about.

I open the shoebox next. Unlike Ariel, I've never experienced an emotional connection to stuff I wear on my feet (except if I hid a magical prop in it somehow), but this time, I nearly get a shoegasm. Shimmering silver, with a delicate clasp around the ankle, they fit me as perfectly as the dress.

I sigh and shake my head before moving on to the necklace. It's composed of a dozen large diamonds, with the truth-demanding stone as a centerpiece. When I put it on, it drapes beautifully over my chest, framed by the low décolletage of the dress.

Unless the diamonds are fake, Nero must've spent a small fortune on this outfit.

"You look fabulous," the saleswoman says when I exit the dressing room. "Mr. Gorin wanted me to tell you that everything in this ensemble is a gift, including the necklace."

I dumbly bob my head, unable to stop staring at myself.

The saleswoman hands me a card. "Mr. Gorin made you an appointment at a hair salon nearby. You're to ask for Sally when you get there."

And so the weirdness continues. I go back into the fitting room and change back into my regular clothes. The saleswoman takes the dress from me and assures me that she'll bring everything to the fund for the event tonight.

It's official. Nero is playing fairy godmother today.

Is that the kind of Cognizant he is? A fairy?

I find that hard to believe.

When I get to the hair salon, it turns out Nero booked me a thousand-dollar haircut. From there, I play a makeover Easter egg hunt throughout the city, receiving fancy mani-pedis, a facial, and posh makeup.

By the time I return to the fund, it's already past six, so I'm late for my own Jubilee. The saleswoman from the store is there with my dress, shoes, and necklace, as promised, and she quickly helps me put it all on. Still, it's 6:30 when I finish, but she assures me it's okay to be fashionably late.

Walking as quickly as possible while wearing my

new pumps, I ignore the incredulous looks from the traders and analysts I pass by on my way to the elevator.

When the elevator opens on the ballroom floor, I strut out, ready for this new Cognizant ordeal. Hopefully, this time they won't need to drag me to a healer after the festivities.

A server with champagne greets me with a smile, so I grab a glass and walk into the big room.

Nero went all out here as well.

A buffet for hundreds of people is overflowing with delicacies, multiple flower arrangements, balloons, and even an ice sculpture in the shape of a hooded figure with a mask, like the one I wore at the Rite. There's also a DJ in charge of the music, a smoke machine on the dance floor, an open bar, and a horde of waiters running around with trays of hors d'oeuvres.

Unfortunately, all this opulence highlights how few people are actually here for the Jubilee. I count less than a dozen. In addition to Ariel and Felix, I spot Kit (the Councilor who can change her face), Pada (the dead body disposal guy), Darian, Gaius, and a couple of other vampire Enforcers I saw at the TV studio and at the *Bodies* exhibit in Vegas. The rest are folks from the fund whose names I barely know but who apparently are also Cognizant.

To my surprise, Lucretia, our shrink, is among them.

Ariel and Felix come up to me first, both dressed up as though for a red carpet premiere.

"Wow," Ariel says and imitates a cartoon wolf whistle. "Who are you and what have you done with Sasha?"

Felix's jaw is slack, and I think I see drool as he looks me up and down.

"You look incredible," he says breathlessly. "How? I mean, why? I mean... never mind. You look incredible."

I thank him, and we chat for a while. He tells me about his power over computers and how it works, though I only comprehend every other word because of the loud music and my lack of a computer science doctorate degree.

"Everything has a transistor nowadays," he says in conclusion. "So, by having control over them, I'm basically a technomancer."

He then explains to me what a technomancer is, and it sounds a lot like what he's been to me all these years anyway—someone who can bend technology to his will.

"I have to tell you something," Felix says, ending his explanation when Ariel starts yawning. A grave expression replaces the excitement on his face. "You have to promise not to get mad, though."

"Ah. It sounds like I'm right on time," Darian says, approaching. His sharp tuxedo and black tie somehow make his British accent more pronounced. "So, dear Felix, you were about to finally grow some balls and fess up?"

Startled, Felix gapes at Darian, then looks back at

me with a guilty expression—and a kernel of suspicion awakens in my mind.

"It was you," I say to Felix. "You put me on Darian's radar, didn't you?"

I must sound accusatory because Felix winces and defensively says, "You started predicting things left and right, and kept talking about your TV career. I figured that if you *were* a Cognizant, someone should send a Herald to speak with you. When Darian hired me to hack into Chester's Cayman bank account, I mentioned your situation to Darian, since he's a seer, and you seemed to be one too. I never suspected he'd turn around and facilitate your TV performance. You're both seers, and I know he values that, so I didn't think he'd almost get you killed."

"I did *not* almost get her killed." Darian carelessly sips the cocktail in his hand. "If anything, I saved her life."

"You saved my life?" I resist the urge to pour my glass of bubbly on his head, and take a healthy sip instead. "What would it have looked like if you'd wanted me dead, then?"

"Oh, come now." Darian's green eyes focus on me, and I get the sense he's divining my future at this very moment. "Surely you remember the text I sent you? 'Amazing job last night,' it very succinctly said."

"Yes," I say hesitantly, taking a bigger sip of my drink. Then it hits me. "That text prevented me from entering the elevator," I say in amazement. "It made it possible for Rose to yell out to me, which led to the trip to the vet and fainting at my job and all the rest of it."

"Exactly," Darian says proudly. "If you didn't get my text, you wouldn't have taken the cat, and would've gone to work in a cab instead of your dearly departed Vespa. Your driver would not have had your reflexes and foresight, and you would've died in one of the car accidents Beatrice so kindly prepped for you. And if by some miracle you survived, you would've perished in that hallway without Vlad's rescue. Remember, you only met him because you delivered the cat back. You're welcome."

My head spins.

Could it be true?

Could Darian's power allow him to play such an intricate long game?

The fact that he knows about every one of those attacks seems to corroborate that. Ariel is the only person I've told the whole story to, and I doubt she's confided in him.

"But what about my visions?" I ask numbly. "I saw myself die."

"So soon?" His whole demeanor changes, and I become the center of his undivided attention. "Do share."

"Don't tell him anything." Ariel gives her empty glass to a passing server. "Not before he explains why the first cadaver attacked you during the TV show. Doesn't that imply Chester knew about you even before you got famous? Before that show, only Darian,

Felix, and I knew you might be a new seer, and we didn't tell Chester. Did we, Felix?"

"No," Felix says indignantly. "I'm not a complete idiot."

"You forgot Nero," Kit says from Darian's left. She must've joined us when I wasn't looking. "I suspect he knew of Sasha's powers."

Darian frowns.

Felix swallows a black caviar cracker and says, "I have a theory."

Everyone looks at him with varying degrees of curiosity.

"Darian and Chester spy on each other incessantly," Felix says, looking down. All the attention is clearly making him uncomfortable. "I bet as soon as Darian spoke to one of his people about Sasha, one of Chester's assets in Darian's inner circle overheard it and reported it back."

"Preposterous," Darian says, but he doesn't look too sure of himself. "My people are loyal."

"Everyone can be bribed and bought," Kit says matter-of-factly. "And, if there was even a slight chance for such an eavesdropping opportunity, Chester's power would've helped his agent exploit it."

"Be that as it may," Darian says. "His powers didn't help him in the end. We saw who won when it comes to Sasha."

"Yes, we most certainly did," Kit says with a smirk. "Nero."

Darian gives her a seething glare. "I better get

myself another drink," he says tightly, then turns toward me. "Cheers, Sasha. My Jubilee gift to you is in the post. I'm sure our paths will cross soon."

I'm tempted to ask about the gift, but Darian leaves too quickly to give me a chance. He must be upset that Nero got to be my Mentor, though I don't completely understand why.

Speaking of Nero, I don't see him anywhere, though I guess he's still in his office, working. The rumor around the fund is that he rarely leaves the office for the night, which is why he often expects all-nighters from the rest of us.

"I'm going to go mingle," I say and extract myself from the little circle we'd formed. "Excuse me."

I look around as I stroll. There's even more food around us now, but the same small group of people remains. The ice sculpture is melting and the dance floor is almost invisible in the heavy fog the smoke machine has put out, creating a magical forest feel in that part of the room.

Grabbing a tiny salmon tartare sandwich, I make my way toward Lucretia, who's speaking with Gaius on the edge of the fog.

She's wearing a black dress with a white square on top, looking as stunning as usual. He, on the other hand, doesn't look all that different from usual; his black tux looks a lot like the black suits he and the other Enforcers always wear. I do notice that his Mandate aura is different from everyone else's; it's fainter and of a different color—must be something to do with being a Herald.

"So, you're a Cognizant," I say to the shrink, examining her very regular-looking Mandate aura.

"Indeed." Lucretia smiles.

"And—and this is just a guess—you're the same type of Cognizant as he?" I look at Gaius. "Or is it erroneous to judge a Cognizant by their pale skin?"

"In my case, you're not far from the truth. I'm a pre-vamp," Lucretia says, and as though to highlight her point, she slurps up the giant raw oyster in her hand.

Gaius looks at her with a disgusted look. I guess vampires are very particular about their legendary liquid diet.

"What is a pre-vamp?" I ask, though I can guess based on the context.

"Pre-vamps are a type of especially long-lived Cognizant," she says, snatching another oyster from a nearby tray. "They turn into vampires when they die."

"What's long-lived for a Cognizant?" I ask. "How long do regular Cognizant live?"

"If I may," Gaius says, sipping from a cup containing a viscous dark liquid that brings to mind images of hospital plasma bags and bleeding human sacrifices. "As a Herald, I answer these questions all the time."

"Splendid." Lucretia wolfs down the morsel in her hand. "I need to go get some of that lobster salad."

"All Cognizant live much longer than humans," Gaius says in his professorial tone. "But the exact number of years varies for each of us. For example,

309

Lucretia"—he points at the food-foraging shrink—"has been around longer than this country."

"You're kidding." I look at the stunning woman with disbelief.

"Not at all. I'm dead serious." He grins.

"Wow." Either the alcohol or the information is making me giddy. "What about seers? How long do we live?"

"I'm not sure how old Darian is, but I heard him tell a story of how he tried to warn King George III about his American colonies and their pesky ambition to declare independence—which was Chester's scheme to stir up discord among humans as usual," Gaius says. "Your own longevity would depend on your parentage, but no one has any idea who your parents are—and not for a lack of trying, believe me."

A torrent of questions about my biological parents is about to spew from my mouth, but I feel someone behind me and spin on my high heel to face the potential danger.

"I hope I'm not interrupting," Nero says and smiles —something he almost never does.

My cheeks heat for some reason. He must've been lurking in the depths of the dance floor fog until now— that or he can turn invisible.

Trying to keep my cool, I take in his appearance.

He finally shaved and is wearing a bespoke suit.

Aside from that and the smile, something about my boss-turned-Mentor doesn't seem quite right, and it takes me a few moments to figure out what that something is.

He looks *relaxed*, his usual intensity muted for the moment.

"I'll let you two discuss important Mentor-Mentee business," Gaius says, bowing, and heads toward Ariel.

"May I have this dance?" Nero murmurs, extending his hand to me in a gentlemanly gesture.

As though in response, the fog envelops us and the DJ starts a slow song.

Inhaling water and glycol fumes like a vape enthusiast, I gape at Nero and his hand long enough to recognize the first words to "I Don't Want to Miss a Thing" by Aerosmith.

In a very un-Nero-like fashion, my usually impatient boss stands serenely, waiting for my answer.

I take a step back, the fog swirling around me, and find my voice long enough to say, "I don't—"

"Come on," Nero says, showing more emotion in this exchange than I've ever seen from him. "You can't have a Jubilee without a dance."

He closes the distance between us and wraps his hand around mine.

Besides truth-telling, his Cognizant power must also be hypnosis, because I allow him to lead me toward the dance floor. The fog around us brings to mind fairytales of travelers following a light until they get bogged down in a swamp.

I bump into a waitress, who comes out of the fog like a

ghost, and I profusely apologize before grabbing another glass of champagne. Quickly downing it, I hand the empty glass back to her, and she disappears into the fog again.

Nero watches me with mirth in the corners of his eyes—another first.

I look away and catch a glimpse of Gaius slow-dancing with Ariel nearby, then lose sight of them just as quickly. Even though they were standing much too close to each other for my liking, I'm encouraged by the fact that Nero and I won't be the only dancers in the room.

We make our way deeper into the fog until the rest of the room is completely obscured.

We stop.

Nero faces me.

Confusion and embarrassment make my heart flutter as we stare at each other—me awkwardly, and him like a predator preparing to leap for his prey.

He takes my right hand into his left and steps close enough that I can smell his cologne, spicy and peppery with floral undertones.

Before I can exhale, his right hand lands on my back once more.

Just like the previous times when Nero touched my back, I feel like I'm about to faint.

He pulls me closer, and soon, we're swaying to the music, with the fog swirling majestically around us. I've never considered myself small, but I feel tiny in his arms. His muscular frame exerts a gravity-like magnetism, and I constantly have to force myself to pull back before I end up clinging to him like a sloth to a tree.

He leans down, his lips close to my ear. "Now that I'm your Mentor, our interactions will be different," he murmurs, and I can feel his breath on my earlobe. "I'm sorry if I was cold and distant before."

Dumbstruck silence is the best response I can manage.

He draws me even closer then, and for some unfathomable reason, I don't pull away.

What is wrong with me?

This isn't another dream.

This is my *boss*.

If something were to happen between us, I'd never live it down at the fund. And it's not just this job that would be in jeopardy; the Mentorship, whatever that entails, would be endangered as well.

And what is *he* thinking? Sexual harassment—assuming I'm not imagining what better be a flashlight in his pocket—is not something to mess with.

"Don't think too much," Nero murmurs, gazing down at me, and before I can blink, he dips his head and kisses me.

On the lips.

A moment passes with our mouths locked together, and I can't believe I'm not pushing him away, or kicking him in the flashlight, or doing any of the things I would've predicted I'd do in this situation.

Clearly, I'm a lousy seer after all.

Then it hits me.

I'm not a lousy seer.

I dreamed about kissing Nero even before the TV show boosted my power. I'd written it off as just an inappropriate fantasy, but now it seems like that dream was a vision of this very moment.

If I needed proof that I've always been a seer, here it is.

In the flesh, so to speak.

My heart pounds, and my breath shudders in my chest as I feel his tongue. I should be pushing him away, should be making sure this doesn't go any further, but instead, I kiss Nero back with all the ferocity of someone who's been abstinent for the past two years. Chills race over my back, and my skin feels overly warm and tight.

The fog-obscured lights in the room dim, the sounds of the song fade, and the world around us dissipates as I lose myself in the oxytocin overdose.

It's as though I'm floating in a cloud, which must surely be a side effect of all this damned vapor.

Something changes about the kiss then.

Nero's masculine lips become soft, and his tongue turns tiny and delicate. He also suddenly tastes and smells like cherry blossoms.

I jolt in shock, but then I get it.

This is yet another dream—the strangest one of my life.

I open my eyes, ready to wake up, but I'm still awake, and still at the Jubilee.

My brain does, however, have trouble making sense of what I'm looking at.

It's not Nero I'm kissing.

Or, more accurately, it's no longer Nero... or even a man.

Are there hallucinogens in the fog machine juice?

Gathering my scattered wits, I push the woman away—and then I recognize her.

It's Kit, the Councilor who can change her face—and apparently her whole body, right down to flashlight, masculine scent, clothes, and all.

Heartbeat spiking, I step back. "That was you all along?" My voice rises. "You made me think I was dancing with Nero? That I was *kissing* him?" I furiously touch my swollen lips.

"Gifts are expected from any Council member who attends the Jubilee," Kit says in Nero's voice. "This is only the beginning of my gift, of course. I have the penthouse booked at the Four Seasons. We can leave to spend the night there as soon as you're ready."

I gape at her, unable to believe what I'm hearing—and what just happened.

I kissed Nero back. Fake Nero, but still.

Maybe it's not hallucinogens but Cognizant sex pheromones in this stupid fog?

I don't think I was this freaked out when I learned about vampires and zombies.

Did this woman, who barely knows me, expect me to react as I did? If so, did she figure it out using her

Cognizant powers, or am I pathetically transparent to everyone but myself?

"So," Kit says, changing her voice back to sound like an anime girl. "What do you say?"

"No." I take another step back and debate escaping into the fog. Then I recall that Council members are powerful and not to be insulted or messed with, and I hastily add, "Thank you, though. This is already a great gift. I can now cross kissing Nero off my bucket list. And dancing with him. And kissing a girl."

"Is my gender the reason for your reluctance?" She makes herself look like a hot Asian guy who could easily be her brother. "Or is it my race?" The guy turns Caucasian.

I shake my head vigorously. "I'm not being racist or sexist. Plus, isn't that a moot point, given that your plan was to look like Nero anyway?"

"I don't have to look like Nero," Kit says. Her black eyes turn green, her nose grows stronger, and a goatee sprouts around her mouth as she morphs into Darian.

He/she gives me a promising smile.

My pulse jumps again. "Really, I'm honored," I manage to say, taking yet another step back. "But no. Thank you."

"So long as you're certain," Kit says, and now she looks like Felix. Only this Felix is naked and unexpectedly buff.

Did she take liberties with his appearance, or does he actually look like that without clothes?

"I'm pretty confident," I choke out, thanking my

lucky stars that the real Felix can't see this through the fog. "But thank you again."

"Last chance." She makes herself look like Ariel— one dressed (and I use this term loosely) in Princess Leia's iconic slave-girl bikini.

How did she know I always try to convince my roommate to wear that for Halloween? And what is she trying to say with this?

"Still no, thank you," I say in a firmer tone. "It's not the shape you take. Or you. I just need an emotional bond before I can enjoy intimacy. And no offense, but I barely know you."

"A raincheck then?" she says, her face turning back to her usual self. Her body, however, retains Ariel's distinct perfection, along with the slave-girl bikini. "After we get to know each other better, perhaps?"

"Perhaps," I say as noncommittally as I can. "I would certainly be more receptive to such an idea in the far, far future if you don't pull a stunt like this again."

"Say no more," she says, turning her body back to its kimono-clad self. "Now if you'll excuse me, I have to go give a speech in your honor."

She winks and stalks through the fog in the direction of the DJ's podium.

Soon after she's gone, the hiss of the fog machine recedes, and the music stops.

My phone dings with a message notification.

Glad to be distracted from my tumultuous feelings, I take a look.

It's a text from Nero.

The real Nero.

Something's come up, and I won't be able to come down to the Jubilee. As a Council member and your Mentor, I do have a gift for you. Your raise for the year is fifty percent of your salary, and a mid-year bonus of fifty grand should hit your account tomorrow. And speaking of tomorrow, I need you to research two new biotech stocks for our portfolio. I need it done by 11 a.m.

I reread the words a couple of times and marvel at how I could've possibly kissed my boss. Maybe it wasn't the fog. Maybe Kit herself produces some sort of magic pheromones as part of her power, some kind of substance that overrules common sense.

Alternatively, this could be a side effect of severe stress, and if so, I should consider therapy from Lucretia after all. Though I don't think I could discuss kissing Nero with her—or anyone, really. I'm just going to do my best to put this incident out of my mind.

The fog recedes enough that I can see the people in the room again. Kit clears her throat through the giant speakers.

"If I could get everyone's attention," she says into DJ's mic, and everyone looks at her with genuine excitement. "As a member of the Council, I want to officially welcome Sasha into the ranks of the Cognizant."

Everyone loudly claps, cheers, and heads toward me with two drinks. I soon learn one drink is for me, and one is for them.

Alcohol-induced amnesia sounds great right about

now, so I sip every drink while Kit waxes ecstatic about how great it is to be a new Cognizant.

"Just wait and see, Sasha," she says at the end of her spiel. "You have no idea how exciting your life will be from now on."

I wave and thank her and everyone else, trying to look as jubilant as I imagine one should be during a Jubilee. But my emotions are turbulent and my thoughts scattered, with one in particular souring my mood.

The last thing she's said sounds suspiciously like an ancient Chinese curse: "May you live in interesting times." Perhaps it was payback for not getting me into bed, perhaps she didn't mean it that way, but I can't help thinking one thing, over and over.

If the last few days are representative of the excitement I'll enjoy as a Cognizant, I hope I can survive the week.

SNEAK PEEKS

Thank you for reading! I hope you loved Sasha's story! Her adventures continue in *Misfortune Teller (Sasha Urban Series: Book 2)*. Description below:

So I'm a seer. A Cognizant under the Mandate.

Life should be easy now, right?

Wrong.

With all the "accidents" that keep befalling me, I'll be lucky to survive the week. That is, if my crazy boss doesn't work me to death first...

Visit my website at www.dimazales.com to get your copy today!

Do you want to be notified of my new releases? Sign up for my email list at www.dimazales.com!

Love audiobooks? This series, and all of my other books, are available in audio.

Want to read my other books? You can check out:

- *Mind Dimensions* - the action-packed urban fantasy adventures of Darren, who can stop time and read minds
- *Transcendence* - the thrilling sci-fi tale of Mike Cohen, whose new technology will transform our brains *and* the world
- *The Last Humans* - the futuristic sci-fi/dystopian story of Theo, who lives in a world where nothing is as it seems
- *The Sorcery Code* - the epic fantasy adventures of sorcerer Blaise and his creation, the beautiful and powerful Gala

And now, please turn the page for a sneak peek at Chapter 1 of *Misfortune Teller* and an excerpt from *The Thought Readers (Mind Dimensions: Book 1).*

SNEAK PEEK AT MISFORTUNE TELLER

So I'm a seer. A Cognizant under the Mandate.

Life should be easy now, right?

Wrong.

With all the "accidents" that keep befalling me, I'll be lucky to survive the week. That is, if my crazy boss doesn't work me to death first...

———

I groan, opening my eyes.

The bedroom is spinning, and a horde of drummers are using my brain to practice "Death Metal's greatest hits."

How much did I drink at the Jubilee?

All I recall is people with two glasses of alcohol, onc

for them, one for me—and me giving in to peer pressure.

Sitting up, I slide my feet into my slippers. Moving makes my skull feel like a white dwarf star about to explode into a supernova.

With superhuman effort, I somehow manage to navigate my way to the bathroom.

If walking with a hangover were a sport, I'd get a gold medal.

A pale ghost of my already pasty self looks out of the bathroom mirror with huge bloodshot eyes and a jet-black mop of hair.

Looking at the toilet generates flashbacks of me hugging the white marble, and I vaguely recall Ariel and Felix fighting for the honor of holding back my hair.

After a thorough shower and five minutes of brushing my teeth, my mind clears enough for me to decide that this hangover is the worst of my life.

I'm never drinking again.

At least I had a good reason to get so trashed—the Jubilee is a big deal. It was my entry into Cognizant society, the secret race that includes psychics (like me), vampires, descendants of Hercules like my roommate Ariel, and whatever techno-thing Felix is.

I stumble back into my room and strongly debate skipping work. The problem with this idea is that my boss Nero is now my Mentor in the Cognizant world— a role with as-yet-unclear meaning. Last night, after informing me about a raise, he demanded I research two new biotech stocks for our portfolio by 11 a.m.—and it's already 7:45, so I don't have much time.

Figuring I should break the problem into smaller chunks, I decide to go to the kitchen and jam some liquids and electrolytes into myself, to see if that makes me human again. Though maybe the expression should now be "Cognizant again," since we don't seem to be human.

Dressing in my most comfortable work clothes, I waddle into the kitchen and find Felix there.

"Morning, party girl," he says with an annoyingly cheerful smile as he points at the stove. "Do you want eggs or oatmeal?"

Felix's face is a melting pot of Slavic, Asian, and Middle Eastern features, and he's the only person I know who looks endearing when wiggling a bushy unibrow.

"Whichever works better for a hangover," I croak, the smell of food failing to entice me for once.

Felix nods and fusses over the stove as I watch the kitchen spin.

"I've put some salt and bananas into your oatmeal," he says a moment later, his voice much too loud for my comfort. He sets the bowl in front of me with a skull-shattering bang. "Let me also pour you some juice and tea."

When he hands me the liquids, I guzzle the juice in one gulp, like medicine, and slurp the tea while I wait for the oatmeal to cool.

"Did you see Ariel dancing with that vampire?"

Felix says conspiratorially, putting his own plate of eggs on the table with another too-loud smack. "What was she thinking?"

"You mean Gaius?" I catch some banana with my spoon. "She says they're just friends."

"Just friends," Felix mutters. "*We* are just friends, and if I rubbed against her like that, she'd probably break my neck."

He blushes as he says this. Then he looks at the door and turns beet red.

Ariel jauntily sashays into the room. Though her Jubilee makeup is gone, she still looks like she could pose for a cover of *Maxim* magazine. Batting her perfect eyelashes at Felix, she asks, "Who would break your neck and why?"

"No one. No reason." Felix stuffs food into his mouth.

"All right," Ariel says and blitzes through the kitchen like a sultry Tasmanian devil from the cartoons. Cabinet doors slam, plates thump against the counter, and dishes rattle in the sink. I'm pretty sure I see a crack appear in the cup she's holding as she bangs it against the kitchen faucet in an effort to get water. Before I can beg her to stop making such a clamor, she grabs a plate of eggs and a cup of coffee, and heads for the table.

"Would you sit down," Felix says to her as she jumps up a second later to grab milk in the same frantic manner. "What, is this your tenth cup of coffee?"

Actually, Ariel is acting like she's on amphetamines,

but I don't say it out loud because that would just upset her. My roommate takes a range of legal and, I suspect, some not-so-legal drugs to help her cope with the PTSD she denies having. Felix and I generally don't give her a hard time about that because taking those pills seems to improve her quality of life.

"I'm just excited after having so much fun last night." Ariel's megawatt smile blinds my hungover eyes.

"So much 'fun.'" I make air quotes to make sure no one misses my sarcasm. "I could use a guillotine right about now."

"Is your hangover really that bad?" Ariel's smile dims slightly. "I can hook you up to an IV, if you'd like. They say it helps with dehydration symptoms."

"I think I'll pass," I say, sipping my tea. "But I will take enough Tylenol to cure or kill an elephant."

Ariel jumps up and beelines for the medicine cabinet. Almost instantly, she's back with a bottle of painkillers and a glass of water.

I gratefully shove a pile of pills into my mouth and chase them down with water. Hopefully, my liver can take it.

"You better recover soon. The Jubilee was just the first step in our celebration," Ariel says as I resume eating.

I nearly choke on my oatmeal. "More celebration?"

"Of course." She beams at me again. "I'm taking you to Earth Club."

I picture loud club beats, and my left eye twitches

involuntarily, the headache gleefully pulsing at the base of my noggin.

Felix looks me over. "Are you sure it's a good idea to take her there so soon?"

"No. Not a good idea," I say, clearing the knot in my throat. "I'd rather go to a shooting range and let someone shoot me in the head."

"I'm not saying we go today," Ariel says, her hyper manner undiminished. "We don't even need to go tomorrow. We'll go on Saturday—that's when everyone's going to be there, anyway."

"What do you mean, everyone?" I massage my throbbing temples.

"The Cognizant," Ariel says and spears a piece of egg on her fork. "Earth Club is where we hang out without having to hide our natures."

"That does make it a little more interesting," I say cautiously and eat half a spoon of oatmeal. "Maybe in a few years, when this headache is gone—"

"It's located in the Otherlands." Ariel's smile threatens to break her face. "It's your chance to officially go there—I know you'd want that."

"I'll think about this," I say and sip my tea again. "But no alcohol at the club if I go. No alcohol for me ever."

"Sure." Ariel shoves her fingers through her hair in a jerky motion, still beaming like a lunatic. "They have every drug known to man—and some not known to man."

My earlier concerns about Ariel's sobriety return

with a vengeance. I catch Felix staring at me intently—his thoughts must echo mine.

"Are you going with us?" I ask Felix. What I leave unsaid is, "Maybe you can help me keep an eye on her?"

Felix hesitates, then nods. "Yes. All right. I'll go."

Ariel all but jumps up and down in her chair. "This is going to be so much fun, you guys."

In the momentary silence that follows, I hear the pitter-patter of fluffy feet. With a wave of guilt, I realize that in my hangover misery, I completely forgot to feed Fluffster—my pet chinchilla.

Fortunately, Fluffster doesn't look particularly grumpy, so hopefully, he just woke up and didn't realize I forgot about him. In fact, he looks extra bright eyed and bushy tailed today, his tiny nose wrinkling in the middle of majestically long whiskers and his large ears standing up like radio antenna dishes ready to receive alien transmissions.

My roommates exchange a strange look, then stare at me.

I look at them, then at Fluffster worriedly—and then I see it.

Fluffster has a tiny aura.

The glow is similar to the one both of my roommates possess—which in their case means they are under the Mandate, like me.

In other words, Cognizant.

"Felix. Ariel." I point at the aura. "Are you also seeing the glow that's supposed to indicate *people* under the Mandate? Do you know why my cute rodent has one?"

"It's a long story." Felix puts down a butter knife and looks at Ariel.

"Fluffster isn't what or who you think he is," Ariel says, her smile as bright as ever.

Fluffster scurries closer, jumps onto my knee and then onto the table. He's never displayed this much dexterity before. He then looks very intently at Ariel with his pretty black eyes.

"No," Ariel says, seemingly to Fluffster. "It's better if you tell her." Fluffster looks at Felix in that same way—as though he wants to hypnotize him.

"Don't look at me," Felix says. "I think it should come from the horse's mouth. Or chinchilla's brain. Or whatever."

"*Tell* me?" The room starts to spin again, and it's no longer because of the hangover. "Guys, please. This is the worst day for jokes."

Fluffster stands on his haunches on the table, and it could be my imagination, but did he just gesticulate with his little hand-like paws?

"I wouldn't know where to start." Ariel puts down her fork with a loud clank, her smile disappearing as she full-on glares at my pet. "It's your charade; you deal with it."

Fluffster begins to pace the table. From time to time, he looks at Felix or Ariel, then at me.

"Okay," Felix finally says to my pet. He then turns to me. "You ever hear of the domovoi?"

"Yes," I say, my headache very quickly evolving into a full-on migraine. "It's some kind of a Russian house spirit or something like that, right? Vlad and Pada called Fluffster by that word, so I looked it up."

"Correct," Felix says. "The domovoi feature prominently in Slavic folklore. And, according to my dad, they are a group of powerful Cognizant within their own realm of influence, and he"—Felix points at Fluffster—"is one of them."

I gape at the little animal. "But he's a chinchilla. A rodent native to the Andean Mountains in South America—as far from Russia as you can get. I bought him at the pet shop. This makes no sense."

Both Felix and Ariel look at Fluffster, avoiding my gaze.

"This isn't funny," I say. "Are you seriously about to tell me Fluffster is a were-chinchilla? Or is he supposed to be a chinchilla who got bitten by a rabid guy from Siberia, making him a were-man—a cute furry creature who turns into a hairy Russian dude during a full moon?"

"Having grown up in the States, I don't know that much about the way the domovoi work," Felix says. "What I do know is based on what my dad told me. The domovoi usually stay in an insubstantial form, but sometimes, they take the shape of a passed-away pet— usually a dog or a cat..."

I stare at everyone in turn, the hair on the back of my neck standing up.

Fluffster walks over to my oatmeal bowl, stands on his haunches again, and stares directly into my face.

My eyes widen, and I blink repeatedly.

There's always been intelligence in Fluffster's gaze, but never this deep. Never this intense.

"I'm so sorry you had to find out this way," says a soft voice in my head—and though it's purely mental, it has a hint of a Russian accent.

———

Visit www.dimazales.com to learn more!

SNEAK PEEK AT THE THOUGHT READERS

Everyone thinks I'm a genius.

Everyone is wrong.

Sure, I finished Harvard at eighteen and now make crazy money at a hedge fund. But that's not because I'm unusually smart or hard-working.

It's because I cheat.

You see, I have a unique ability. I can go outside time into my own personal version of reality—the place I call "the Quiet"—where I can explore my surroundings while the rest of the world stands still.

I thought I was the only one who could do this—until I met *her*.

My name is Darren, and this is how I learned that I'm a Reader.

———

Sometimes I think I'm crazy. I'm sitting at a casino table in Atlantic City, and everyone around me is motionless. I call this the *Quiet*, as though giving it a name makes it seem more real—as though giving it a name changes the fact that all the players around me are frozen like statues, and I'm walking among them, looking at the cards they've been dealt.

The problem with the theory of my being crazy is that when I 'unfreeze' the world, as I just have, the cards the players turn over are the same ones I just saw in the Quiet. If I were crazy, wouldn't these cards be different? Unless I'm so far gone that I'm imagining the cards on the table, too.

But then I also win. If that's a delusion—if the pile of chips on my side of the table is a delusion—then I might as well question everything. Maybe my name isn't even Darren.

No. I can't think that way. If I'm really that confused, I don't want to snap out of it—because if I do, I'll probably wake up in a mental hospital.

Besides, I love my life, crazy and all.

My shrink thinks the Quiet is an inventive way I describe the 'inner workings of my genius.' Now that sounds crazy to me. She also might want me, but that's beside the point. Suffice it to say, she's as far as it gets from my datable age range, which is currently right around twenty-four. Still young, still hot, but done with school and pretty much beyond the clubbing phase. I hate clubbing, almost as much as I hated studying. In any case, my shrink's explanation doesn't work, as it doesn't account for the way I know things even a genius wouldn't know—like the exact value and suit of the other players' cards.

I watch as the dealer begins a new round. Besides me, there are three players at the table: Grandma, the Cowboy, and the Professional, as I call them. I feel that now almost imperceptible fear that accompanies the phasing. That's what I call the process: phasing into the Quiet. Worrying about my sanity has always facilitated phasing; fear seems helpful in this process.

I phase in, and everything gets quiet. Hence the name for this state.

It's eerie to me, even now. Outside the Quiet, this casino is very loud: drunk people talking, slot machines, ringing of wins, music—the only place louder is a club or a concert. And yet, right at this moment, I could probably hear a pin drop. It's like I've gone deaf to the chaos that surrounds me.

Having so many frozen people around adds to the strangeness of it all. Here is a waitress stopped mid-step, carrying a tray with drinks. There is a woman about to pull a slot machine lever. At my own table, the dealer's hand is raised, the last card he dealt hanging unnaturally in midair. I walk up to him from the side of the table and reach for it. It's a king, meant for the Professional. Once I let the card go, it falls on the table rather than continuing to float as before—but I know full well that it will be back in the air, in the exact position it was when I grabbed it, when I phase out.

The Professional looks like someone who makes money playing poker, or at least the way I always imagined someone like that might look. Scruffy, shades on, a little sketchy-looking. He's been doing an excellent job with the poker face—basically not twitching a single muscle throughout the game. His face is so expressionless that I wonder if he might've gotten Botox to help maintain such a stony countenance. His hand is on the table, protectively covering the cards dealt to him.

I move his limp hand away. It feels normal. Well, in a manner of speaking. The hand is sweaty and hairy, so moving it aside is unpleasant and is admittedly an abnormal thing to do. The normal part is that the hand is warm, rather than cold. When I was a kid, I expected people to feel cold in the Quiet, like stone statues.

With the Professional's hand moved away, I pick up his cards. Combined with the king that was hanging in the air, he has a nice high pair. Good to know.

I walk over to Grandma. She's already holding her cards, and she has fanned them nicely for me. I'm able to avoid touching her wrinkled, spotted hands. This is a relief, as I've recently become conflicted about touching people—or, more specifically, women—in the Quiet. If I had to, I would rationalize touching

Grandma's hand as harmless, or at least not creepy, but it's better to avoid it if possible.

In any case, she has a low pair. I feel bad for her. She's been losing a lot tonight. Her chips are dwindling. Her losses are due, at least partially, to the fact that she has a terrible poker face. Even before looking at her cards, I knew they wouldn't be good because I could tell she was disappointed as soon as her hand was dealt. I also caught a gleeful gleam in her eyes a few rounds ago when she had a winning three of a kind.

This whole game of poker is, to a large degree, an exercise in reading people—something I really want to get better at. At my job, I've been told I'm great at reading people. I'm not, though; I'm just good at using the Quiet to make it seem like I am. I do want to learn how to read people for real, though. It would be nice to know what everyone is thinking.

What I don't care that much about in this poker game is money. I do well enough financially to not have to depend on hitting it big gambling. I don't care if I win or lose, though quintupling my money back at the blackjack table was fun. This whole trip has been more about going gambling because I finally can, being twenty-one and all. I was never into fake IDs, so this is an actual milestone for me.

Leaving Grandma alone, I move on to the next player—the Cowboy. I can't resist taking off his straw hat and trying it on. I wonder if it's possible for me to get lice this way. Since I've never been able to bring back any inanimate objects from the Quiet, nor otherwise affect the real world in any lasting way, I figure I won't be able to get any living critters to come back with me, either.

Dropping the hat, I look at his cards. He has a pair of aces—a better hand than the Professional. Maybe the Cowboy is a professional, too. He has a good poker face, as far as I can tell. It'll be interesting to watch those two in this round.

Next, I walk up to the deck and look at the top cards, memorizing them. I'm not leaving anything to chance.

When my task in the Quiet is complete, I walk back to myself. Oh, yes, did I mention that I see myself sitting there, frozen like the rest of them? That's the weirdest part. It's like having an out-of-body experience.

Approaching my frozen self, I look at him. I usually avoid doing this, as it's too unsettling. No amount of looking in the mirror—or seeing videos of yourself on YouTube—can prepare you for viewing your own three-dimensional body up close. It's not something anyone is meant to experience. Well, aside from identical twins, I guess.

It's hard to believe that this person is me. He looks more like some random guy. Well, maybe a bit better than that. I do find this guy interesting. He looks cool. He looks smart. I think women would probably consider him good-looking, though I know that's not a modest thing to think.

It's not like I'm an expert at gauging how attractive a guy is, but some things are common sense. I can tell when a dude is ugly, and this frozen me is not. I also know that generally, being good-looking requires a symmetrical face, and the statue of me has that. A strong jaw doesn't hurt, either. Check. Having broad shoulders is a positive, and being tall really helps. All covered. I have blue eyes—that seems to be a plus. Girls have told me they like my eyes, though right now, on the frozen me, the eyes look creepy—glassy. They look like the eyes of a lifeless wax figure.

Realizing that I'm dwelling on this subject way too long, I shake my head. I can just picture my shrink analyzing this moment. Who would imagine admiring themselves like this as part of their mental illness? I can just picture her scribbling down *Narcissist*, underlining it for emphasis.

Enough. I need to leave the Quiet. Raising my hand, I touch my frozen self on the forehead, and I hear noise again as I phase out.

Everything is back to normal.

The card that I looked at a moment before—the king that I left on the table—is in the air again, and from there it follows the trajectory it was always meant to, landing near the Professional's hands. Grandma is still eyeing her fanned cards in disappointment, and the Cowboy has his hat on again, though I took it off him in the Quiet. Everything is exactly as it was.

On some level, my brain never ceases to be surprised at the discontinuity of the experience in the

Quiet and outside it. As humans, we're hardwired to question reality when such things happen. When I was trying to outwit my shrink early on in my therapy, I once read an entire psychology textbook during our session. She, of course, didn't notice it, as I did it in the Quiet. The book talked about how babies as young as two months old are surprised if they see something out of the ordinary, like gravity appearing to work backwards. It's no wonder my brain has trouble adapting. Until I was ten, the world behaved normally, but everything has been weird since then, to put it mildly.

Glancing down, I realize I'm holding three of a kind. Next time, I'll look at my cards before phasing. If I have something this strong, I might take my chances and play fair.

The game unfolds predictably because I know everybody's cards. At the end, Grandma gets up. She's clearly lost enough money.

And that's when I see the girl for the first time.

She's hot. My friend Bert at work claims that I have a 'type,' but I reject that idea. I don't like to think of myself as shallow or predictable. But I might actually be a bit of both, because this girl fits Bert's description of my type to a T. And my reaction is extreme interest, to say the least.

Large blue eyes. Well-defined cheekbones on a slender face, with a hint of something exotic. Long, shapely legs, like those of a dancer. Dark wavy hair in a ponytail—a hairstyle that I like. And without bangs—

even better. I hate bangs—not sure why girls do that to themselves. Though lack of bangs is not, strictly speaking, in Bert's description of my type, it probably should be.

I continue staring at her. With her high heels and tight skirt, she's overdressed for this place. Or maybe I'm underdressed in my jeans and t-shirt. Either way, I don't care. I have to try to talk to her.

I debate phasing into the Quiet and approaching her, so I can do something creepy like stare at her up close, or maybe even snoop in her pockets. Anything to help me when I talk to her.

I decide against it, which is probably the first time that's ever happened.

I know that my reasoning for breaking my usual habit—if you can even call it that—is strange. I picture the following chain of events: she agrees to date me, we go out for a while, we get serious, and because of the deep connection we have, I come clean about the Quiet. She learns I did something creepy and has a fit, then dumps me. It's ridiculous to think this, of course, considering that we haven't even spoken yet. Talk about jumping the gun. She might have an IQ below seventy, or the personality of a piece of wood. There can be twenty different reasons why I wouldn't want to date her. And besides, it's not all up to me. She might tell me to go fuck myself as soon as I try to talk to her.

Still, working at a hedge fund has taught me to hedge. As crazy as that reasoning is, I stick with my decision not to phase because I know it's the gentlemanly thing to do. In keeping with this unusually chivalrous me, I also decide not to cheat at this round of poker.

As the cards are dealt again, I reflect on how good it feels to have done the honorable thing—even without anyone knowing. Maybe I should try to respect people's privacy more often. As soon as I think this, I mentally snort. *Yeah, right.* I have to be realistic. I wouldn't be where I am today if I'd followed that advice. In fact, if I made a habit of respecting people's privacy, I would lose my job within days—and with it, a lot of the comforts I've become accustomed to.

Copying the Professional's move, I cover my cards with my hand as soon as I receive them. I'm about to sneak a peek at what I was dealt when something unusual happens.

The world goes quiet, just like it does when I phase in... but I did nothing this time.

And at that moment, I see *her*—the girl sitting across the table from me, the girl I was just thinking about. She's standing next to me, pulling her hand away from mine. Or, strictly speaking, from my frozen self's hand—as I'm standing a little to the side looking at her.

She's also still sitting in front of me at the table, a frozen statue like all the others.

My mind goes into overdrive as my heartbeat jumps. I don't even consider the possibility of that second girl being a twin sister or something like that. I know it's her. She's doing what I did just a few minutes ago. She's walking in the Quiet. The world around us is frozen, but we are not.

A horrified look crosses her face as she realizes the same thing. Before I can react, she lunges across the table and touches her own forehead.

The world becomes normal again.

She stares at me from across the table, shocked, her eyes huge and her face pale. Her hands tremble as she rises to her feet. Without so much as a word, she turns and begins walking away, then breaks into a run a couple of seconds later.

Getting over my own shock, I get up and run after her. It's not exactly smooth. If she notices a guy she doesn't know running after her, dating will be the last thing on her mind. But I'm beyond that now. She's the only person I've met who can do what I do. She's proof that I'm not insane. She might have what I want most in the world.

She might have answers.

———

Visit www.dimazales.com to learn more!

ABOUT THE AUTHOR

Dima Zales is a *New York Times* and *USA Today* bestselling author of science fiction and fantasy. Prior to becoming a writer, he worked in the software development industry in New York as both a programmer and an executive. From high-frequency trading software for big banks to mobile apps for popular magazines, Dima has done it all. In 2013, he left the software industry in order to concentrate on his writing career and moved to Palm Coast, Florida, where he currently resides.

Please visit www.dimazales.com to learn more.

Made in the USA
Lexington, KY
29 August 2018

He has the kind of pretty face that some women swoon over, but I'm not a fan. His eyes are the color of arctic sky. Then they start to change. The pitch-black pupil turns reflective silver and begins to expand, first covering the iris, then the white of the sclera.

My breath evens out. The mirrored orbs that are Gaius's eyes each reflect a distorted image of me, my face translucently pale and my pupils the size of dimes.

A drunken serenity steals over me. Analytically, I know it's something to do with his gaze, but no matter how hard I try, I can't close my eyes or look away.

My consciousness sinks into a dark, underground place. The closest I've ever come to feeling this way was when I was drunk on a dozen shots of tequila.

Through the haze, I register only slices of events.

The guards, if that's what they are, finish their odd stare-down of every person in the crowd. Gaius picks me up like a feather, and a blink later, I'm half-lying in a limo that's zooming down West Side Highway.

Just as my mind begins to clear, Gaius peers into my eyes again, and the haze envelops me once more.

When I next come to my senses, I'm inside my building's elevator, propped up by a body so hard it might as well be made of marble.

"Almost home," says the familiar hypnotic voice as the mirrored eyes stare into mine. "You're amazingly resilient to glamour. I'm truly impressed."

I must black out again, because in the next instance, I'm standing by my apartment door with a strong arm holding me upright. Gaius's pale finger is on the doorbell, and I'm too out of my mind to chastise him for waking up my roommates when I have the key to the place.

The door opens, revealing Ariel in her silk nightgown.

The arm around me tenses, and I can't blame Gaius for his reaction. Even when she's wearing hospital scrubs—clothes designed to make nurses look less sexy—Ariel looks like a supermodel, and in this skintight nightgown, men would gobble fish oil with a spoon for her attention.

When I look at beautiful people, I often philosophically ponder what it is about a person's face and body that makes it so appealing. Is it symmetry and proportions? If so, Ariel's is among the most symmetric faces I've ever seen, and her body's 0.7 waist-to-hip ratio is pure mathematical perfection. On top of it, her skin is melted-candy smooth, even now, when she's not wearing any makeup. And, whereas more traditionally pretty faces have infant-like, small facial features, Ariel's Greek nose and jaw are strong, yet both are sublime on her face, giving her a touch of the exotic.

Her dark brown eyes stare at me with worry, then focus on my chaperone with undisguised hostility.

"What's going on? What are you doing with her?" Ariel's voice is melodious even when angry.

"Sasha isn't feeling well." Lowering his shades a couple of inches, Gaius scans Ariel up and down, his gaze lingering on her ballerina-long neck instead of her breasts. "I'd like to put her to bed. Why don't you invite me in?"

"Hell no. I've got it from here, thanks." Reaching for me, she loops a toned arm around my back.

"Suit yourself," Gaius says and steps back, letting Ariel support me fully.

She's about to drag me into the apartment when he says, "Just one other thing." Reaching out, he winds a hair from my head around his finger, and before Ariel or I can protest, he yanks it out.

I flinch but feel nothing—I must be too flabbergasted to feel such minor pain.

Pocketing the hair, he says, "She isn't likely to remember any of this in the morning, so you might not want to cause her unnecessary grief by reminding her."

Instead of answering, Ariel pulls me into the apartment and slams the door shut, almost hitting the pale man in the face.

"What happened?" she asks, turning me to face her. Her eyes hone in on my neck as though looking for a hickey. "Did he—"

I sway on my feet. "I just need to sleep so I can wake up."

"Good idea," Ariel says, and though we're nearly the same size, she picks me up like a bridegroom and carries me to my bedroom without a hint of effort.

Anyone watching this would be amazed, but I'm used to this sort of thing with Ariel. She likes to call herself "Army Strong," and I sometimes half-jokingly wonder if the Army gave her special drugs to turn her into a super soldier.

"Do you need help with your clothes?" she asks once she lays me on the bed.

Unable to think of a good reply to such a difficult conundrum, I blink at her and plummet into sleep as soon as my head touches the bliss of my memory foam pillow.